TIENKUO

The Heavenly Kingdom

Li Bo

ISBN: 1542660572
ISBN 13: 9781542660570
Library of Congress Control Number: 2017900969
CreateSpace Independent Publishing Platform
North Charleston, South Carolina

A NOTE ON TRANSLATION

In keeping with recent transliteration practices, this revision of *Tienkuo: The Heavenly Kingdom* has been converted from the older Wade-Giles system to the newer Hanyu Pinyin system, except in a few places to avoid confusion or to facilitate research by those interested in learning more about the many historic individuals discussed in the novel.

CHAPTER 1

HONG KONG

"Jason, come in at once!" He heard the call, but snug in his hiding place behind the church, Jason knew his father, Reverend Brandt, wasn't likely to find him. The young man sat quietly, hoping to remain hidden as the others went in to services. It would be depressing to go in. Paul Li would be there and perhaps some beggars hoping for a bowl of rice in reward for reciting praises to the Western god. However, no more than that and Jason's father would scowl as he viewed the sparse turnout. When it became obvious that no more converts were coming, he would begin the service.

Li Lao T'ai-t'ai might come, but that would hardly please the stern New England minister. Her only interest was to beg her son, Li Yueming, who now called himself Paul, to return to the Li family. There had been a long-running feud between the taciturn Massachusetts minister and Li Lao T'ai-t'ai, the mother of his star convert. Jason wanted to escape such tensions.

Hearing his father reenter the chapel and the sounds of the first hymn, Jason took off at a run. Hong Kong's harbor was as exciting as ever. There were always scores of junks to watch, as well as the occasional docking of a steam gunship. Sometimes Jason would sit for hours, watching the coolies carry their loads into the warehouses. Later, between loadings, the coolies would squat and chatter. Jason loved listening to the lyrical sounds of the coolies' conversations. He was often amused by their comments on the strangeness of the cargo they carried.

At the wharf, Jason could forget his father's futile but constant attempts to save souls, as well as his continuous stories of Boston and America. Only China, and especially Hong Kong, mattered to Jason. And now there was excitement in the air. More and more English and French naval frigates were arriving as the year 1857 drew to a close. It was rumored that the Western forces were planning to storm Guangzhou. Jason hardly understood the political issues behind the tension, but he had heard how Governor Ye Mingchen had outraged the foreigners by refusing their demands to enter the walled city of Guangzhou.

Jason tried to remember what the old-timers had told him about the first Opium War. Even then, they said, the Chinese had been unable to resist the power of the English guns. And now, France had joined Great Britain against the Middle Kingdom, as the Chinese called their land.

As he sat on the edge of the stone pier, Jason spotted several ships flying French colors. It was clear that something would happen soon. He wondered if his father would go north. Certainly fighting near Guangzhou would require the presence of a minister, if only to offer solace to the wounded. But what if the reverend planned no trip north? Would a battle occur, so nearby, and Jason miss it? That would be too much, reflected the young American.

He knew that if his father refused to go, he would travel north by himself. The soldiers could hardly turn down the chance for an interpreter, even a sixteen-year-old. Maybe he wouldn't have to defy his father; maybe the reverend would agree. One could always point out the chance to seek more converts. Guangzhou certainly had more potential than Hong Kong. Even his father often said that only the gentry and their leader, Governor General Ye, really opposed Christianity. The local people themselves, the old man would proclaim regularly, had always been receptive to the Lord. Or at least that was what his father thought.

Jason himself had never found the words necessary to tell the older man what the Chinese said about the missionaries among themselves. No, that would hurt the reverend too much. Since his mother's death six months before, that was the last thing Jason wanted to do to wound his father. Half watching the fleet, half lost in his own thoughts, he sat thinking of his mother and staring, at the same time, at the stunningly beautiful waters of Hong Kong Bay, spread out before him. His father often claimed that Boston's harbor was just as impressive, but he doubted it. Watching the waves lap against the shore and the graceful sails of the junks always captivated him, in a way his father could simply not understand. For the older man, China was an assignment—a godless region to save. For Jason, it was something else, though precisely what, he did not know. Was it home? He sometimes wondered. He didn't think so. Boston was home, or at least that is what his father told him over and over. Jason reflected, as he looked across the harbor, at how distant he really felt from his father's world.

"Little translator." The call roused him from his thoughts. It was Xu Pakwah, a local merchant. "Your father is looking for you, little one." Merchant Xu had known Jason since he was a child. It was from his stall that the missionary family had long purchased their vegetables.

"I am going back soon," said Jason, looking up at the old man. "Merchant Xu, do you know what is happening at Guangzhou?"

"What do you mean, little one?" Xu asked, looking closely at the boy.

"The soldiers, the French and English—will they attack the city?"

"This one doesn't know. I am only a poor merchant, with no degree holders in my family. I know that Viceroy Ye won't be very happy with the arrival of these troops. The foreign soldiers have been hiring coolies to carry their equipment toward the city. But what has that to do with us? Enough of this; go to your father."

After giving him a stern look, Xu marched off. Pulling himself to his feet, Jason started toward his father's church, his head full of thoughts of what might even now be happening in Guangzhou. As he walked, Jason wished he had wandered farther. He'd be home in minutes, he thought unhappily. Somehow the thought of sitting opposite his father at supper depressed him.

Of late his father had become increasingly bitter. Jason knew it was difficult for his father to stay on in Hong Kong, particularly since Jason's mother's death. He understood as well, though, how fearful his father was of starting over again in New England. Reverend Brandt was almost fifty. He made it sound practically impossible. Nevertheless, the reverend awaited every ship from Boston with the hope that his query letters might have been favorably answered.

The letters had gone off regularly since Jason was thirteen. The boy, though, had long since realized that nothing was likely to ever come of them. Perhaps it was too late for his father to establish a "real" congregation, as the older man called a Massachusetts pulpit. Even his father believed only halfheartedly that they would ever be able to return to America. The older man's anxiety seemed to have quickened of late. In fact, he talked of almost nothing else.

"It's time for you to start college, to learn to be a gentleman. I've let you become half Chinese. If I weren't certain you'd received the Lord's teachings, I'd be even more concerned." Jason could almost recite their supper conversations, and he knew his father had begun to ask his mother's relatives to seek an appropriate college. But all that seemed very far away. Guangzhou was only a few score leagues to the north. And there might be fighting there! Jason could hardly contain his frustrations.

His father was standing at the door as he came into sight, clearly watching for him.

"You missed services, Jason Randolph Brandt." His father looked at him coldly; then, warming a bit, he said, "Son, you know it makes it more difficult for me to convince the Chinese to come if I can't even keep my own son in church."

"I'm sorry, Father. I just forgot," Jason mumbled, looking down and feeling guilty about lying. He expected his father to challenge his flimsy excuse, but the older man's thoughts were elsewhere. The reverend put a hand on Jason's shoulder, his features now crowded with love, concern, and glad tidings. "The mail arrived, and we've good news. Your aunt has found a college for you, Oberlin, in Ohio. They have agreed to have you for next term."

Jason froze in his tracks. His throat felt drier than he ever remembered.

"Uh…that's very good news, Father," he said, the words difficult to mouth. He looked up striving to appear grateful. "Where's Ohio, Father?"

The reverend peered at him, a bit taken back.

"It's in the Midwest, just past Pennsylvania. Not Boston, but it is a God-fearing region, and the college is a respected one. They've offered space for you and even work on the campus."

"When would I leave?"

"Why, on the next ship. You'll want to spend some time with your mother's relatives in Salem before you go on to college." He removed his hand from Jason's shoulder and turned away, closing the subject. "Supper must be ready by now." Reverend Brandt set off for the family home.

Jason slowly followed his father, though the older man's brisk steps left him farther behind with each lengthy stride. His mind was racing. He would miss everything. He did not want to be a college student in some place called Ohio while a war raged in China. He had to find a way to go north, to put off until next year the trip to America. Jason barely noticed the smell of supper as they walked into the Western-style house his father had built near the coast.

"Father," he began, starting the conversation anew, "couldn't I go next year? Is it that important that I go now? They'll be needing you in Guangzhou when the war comes. And you'll want me there for translating and passing out literature."

The older man did not reply. Jason bowed his head as his father intoned, "Bless this food and all those who partake of it." Then, turning toward Jason, he said, "No. You won't wait till next year. You will go now. There is no way of knowing whether you'll receive as good an offer again. I'll not have you wasting your life here in Hong Kong."

"But you live here, Father."

A spasm of anger briefly contorted the reverend's face. His glance raked Jason with a familiar expression of righteous impatience.

"That's different. I'm here to do the Lord's work. And that's important work. But you will do something else. I want you to be a lawyer or, if you want, a man of the cloth, but with a proper flock, not these heathens. I won't need you here, anyway. I'll not be going up to Guangzhou, and you shouldn't be so interested in going, either. That's final."

The reverend turned back to his meal. Jason knew him too well to bother continuing the discussion. They ate in silence, and Jason's mind raced, trying to find a way to change his father's mind.

Much later, as they prepared for bed, Jason grew almost desperate. He had tried, unsuccessfully, to broach the subject throughout the evening. He knew from the beginning, however, that his father would not relent. Jason was expected to leave on the next boat, and that could be any time. Money for his passage was already set aside, and he knew he would be on the next boat—if, he chilled at the thought, if he were still in Hong Kong.

Later, Jason was shocked at how quickly he had made his decision, surprised it had come so easily.

Waking before dawn, he quietly lit a candle and began the following note to his father:

> Dear Father:
> Please understand. I am certain you are right about my going to Ohio. I do promise you that I will go but not now. I am not ready to leave. I hope that when I see you again, you will understand.
> Faithfully,
> Jason
> This day, December 27, 1858

He signed it and proceeded to the second part of his plan—the part he was less sure about. Groping in the darkness, he finally located his father's strongbox. Quietly, using the key he'd set aside earlier, he opened the musty container. There, as it had always lain, was the special pouch that contained the money his parents had long set aside for his education. It was heavy with Mexican dollars, a currency commonly in use on the coast. His father had planned to use the money to ease Jason's return to America and for tuition. How would the reverend react to his son taking the money? Certainly not well. Nevertheless, he had gone this far; taking the money was absolutely necessary if he was going to carry out his plans. All he could do was to hope that his father would one day understand. It would now be Jason's own responsibility to earn the money for college. With that thought slightly easing his conscience, he quietly closed the strongbox and crept out the door afraid of discovery. The reverend had not slept well lately and might awaken at any moment. It was time to leave.

Twenty minutes later, he was at the harbor. From there it would be more difficult. The waterfront was filled with the usual Chinese junks, merchant ships, and even more Western gunships than the previous day. From Jason's vantage point, he could dimly see the colors of America, Britain, France, and Holland. Among the naval vessels, British and French colors shone brightly. But how could he get them to take him north? He'd spent part of the previous evening trying to come up with an appropriate approach. Now he had only to attempt it. He stood a few yards from one group of sailors standing on a dock arguing with some coolies. Apparently in charge was a young Englishman about twenty, clearly a class above the sailors. The argument seemed quite heated, both from the negotiations and the young officer's inability to communicate. One of the coolies spoke the sort of pidgin English common on the wharves, but the young officer, obviously new to China, couldn't understand a word the man said. It seemed the opening Jason was looking for.

"Excuse me, sir, could I be of service? I speak the language," Jason began as he pushed himself into the crowd.

"Speak the language—I'd not grace this heathen gibberish with the term," the young lieutenant shot back in irritation, and then, thinking again, he said, "Well, tell these heathens we'll give them two shillings a day, whatever that is in the local species, if they come aboard for a week." Jason explained the offer to the coolies, several of whom he'd seen working on the wharves since he was a child. As he spoke, he knew the young lieutenant was watching him carefully. Jason hoped he was coming to the desired conclusion.

"They want to know where they'll be going and what they'll be doing."

The lieutenant frowned. "Just tell them they'll work like the coolies they are, damned heathens, hauling our equipment around Guangzhou." Then, more to Jason than for translation, he said, "There's no telling what we'll find up north. They say the Cantonese really hate us, the devils."

Trying to convince the coolies to board the ship was not easy. Their leader wanted assurances from Jason that the foreigners only required haulers for the week. Jason understood their hesitation. He, too, had heard about coolies being kidnapped to work overseas. Men, sometimes even young scholars, were simply grabbed off the streets and crammed into the ship hulls until enough coolies were collected to make a run for Peru or Cuba.

"I understand your concern, but I think they are sincere. These are soldiers looking for temporary workers, not coolie merchants," Jason said.

Jason wondered if they would have believed him had they not seen him grow up around the wharves. For a fleeting second, he wished his father could see him negotiating, but then he thought again. The reverend could not possibly appreciate such an accomplishment.

A few moments more and the transaction was arranged. Fifteen coolies agreed to board the ship. As they marched aboard, the young officer turned to Jason.

"Who are you, boy, and where'd you learn the lingo?"

"My family's in the trade, sir. We arrange tea cargoes for the New England market. I'm just now on my way north to meet my father at the factories off Guangzhou." Jason hoped the lieutenant would believe him. The man was new to China and could hardly question him further. That would have been a problem, since Jason had never actually been north to see the warehouses used by those merchants involved in the Canton trade.

"You wouldn't be interested in sailing with us, would you? We're leaving for Guangzhou in an hour or so. We could use someone who knows the lingo. I'm sure the captain would consider it a fair trade—translations for your passage and board."

"Well, I suppose I could, sir. Would it be a bother?" Jason asked, delighted that his purse would remain sealed, at least for the moment.

"On the contrary, I'll just go have a talk with the captain myself." He walked off, delighted to share his discovery with the ship's captain. Nervously, Jason stood about in the morning cold. It had been some time since he left the house. His father might already have awakened and found the note. It wouldn't do to have a family acquaintance spot him leaving on the ship, either. The community was small, and Reverend Brandt's son was not unknown. Happily, his thoughts were interrupted by the lieutenant's whistle.

"Come aboard. So what is your name, anyway? We're to board together, the captain says." With enthusiasm, Jason bolted up the plank.

He often wondered later if, at that critical moment, he'd felt any ambivalence. But as far as Jason was ever able to remember, he'd felt nothing of the sort, only an incredible sense of exhilaration at the prospect of going to Guangzhou, and with work, as well. Once on board, he was required to direct the coolies toward their quarters for the upcoming trip. Actually, "quarters" was probably the wrong word, since the sailors had merely roped off a few square feet of deck space for them to huddle in during the voyage. Once that was arranged, Jason was forgotten by the young lieutenant and the rest of the crew.

He lay back on a pile of canvas and waited for the ship to cast off. Nervously Jason remained concerned that, having gotten so far, he'd be spotted before they left. He need not have worried. The crew was even more anxious to set off than he. Within an hour, the ship pulled slowly away from its mooring.

Once free of the island, Jason felt secure enough to explore the ship. It seemed far smaller than he had imagined. The crowd of men on deck made it seem even more packed. The English sailors were much like those he'd seen since childhood wandering the beaches and bars of Hong Kong. The sounds of the Cantonese gambling on deck hardly aroused his curiosity, either. Those images were far too familiar.

After a time, he decided to settle down for a nap, exhausted after the excitement of the morning. Before drifting off, he studied the faces of the Cantonese, whose presence had made possible his own passage. Although he had never actually spoken to any of them before, several were quite familiar to him. He'd often seen them working along the coast. Studying them now, more closely, he realized that something was unusual about one of them. Clearly a loner, yet dressed no differently than the others, one sat slightly to one side. It was clear he felt no kinship with the others. They in turn seemed to be ignoring him. From the fifteen feet or so that separated Jason from the coolies; he could still tell that the young man's hands and manner were quite different from the others, perhaps a man from the literati, from the intellectual elite. Yet if that were so, why was he here, living as a coolie? Jason wondered to himself, even as the growing heaviness of his eyes forced him to sleep. There would be time to speak to the boy later.

CHAPTER 2
ABOARD SHIP

J ason did not awaken until they were far north of Hong Kong and the sun so bright above as to make sleep impossible. Little seemed to have occurred while he slept. The English sailors and their Indian assistants had gone about their tasks, checking the various ropes, rummaging through storage bins on deck, and mopping the surface. Jason stood to one side by a cabin house, his presence for the moment unimportant. As he watched, he saw a large number of crates, unambiguously labeled "1 lb. shot"—obviously ammunition for small cannon, being prepared for disembarkation. It surely seemed they were expecting battle. The coolies still sat huddled in a corner created by the aft cabin and a small shed. A lively gambling circle had developed.

As Jason watched, it was all the more obvious that one fellow stood apart. He walked over to the boy and, leaning against the railing, tried to introduce himself.

"Excuse me, but you don't look like a Hong Kong laborer. Where are you from?" Jason asked, addressing the boy directly. The response was less than he had expected, much less. The boy merely leaned forward, grunted something, and proceeded to ignore him. He tried again:

"Excuse me, my Chinese is very poor and perhaps difficult to understand. My name is Jason. I am travelling north to Guangzhou, as you are. I am to serve as translator and should at least introduce myself." The boy didn't respond. Jason, for reasons he never quite understood, kept talking. "I am the son of a missionary from Victoria. I really shouldn't be here, but my father was about to send me off to America...so I just left."

Why had he said that? It was really stupid to advertise what he was doing even to the Chinese. But he had made an impact, an unexpected one. At the mention of his father, the young man shuddered to himself and appeared to try to make his body even smaller, crouching even lower on the deck.

"That one won't talk at all." It was one of the other coolies, an older man Jason had seen working on the wharves for years.

"He's not one of us, but we know his type. A gentry brat, though what this one's up to, we don't know." The young man sat unmoving, seemingly oblivious to the discussion. Jason remained there for another moment, and then returned to his own small territory across the deck. Dishonored over something, he assumed, but what?

For the rest of the voyage, Jason had little opportunity to approach the boy. Rather, his attention was demanded by the young officer whom he had originally approached and who now insisted on plying him with questions about China. Jason answered with enthusiasm. At home, his knowledge of Chinese customs had seemed more a point of shame than of pride to his father. Jason knew his father felt his son was not becoming the young New Englander he was meant to be. But here, at least this one officer, Hedrick Richards, seemed fascinated. Jason was particularly amused as the young man gingerly approached the subject of Chinese women and specifically of foot-binding. Jason's own knowledge was actually quite limited. Still he had managed a few close glances from time to time and now and then heard comments by the local Chinese.

13

Hedrick, however, was not in a position to question his information and eagerly passed on his own tales of India, where the young officer had recently served. Jason was particularly amazed by the tales of the Sati.

"It's outlawed, you know. But they still do it. Imagine the buggers actually burning their widows alive!" the young man exclaimed, partly horrified, partly fascinated. Jason himself was amazed, wondering if his father had heard of such things. For the rest of the voyage, forgetting the Chinese, Jason studied the Indians, wondering how they would explain the custom.

Finally, China recaptured his attention as the ship approached Guangzhou's walls. From the scene, it was obvious that the struggle was about to begin. The entire river was filled with English and French naval frigates. Huge amounts of equipment were being unloaded and carted inland by coolies. Jason could see that his ship was not the only one that had hired laborers in Hong Kong. He wondered how well the others would fare communicating with their temporary workers.

As it turned out, he did not have much time to speculate. The senior ship's officers soon emerged from below and gave him instructions. It would be many hours before he had a moment to himself. The morning was spent unloading the ship's equipment and carrying it to a depot established by the English and French officers who commanded the flotilla. As he supervised the coolies, Jason tried to remember what little French his father had taught him, for he soon realized that he would be more valuable as a translator if he could offer himself to the French, as well. With irritation, he thought of the many sessions with his father and old Jacques, a tutor his father had hired. The reverend had insisted, even as he had practically disdained Jason's Chinese language skills, that French would be invaluable back in college in New England. If only that hadn't been the reasoning, Jason thought to himself, he might have worked harder.

As he watched the coolies, though, Jason realized that he really wasn't sure what his plans were. He knew it was more than simply missing the boat for Boston or seeing the upcoming battle. What it was, however, he could hardly speculate. He only knew for certain that he would probably not see Boston, or for that matter Hong Kong, for a long time.

Suddenly, quite unexpectedly, for Jason's status hardly made him privy to military planning, the flotilla started to bombard Guangzhou. One shell after another crashed into the walled city. From Jason's vantage point, it was difficult to judge their impact. The noise was tremendous, though he had little time to contemplate the allied display of military might. He was kept busy most of the day translating for the several officers responsible for seeing that the coolies handled well the enormous amount of supplies shipped from Hong Kong. Jason was not the only one who spoke enough Chinese to communicate with the locals, but it was clear that his services were sorely needed.

One of the few memories of that day he later retained was of the young Chinese he'd approached on the boat. Working alongside the others and yet always somehow apart—something in the young man's look continued to attract Jason's interest. He had convinced himself by this time that the boy, like himself, was running away from home. Feeling thus that the two were under similar pressures, a kinship of circumstance, Jason tried several times to speak to the young Chinese, but each effort was rebuffed. That night, overcome with fatigue, Jason fell asleep curled on the ground in a blanket supplied by one of the ship's officers. Even the continuing thunder of the bombs failed to keep him from sleeping. After more than twelve hours of such noise, he'd become quite used to it.

The next morning, waking with a start, Jason realized that large numbers of fully armed soldiers were silently marching toward the city's walls. It was time. The assault was about to begin. His services not immediately required, Jason sat quietly watching the soldiers,

French, British and Indian troops, approaching the walls. Without thinking, Jason started to rise. No one seemed concerned by his action. Each man was involved with his own thoughts.

Jason moved slowly, occasionally half squatting in the dirt, gradually falling farther behind the soldiers. Yet he felt drawn forward by the deliberate, inexorable movement of the body of armed men. The troops' demeanor was spellbinding to Jason. They seemed almost casual, their weapons still slung over their shoulders, yet each walked with care, their bodies not quite upright, only somewhat crouched. It was hard not to follow them as they moved toward the walls, listening, no doubt, to the continuing sounds of artillery, which had shattered the eardrums almost incessantly since Jason had arrived. Suddenly, Jason bolted upright. This was why he had come. There was no reason to hang back, so off he went trying to catch up with the closest squad of soldiers. As he scuttled forward, he was aware that scores of Chinese civilians watched them. Not menacingly, but with considerable interest. He wondered if their neutrality would continue if the allied contingents were beaten back. He had already heard rough figures about the numbers of troops who had gathered for the assault. Some six thousand, they said, mostly British. And that against a city of more than a million! From the previous day's fighting, it was clear that if the Chinese soldiers weren't very energetic about fighting, the emperor's kinsmen, the Manchu troops, had been a formidable enemy, and the Europeans were fast coming to respect them.

But what would happen that morning was unclear. Would they be able to scale the walls, as was obviously planned? Even from his position a few hundred yards behind, Jason could see that many carried climbing ladders. Would they be long enough? The walls looked to be at least twenty-five feet high. If the ladders failed, it would be a bit late to call off the assault.

Without warning, Jason was slammed to the ground, his breath knocked out of him. His only sensation was that of a body lying on top of him. He began to cry out, but the ground exploded around him. His ears ringing with pain, Jason realized he was in the center of an artillery barrage. As he lost consciousness, he wondered if the guns were Chinese or European. "The little translator awakens." Those were the first words Jason was aware of as he regained consciousness.

"What happened? Where am I?" he asked as his vision cleared. There, seated before him, was the young Chinese loner from the coolie squad. His demeanor had changed.

"Are you all right?" the young man asked Jason with concern. "I thought you had gone to see your ancestors."

"I am fine. Did you push me down?"

"No…it was one of them." He pointed to one of the other coolies, now sitting, eating noodles a few feet away. "We followed you. It wasn't too smart to follow those soldiers. You could have been killed."

"Thank you. Why are you suddenly so friendly?" Jason asked, intrigued with the sudden change in the young man's manner.

"Maybe because everything has changed. My small problems, even my having dishonored my family in the civil service exams, seem of minor importance in the face of all this. That's why, you know, I was with the coolies when you saw me. I couldn't go home, having failed my family."

Their discussion was interrupted by the approach of another shell. It exploded not more than a hundred feet from them, sending dirt and other materials into the air. Lowering their heads, the two scanned the city, trying to understand what was going on. Had the English and their French allies already scaled the walls? Were they inside? There was no way of knowing.

Jason got up and started slowly forward. He had to see. His new acquaintance reluctantly followed alongside.

"You're going to get both of us killed," the Cantonese youth whispered into his ear.

"You're probably right," Jason responded and kept going. If he were going to hold back, he might as well have stayed with his father in Hong Kong. The thought of Reverend Brandt caught him by surprise. His father surely knew by now of his departure and would perhaps already have made plans to follow. Jason wondered if the old man would arrive in Guangzhou to confront him. What would he say? He'd much rather tell him of the previous day's events than argue over going to America. Jason knew by this time that would be impossible. Next year, maybe, but for the moment there was nothing his father could say sufficient to persuade him to turn back.

As they approached the walls, Jason was startled from his thoughts. "Halt there. Who are you, boy? What's that Chinaman doing with you?" It was an English soldier, fat and drunk.

"There's nothing to see here, boy. We've taken the walls, and these precincts have been plucked clean. Now there's nothing worth grabbing till we get inside."

Apparently, the fighting was over for the moment. The soldiers, some of them with minor wounds, were anxious to loot. Jason, aware that his presence now seemed to make the young Cantonese feel more secure, nodded at the soldier and kept walking. They were within view of the city walls. He could see scores of soldiers standing on them, staring down into it. Would they now lower themselves into the city?

"Ho there. Young Jason, that be your name, isn't it?"

Jason looked up to see the young officer, Hedrick, hailing him from the walls.

"You down there! Let the boy up. We can use him," he yelled to those below. It was obvious that he was to climb the ladders. Jason turned back to his friend, but the young Cantonese had disappeared. Jason looked around for a moment, glancing at the piles of military equipment, milling soldiers, and the occasional wounded. It was clear that few Europeans had been hurt in the assault.

"Jason, hurry up. We've a city to capture." Forgetting the Cantonese boy for the moment, Jason scurried the last steps to the walls and climbed up a ladder. Once on the top, the entire sweep of Guangzhou lay before him. The walls were easily thick enough to hold the scores of men who stood upon them, gazing below. Most of the buildings, save those few that looked a bit more official, were single storied. Although most of the streets were terribly narrow and confined, Jason could see several open spaces. The sellers and pedestrians one might expect were nowhere to be seen. Obvious damage from the days of shelling was visible.

"Jason, if you still want work, there will be plenty for you in the next few months. There are millions of these heathens, and if I'm right, we've hardly anyone who speaks this dog lingo. I've seen only one of the diplomatic people translating, and I doubt there will be more." Hedrick spread his arms wide, as if to express the dimensions of the situation.

"We could be here for months. Someone of your talents will be needed, if your father can spare you. Do you want me to talk to my captain?"

It was the offer Jason had hoped for. To have work and possibly even a bed for the following months would allow him to avoid spending the money he'd taken from his father's strongbox. He might, after all, still need it for a trip to America the following year.

"That would be good of you, sir," he answered, trying not to reveal the excitement in his voice. Ohio seemed farther away than ever. Looking down into the city, he wondered how the people felt, looking up and seeing the foreigners on the walls.

Jason had never visited Guangzhou before. All he knew of it was hearsay from foreigners angry that the city's inhabitants had long refused to allow them to enter. And that, in defiance of the treaties signed at the conclusion of the Opium War. As he stared down into the city, Jason thought for a moment about Viceroy Ye. Was he in the city itself? Was he down there, fearing what would happen next to the city for which he had so long been responsible? Then, turning around, Jason stared down among the ruins and military equipment that seemed to fill the space before the city walls. His friend, the young Cantonese, was gone. Where had he disappeared to? Would he see him again? Finally, rousing himself from his thoughts, he turned to the young officer who had asked for his assistance. They were already bringing up material with the aid of the coolies. Jason was needed.

For the rest of the afternoon, Jason helped direct the coolies. More ships were being unloaded and temporary camps set up nearer the walls. As yet, no effort had been made to enter the city itself. For those among them who watched the inhabitants from the city walls, all seemed ominously silent. Only occasionally did one see movement—a figure darting furtively from building to building. No doubt, those below were waiting in considerable anxiety.

"Jason." The voice, Hedrick again, roused him from his concentration.

"We need your language skills. Forget these heathens for a minute and follow me. Captain Tracy wants to speak with you."

Jason stalled for a moment, giving the brightest seeming of the laborers some general instructions, and then set off after Hedrick. It was important, he knew, to make himself as valuable as possible. They did not have far to go. Jason was ushered into a poorly lit tent, where a Manchu soldier squatted on the floor looking frightened.

"Good. You have him. So let's see if he can get anything out of this heathen." Jason had hardly a moment to study the man who spoke. He was an English officer, about forty, with squinty, mean eyes and a patch of jet-black hair. From behind the captain, another officer, apparently French, sat quietly surveying the scene and sipping from a glass. For a moment Jason thought of asking for something to refresh himself but thought better of it. The English officer, Tracy, did not appear to be the hospitable type.

"So you're an American, eh, boy? Lieutenant Richards tells me you speak this dog talk. Tell him we want to know where his boss is. We want to know where that dog Viceroy Ye is, and I'm in no mood for stalling."

"*Néih hóu ma,*" Jason started off in his best Cantonese, hoping an effort at being polite would help. It didn't. The fellow was in no mood for pleasantries.

"The officer says you must tell us where the viceroy is."

The man remained silent, staring deeply into Jason's eyes, with neither anger nor warmth. Jason wondered what he was thinking. Then, from behind him, a loud crack and the Manchu's face twisted in anguish, his body shuddering involuntarily in pain. Tracy had kicked him violently in the kneecap.

"Ask him again!" the officer blurted.

"You can see what is happening. You must tell them what they want." Jason's throat was suddenly parched. "The city is taken. They hold the walls. Tell them where Ye is." Still, the eyes, as black as coal, erased of pain or any other feeling, stared up at him. Captain Tracy had begun to pace angrily.

"*Mon ami,* I have seen this man destroy Russian soldiers at Sevastopol. You better tell him that our campaign in the Crimea has made Captain Tracy very impatient with interrogations." So the Frenchman had more of a role than sipping wine. Jason turned back to the prisoner.

"Crack." Again Tracy's foot struck out, this time at the prisoner's right shin. Once again a flash of agony crossed his face. Then, as he regained his composure, nothing.

"Do you have to do that, sir?" Jason asked, terribly upset with his role in the torture.

"Boy, do your job; get the truth out of him, and there'll be no torture," Tracy answered abruptly.

"Look, you have got to tell them." Studying the prisoner, Jason tried another tack. "Where is your family home? What province are you from?"

The prisoner now, for the first time, looked uncertain. What harm could there be in such a question?

"We're from north of Guangzhou."

"And your home is a prosperous one?"

"We have our stipend from the government and a small business."

"What does the bugger say?" Tracy demanded, hearing the beginnings of a dialogue.

"Wait a moment," Jason replied quietly, intent on continuing his own approach.

"And your father, does he have many sons?"

"Many sons, but only me from his wife. The concubine's offspring hardly count." He was answering, perhaps only to put off continuation of the blows.

"And your father, does he expect you to serve his ghost upon death? To make the appropriate sacrifices, as required by the Master?"

At this, the young man's eyes narrowed. He now understood where the conversation was going.

"Listen to me," Jason insisted, his voice becoming more earnest. "This man will kill you. Your father will have no one to honor him. Your family name will be gone. They ask only that you tell us of the viceroy's location. Is he still in the city?" He could see that he had made his point.

"This one only knows that the viceroy was unable to leave."

"He says Ye is still within the city walls," Jason almost shouted. It was obvious another moment would have seen resumption of the torture. Captain Tracy visibly relaxed. There would be a few moments of lesser tension.

"Ask him where the sonofabitch is now!" shouted the officer.

"I don't know, but he's probably still in his yamen...the official residence." The Manchu was finally talking readily. Within minutes the yamen's location was described on a map drawn on the dirt floor. Tracy, the French officer, and Hedrick, who had remained silent in the background, seemed pleased. The tension was over.

22

"Thank you, boy. We'll be talking later. Hedrick tells me you're looking for work. Is that true?"

"It is, sir."

"Fine. There will be plenty of it, I can assure you. Just stick around."

"Lieutenant. Make sure the boy has a place to sleep, and access to the mess halls." Then, turning once more toward Jason, he said, "There's only one thing, boy. No looting. It's going to stop. I don't care what the men think. Until we leave this place, we're in charge, and we can't keep the entire population under control with such doings. Remember that, boy, because I'm going to start shooting a few people to make my point. You don't want to be one of them. Besides, I need you, for the moment." With that, he indicated the tent flap; Jason exited as quickly as possible.

While he had been in the tent, Jason's eyes had adjusted to the dimmer light of the interior. Now, as he emerged into the bright light of Guangzhou's midafternoon, he was temporarily blinded. Standing there covering his face just beyond the tent, he waited for his vision to clear. A moment later, he was comfortable again and started back toward his coolie gang. Several more had rejoined the group. The rest of the day was spent continuing the work of organizing the baggage handlers.

His young Cantonese friend had returned as well. Though they spoke little that afternoon, Jason had the opportunity to watch him closely. It was obvious that the fellow had little experience at hard labor. Though his fellows easily hauled the boxes from the ships, and carried without difficulty the barrels of provisions, the young man breathed heavily. Even from Jason's distance, it was easy to see that his hands were showing the growth of deep blisters. Again, as on the ship, the young man spoke little with the other coolies. The distance that separated them had not lessened. The only comments Jason heard at all were jokes about the fellow's lack of physical prowess. Nevertheless, though the comments were often cruel, Jason could tell that the others retained a certain awe of the boy. Whatever had occurred to allow such a fall from the world of the gentry notwithstanding, they all understood he was different, and perhaps not to be trifled with. Besides, Jason speculated, perhaps they feared that the fellow might still have powerful friends. Jason himself, though, was powerfully drawn to him on his own account. In Hong Kong, he had known many local workers, certainly more than his father would have liked. Of the gentry, however, Jason knew almost nothing. All he really understood was his father's hatred of them.

According to Reverend Brandt, it was well known that without the animosity of the Confucian leaders, the Chinese masses could be easily converted to the true faith. It was only the stubborn gentry who propagandized against the missionaries, accusing them of activities even his father refused to discuss. According to the reverend, there was simply no way to please the gentry. If one served as a teacher, helped organize social activities, or even protected one's converts, the gentry felt threatened. They simply would not accept the truth of God's teaching that China had to be changed for its own good that otherwise they would all go to hell, to burn in torment forever.

"If the gentry would only accept the necessity of change, all would be better," the reverend had constantly intoned.

As Jason reflected on the many discussions he had heard between his father and his fellow missionaries, he knew there was more to it. Even the coolies found the Christians objectionable. One had even asked him whether it was true Christians forgot their ancestors, and ate blood. Jason remembered being shocked at the question, and at the unusual temerity required to ask it. He sat reflecting for a moment on his effort to justify his, and perhaps his father's attitudes, toward ancestor worship; and with more difficulty to explain the symbolism, rather than literal cannibalism, of the communion. The coolie had listened, but with a look more skeptical than convinced.

But all that had been nothing compared to actually talking with a member of the gentry and learning about his life. Jason looked forward eagerly to questioning the young man. If he were to make it on his own, Jason understood he had to know more of China. It was a way to make himself more valuable to potential employers.

Still he felt it best to avoid approaching the fellow too openly. He had already come to understand that showing too much friendship with the Chinese would raise suspicions among the very English and French officers whom he wished to please. In that, the camp seemed little different from his father's home.

CHAPTER 3

A NEW FRIEND

That evening, after Jason had labored to swallow the hard-tack lieutenant Richards had given him, he set out to look for the young Cantonese. Getting started though had been difficult. Hedrick, as he told Jason to address him, wanted to talk. So Jason had stayed for a time, listening to Hedrick's homesick chatter about England; about how much he loved the small country town near Dover, where he had grown up, and of his family. As they talked, they sat near a group of common soldiers and partially listened to their conversations as well.

"I can tell you, at home I would not speak to such as them, even for a moment," Hedrick commented quietly, gesturing toward the soldiers. "And here, at least, I don't have to socialize with them. They follow orders, and if they're lucky, they can get back to the East End slum that spawned them."

As Jason sat there impatiently, his eyes wandered over the collection of tents and seated groups that dotted the area before the walls. He could hear the lively sounds of French coming from one of the encampments, the voices both humorous and dogmatic. Even closer, the dark Indians brought over from Calcutta sat tightly around campfires, talking quietly among themselves.

For Jason, it was clear that of those groups that surrounded him, he really only felt comfortable with one, and it was certainly not the British; neither the young aristocrat, Hedrick, nor his troops. The Indians were simply a question in his mind, more Western looking than the Chinese but even more mysterious. No, only with the Chinese did he feel any affection or familiarity. After enduring more of Hedrick's homesickness, he finally excused himself and drifted away from the campsite.

It took only a few minutes to accomplish his goal. His own coolie gang had encamped only a few feet from their last assignment. At something of a distance from them sat the young man Jason now knew to be of the family of Wu. He approached him and sat down. The fellow was slowly eating from a bowl of rice and looking out toward the city walls.

Wu looked up with a shy smile. "There is plenty of good rice tonight. No millet for us. Your barbarian friends took what they cared about but left the rice stocks available for the picking. For us, it will be quite enough. Do you want some?" Wu gestured.

Retrieving his bowl from his shoulder bag, Jason took a portion and ate it slowly, savoring the flavor and allowing it to push from his tongue the taste of beef jerky, which had formed the bulk of his dinner.

"So tell me, friend, as you began this morning. Why are you here? You are obviously of the gentry."

Wu stared at him, reflecting for a moment.

"Of the gentry…well, perhaps my family has such pretensions, but not for long. I was supposed to continue my family's place among the literati, but my failure—no, it was worse than that; my most blameworthy carelessness has destroyed everything now. I'll never pass the examinations; never become the respected official everyone in my family expected."

Wu's chin tucked in, and his lips briefly pinched together, an expression of distaste.

"A barbarian like you could never hope to understand. Though you speak the language of the Han, it's the patois of Hong Kong coolies, not of gentlemen."

Jason was put off but started again. "I know my Chinese is not refined, that I speak the language of the uncouth. But I would like to learn. In fact, I would like you to serve as my teacher."

"Your intentions are honorable, but I am not the proper guide. To merely assume such a role is to dishonor it with my identification."

Despite an apparent willingness to continue, the fellow turned away from Jason, seeming to contemplate the scene, rapidly changing in the fading light of twilight. It appeared he was momentarily overcome with emotion. Jason considered asking another question but thought better of it. They sat in silence, both studying a distant pagoda's faint image, which stretched upward, somewhat to their left.

"I'm from a village a few miles from here. My family isn't rich, but there have been several high-degree holders. And once, during the reign of Qianlong, even a jinshi, the highest imperial degree."

Jason listened silently, unsure of Qianlong's era but afraid to interrupt.

"My father is very old. I was the only child. He spent everything on preparing me for the exams, and now…" The voice trailed off.

"Only one child, isn't that unusual for a Chinese family?" Jason asked, hoping to pick up the momentum again.

"Well, only one boy. I have five older sisters. Girls don't count. They can't bring great honor to the family in the exams. They're never really part of the household; they're raised only for some other household. If you can't understand that, you can never see the true path."

Jason blinked, and then bit his lip. If he were to learn from the young man, he would have to be as humble as one expected of a Chinese student.

"Since I was three years old, my family has prepared me for the exams. I can still remember the first characters I learned. Not one more than seven strokes, and their message:

Let us present our work to father.
Confucius himself
taught three thousand…
Seventy were capable gentlemen.
You young scholars,
eight or nine!
Work well to attain virtue,
and you will understand propriety.

Wu then hummed to himself as he traced the characters in the dirt. Jason's verbal skills were impressive indeed, but he had never seriously begun the effort to learn to read and write Chinese. Staring down at the characters, he remembered, for a moment, his conversation the year before, with his father. Jason had come home anxious to learn to write Chinese. The old man would have none of it.

"How many times have I told you, your life's not here! You'll be needing French far more than this gibberish; and besides, the Bible's already been rendered into Chinese by Reverend Morrison. There's no more work to be done on that score." Jason had argued that the Church needed men who could write tracts on the gospels in Chinese, but Reverend Brandt remained steadfast.

"It's just a ruse, boy; you're no more willing to do the Lord's work than to attend services for your own blessed soul." The old man had paused for a moment, as if reflecting. "And for that, I blame only myself. I have kept you in this heathen land too long." The conversation had ended in another of their arguments, and in a renewal of the reverend's letter-writing campaign in search of an appropriate, affordable American college. Nothing had come of Jason's plan. For the young American, the characters remained as much a mystery as ever.

"It makes me sad, even as I remember my training," continued the young Cantonese. "My parents sent me to the clan school. After I had mastered the Primer of a Thousand Characters, we would sit every day in front of Wang Laoshi, Teacher Wang, reciting the *Analects* over and over. With the book closed and open we'd sit, reciting the text. Zhu, my friend, was always inattentive. Sometimes Wang Laoshi would hit him with the fan-shaped ruler, and remind us that 'if education is not strict, it shows the teacher is lazy.' Wang, with his thin moustache and beady eyes, wasn't going to let that be thought of him. He liked to act the great lord over all of us, because he'd passed the first level of exams...but to us, that was nothing. I would achieve glory in Beijing in the final imperial examinations. I wonder what he thinks of me now?" The boy's voice trailed off for a moment.

The light of day was gone. The scatter of campfires among the tents lit groups of men engaged in eating and cleaning equipment.

"So you're one of the missionaries of the barbarian religion?" Wu asked.

"Not me; my father is a missionary." As an afterthought, he said, "I'm not sure what I am, or will be."

"And will your father come after you? I remember what you said on the barbarian ship."

"Maybe. I think so. I am not looking forward to that."

"And will you return home if he requires it?"

"I don't know."

"It is a grave thing to disobey one's father...at least it is among my people," Wu said seriously.

"It is to us as well. But tell me of your efforts in the exams," Jason requested sincerely, with an enthusiasm born of the desire to move the conversation away from his father.

"If you wish. It is a long story, and I suppose not a unique one. From eight to fifteen, I studied constantly, spending most of my time learning the sacred texts of the Master, and practicing the hundreds of new characters we learned day by day."

Hugging his knees, Wu brought his head down at an odd angle, his eyes losing focus overwhelmed by the still-painful memories. Finally, he began again.

"Sometimes I wanted to run away…to spend time in Guangzhou watching the barbarians, your people…and hearing tales of the long-haired rebels fighting to the north. But mostly, I stayed in my place alongside the other students. My family made it somewhat easier. It was said that I was brilliant, that I would bring great honor to the entire household, and someday even build a magnificent ancestral hall in honor of being named a high official." He stopped, seeming lost in some forgotten dream.

"We boys even had a poem we would recite to remind us of what study could make possible.

To enrich your family, no need to buy good land:
Books hold a thousand measures of grain.
For an easy life, no need to build a mansion:
In books are found houses of gold.
Going out, be not vexed by lack of a good go-between.
In books there are girls with faces of Jade.
A boy who wants to become a somebody
Devotes himself to the classics,
Faces the window, and reads.

"Once when we told Wang Laoshi our poem, he scolded us severely. The classics were to cultivate our crude souls, not to lead us to women and pleasure. If passing the exams brought such things, still, he said, no one should pass who could possibly care about such insignificance. He went on and on, but I thought that he, too, had probably liked the poem during his own youth. Did I tell you how old the man was?"

"No."

"Very old! They say he was already a student when the emperor Qianlong still lived." Apparently the age of Qianlong was quite distant. Jason, still not having the slightest idea when that was, merely nodded and tried to look impressed.

"It was terribly important that I begin well. Though my friends bought every preparation book and model answer pamphlet they could find, I hardly ever looked at them. If those model answers could really help, everyone would pass. I knew there was no easy way. I worked as hard as I possibly could. One summer my family even used the proceeds from a good harvest to have me study with a retired official, a jinshi from the fourth year of Daoguang. Everything was going wonderfully. Finally, it was time to start the district exams. I knew I was ready. My only fear was that my grandfather might die before the tests began. I would hardly be allowed to take the exam if I were in mourning."

What I remember most was sitting there in the huge examination hall, not only with my friends and classmates but with a host of other locals whose faces I hardly remembered. The older men had shaved their beards, trying to look as young as possible. It was said that the youngest were given the easiest questions. Those fellows, to a man, had already flunked before, and hardly wanted more difficult questions." His voice was getting more enthusiastic as he told his tale.

Pausing, Wu seemed to look within himself. Gradually his brows came together, and his normally expressive features seemed to pucker, as if he tasted a sour, repressed memory.

"Did you know, they say that the bandit Heavenly King of the Taiping long hairs took the exams five times? And flunked them every time! No wonder he started a revolution!" Wu's mood seemed to lighten. The black eyes flashed in amusement as he commented on the leader of the movement, which Jason vaguely knew to be tearing the country apart in the regions to the north of Guangzhou.

"I remember sitting there with my ink stone, a gift from my *Yeh-yeh*, grandfather, and the brushes, and lunch. I even had a bowl to relieve myself. My *Mei-mei*, little sister, had giggled when she saw it, but one could hardly take the time to relieve oneself. We sat there in incredible tension. Those who accompanied us left. Finally, the first questions were carried around the room on a placard. What I remember most is not the question, for it was an easy one from the *Analects*, but the suppressed sighs of relief or pain as my comrades recognized the question, or not. I, though, could not have been more confident. I started immediately, stalling only for a moment, to remind myself to use my best calligraphy. For, in my enthusiasm for the answer, I might forget the necessity of making my characters as perfect as possible. Almost an hour later, I recall looking up at the face of my cousin, his sheet blank. I hurt a moment for him; still, it was marvelous to feel so prepared myself.

"The rest of the afternoon was made tense only by the incessant humming of one of my neighbors. We were supposed to compose a poem as part of the examination; no doubt his constant mumbling helped him form the work. It is well known that one can be dismissed for such obnoxious habits, but no one from the yamen said a thing. Still, my work proceeded. When it grew dark, and our papers were stamped, I had to wait a long time for a group of fifty to gather so we would be allowed to leave. As we stood there, one sensed both excitement and exhaustion. Among the oldest, especially those newly shaven, there was more tension; and for some, pained discouragement. I was young. There would be other exams to take, but for them, time was growing short. Their chances for an official career grew less each year. Actually, I was only slightly aware of them. I had done well. I could feel it."

Wu leaned back and folded his arms across his stomach. He gazed heavenward, reliving the moment. He straightened, leaned forward, grasping his knees in recalled excitement. In the flickering light of the campfires, Wu's face seemed to provide its own radiance.

"When the results were announced, I was in ecstasy. A rumor had come to our compound. The results would be posted. I could hardly contain myself as I left for the yamen. The women of the household said nothing, merely watching closely as I prepared to go. Only *Yeh-yeh* commented that the family's honor went with me."

Wu paused and directed an imperious gaze at Jason. "The family honor! What can you know of family honor, barbarian!"

Jason masked his irritation. He tried relaxing his rigid form, his hand stroking air in a calming motion. "Family honor is everything, I know, much more so than anywhere else I know..."

Wu relaxed, displaying once again a wry, sad smile. "That was not necessary, for me to suddenly..." He shrugged, "I was rude, forgive me." His eyelids seemed heavy with pain. "A wound occasionally acts up, bringing forth inappropriate sentiments."

Like a dog shaking wet fur, Wu shook himself briefly. Finally, a smile returned and he continued his narrative.

"The crowd was already huge when I arrived, and not only with those of us who had taken the examinations. Many of the candidates were there with their entire families. The lower classes milled around as well, for they knew that at least for some families there would soon be a time of rejoicing certainly an auspicious moment to order gifts from the merchants present. I suppose that some in the crowd were thieves and pickpockets as well, but that hardly mattered. As I got there, the yamen doors opened and out stepped two rotund officials carrying the scrolls. Try as I might, I could not at first push forward enough to see the names posted in the traditional circular fashion on the walls. The sheets were large enough, but the crowd was too enormous. Once those in front found the names they were searching for, a torrent of voices rose. Not just the excited whispering of the previous few moments but real cries of anguish and, more quietly, of pleasure. As always, many had failed, and the usual mumbling about the officials grew rather louder than appropriate. At last, some pulled back, away from the wall; I was able to inch forward. Finally standing before the sheet, being pushed from behind, I stared at the posters, searching throughout the circle for my name and the red dot that indicated success. For a moment I could not find it; I felt the first tremors of panic, and then, hearing my name mumbled aloud, I looked at the top position. I had won first place!"

His voice, after the energy of his exclamation, trailed off. Again obviously reliving, briefly, the feelings of fulfillment, of pride hard earned, that had swept through him at the time. Jason watched him closely, fascinated with the story, with a view of a life so different from those of the coolies he had known.

"I just felt numb...staring for a moment, to be certain...and then falling back into the crowd. I think a few friends, and perhaps some relatives, patted me on the back as I retreated from the wall, but I'm not sure. I had gained first position. My rise had begun. What would *Yeh-yeh* say? As I emerged from the crowd, I saw one of our servants hurrying off. So they would know by the time I returned! That would be even nicer. I walked quite slowly...not really speaking to those who called out to me as I proceeded home to our compound.

Books hold a thousand measures of gain.
In books are found houses of gold.

"I'm not sure why I thought of those lines, but I did. Over the next several days, we took more exams, but they were as nothing. I was as ready as I could be. I remember only praying that I would not make an error on the *Sacred Edicts*, for the works of emperors

Kangxi and Yongzheng could hardly be reproduced with an error. I had often heard that doing so might end your chances of ever taking the exams again. But even that went well. I passed everything and was ready for the qualifying examination. The only question was when the director of studies would arrive. They said he had been in the capitol, conferring at the Board of Rites.

"Still the exams would soon continue. At least for those of us remaining in the competition. Guangzhou is a great city, and we have many fine scholars, so there are many families with capable students. I spent my days studying and listening to the hopes of my family. No fears invaded my nights. The only unpleasantness was on those occasions when I happened to pass some of the older men who had once again flunked, their attempts to hide their graying beards having been of no avail. They now walked about, their faces covered by stubby new growths, which spoke sadly but eloquently of their despair. Many looked far older, weighed down, almost broken. I remember wondering if flunking the third time was easier, or perhaps even more difficult than the first. Such men occasionally gathered in the teahouses and commiserated with each other, making charges about the probable dishonesty of the examination graders. It was well known that sometimes only the least qualified, the least important, were released by their superiors to grade the exams. Sometimes the embittered ones made sure that their voices were loud enough to be heard by those of us practicing *t'ai ch'i* in the courtyards. However, that was only a means of expressing their bitterness toward those of us who had placed well while they had flunked.

"Once the examination official arrived, we successful ones would continue the path toward the *jinshi*. In those days, I indulged in extraordinary flights of fancy. To travel all the way to Beijing, and take the final examinations at the palace! To be honored all over the realm. What, though, did I know?" Jason saw his face twist in pain, his eyes cast down. "This one was too proud."

Jason and Wu were distracted by the sounds of yelling in the distance, the shrill cries of an enraged old woman, screaming at the top of her lungs. Her speech, though Cantonese, was so emotion laden that even Jason had trouble understanding her.

"She says she has been robbed, that the money for her son's funeral is gone. That the foreign soldiers took it." Even as they listened, two English soldiers rushed past them, shushing each other as they ran. There was little either Jason or his friend could have done. It was over in a minute. The two plunderers were long gone, and even the voice of the old woman, whom they had never actually seen, quieted to an occasional groan that cut the night. Within minutes, the earlier hum of conversation from the various camps began again. Everything was as it had been.

"We have a saying, 'You don't make nails out of good iron, nor soldiers out of good men.' Perhaps it is that way among your people as well?" Jason thought for a moment of explaining the difference between Americans and English but thought better of it. Under the circumstances, it seemed a minor point indeed. For a moment, he reflected whether Hedrick was involved in looting as well, but then, remembering the tale, asked again what had occurred at the next qualifying examination.

"They, too, had begun well. The Director of Studies arrived. Many of us students, at least the youngest of us, followed his sedan chair, as he and the prefect visited the Temple of the Master. Once there, with great drama he lectured us on the classics. I don't remember a thing he said, except the date of the official examinations. Four days later, at the third cannon shot, we were ready. It was an event of great commotion. Officials arrived from everywhere, and the yamen clerks started checking through everyone's goods. They were looking for reference books, cheating sheets, even for money one might bribe with. It was already very tense, especially after they found something hidden in the robes of a young man who stood no more than twenty feet from me. I never saw what it was, but the clerks were furious and dragged the young man out by his pigtails. It was scary. It seemed to take forever, but we were finally certified as officially qualified to take the exam. Then I got my answer sheet and seat allocation. I wrote my name, it was sealed, and that was it. Until it was all over, I would merely be a number. I remember putting it into the deepest recess of my sleeve. If I lost the number, all would be lost.

"We sat there as the officials prepared the examination. I already knew I couldn't change seats, hum, or even drop my paper, but now I spotted a special seal indicating that one had been spotted gazing about. It was incredible. The clerks carried a whole set of seals to stamp on our papers. It wouldn't mean a failure, but a judge could hardly ignore an answer with so prominent a seal affixed to it, attesting to the candidate's poor behavior. I was terrified, and did no more than stare straight at my writing table.

"Again, the exams went on for days. I passed the first set and went on to the last part of the series. Finally, the last formal session arrived. I had made it. I was sure of it. We had only to do a section of the five classics, and I had even been told that the results were rarely stressed. Not at that late date in the process. I wrote out the section from the *Sacred Edict* with a light heart, and left the session filled with pride. It was certain that I would go to the provisional examination. It was certain the palace examination would eventually follow. I had visions of myself one day a viceroy," Wu commented.

"My only sadness was that such officials could never serve in their home provinces. How proud my parents would be, in either case. The moments passed slowly while we waited for the crowd of fifty to gather.

"My confidence never wavered during the entire time it took for the graders to make their decisions. Unlike my friends, for me the days passed quickly." Wu raised his palms and face to the sky, the picture of disgust. "I was so stupid! Finally, it was time. The prefect responsible for the announcement left his yamen. He was in full ceremonial robes, and was preceded by the sounds of musicians I remember knowing some of them toward the prefectural school. The three cannon shots were, to me, the sounds of my triumph. But then, the lists, the announcements, I was not among them! Not listed as a *shengyuan*, official student, the first level of the exams! I didn't understand. What had happened? I ran desperately to the one yamen clerk I knew slightly, begging him to discover the error. I couldn't go home until it was cleared up! He took pity on me, or at least he was willing to accept the small sum I had brought with me to buy rice cakes for the celebration. Even as I stood there, feeling my mouth as dry as I had ever felt it, I could see the runners heading toward the compounds of the successful candidates. The messengers had reason to hurry, for they knew a handsome tip awaited them. My own father had been discussing it even as I had set out what seemed like eons before.

"Let me see your seat number again." Wu handed it to the clerk, studying his face for a clue.

"It is as I guessed. It was rumored that someone had miswritten the sacred characters of the emperor. There it is. To have shown such disrespect." He walked off fingering the coppers I had given him. I felt myself sinking to the ground. A rough stone slab brushed my side as I contemplated his words. The *Sacred Edict*, how could I have made such a mistake? I'd practiced the characters a thousand times!"

"But what had you done? I don't understand. Couldn't you just have taken the examination again, the next time?" Jason was thoroughly perplexed.

"You don't understand; with any other error, perhaps something could have been salvaged; but not that. I had miswritten the great Kangxi's own essay. Nothing could be so terrible. It might be years before I could take the exams again they say that sometimes one might never again be able to compete. It's simply not so easy as to try again. My name is marked. I insulted the ancestor of the Sun of Heaven!"

"What did your parents say?"

"I don't know. I had dishonored them all. I never went back. Perhaps they think I killed myself. I have been wandering for months, mostly among the coolies in Hong Kong. I don't really even know why I got on the ship with the other coolies. But I thought that here, at least, I could discreetly learn of my family's welfare."

"Will you contact them?" Jason asked.

"Never."

CHAPTER 4

GUANGZHOU

Over the next several days, Jason spoke little with his friend Wu. The latter was busy with the coolie gang, and Jason himself, concerned about too obvious an association with the Chinese, was careful to remain somewhat aloof in the presence of the other Westerners. Wu seemed to understand and was not resentful during their occasional evening chats under the cover of darkness.

Within a week of the capture of the city walls, the allied commanders decided the time was finally right to enter Guangzhou the city the Westerners knew as Canton. Other reports had confirmed the Manchu soldier's story. It seemed that the Qing officials responsible for the town had delayed too long in departing and were themselves still within the city. On the morning of the fifth, less than a week into the new year of 1858, Jason was approached by Hedrick.

"Ho there, Jason. Did you hear the news? We're going in! Do you want to come along?" he asked loudly.

Jason, delighted that he had been invited, leaped at the chance. "You mean as a translator?"

"No, we'll not be needing you for that. Mr. Parkes—he's with the consular service—will be there, and he speaks the lingo. No,

I mean just come along with me. The others won't mind, and besides you can at least tell us what's going on."

"Let's go." Jason saw no reason to delay and set off after Hedrick, who had already started back toward his billet. The next hours were slow in passing. Jason had nothing to do, save watch Hedrick giving orders to his men and occasionally consulting with the senior officers who stood at the flap of their command tent. Edging closer to the entrance, Jason could hear the voices from within. They were a combination of English and French and what seemed to be a single voice making an effort to translate. They were arguing about tactics for making their entrance. The French were emphasizing the necessity of making a show of it.

"We must not forget…" stressed the French officer, "that we are a mere few thousand men holding captive a city of a million. If the Chinese are not continually awed by our military presence, a disaster could occur." Agreement finally was reached and the voices calmed as more minor details were worked out.

Suddenly the tent opened. A tall officer of the British naval service exited and nodded in the direction of Hedrick and a number of others. Almost immediately several hundred soldiers gathered and started off toward the walls. Among them, near the front, was a young Englishman, clearly a civilian, probably the translator, Parkes. As they moved out, Jason looked to Hedrick, who was frantically trying to catch his attention.

"Come on, stay near the rear but get moving. The fun is about to start!"

Jason, falling in behind the troops, was conscious of the stares of the many Chinese by whom they marched. Most were the Hong Kong coolies whom he had seen for days. Others, clearly locals, now less frightened by the foreigners, crowded near the marchers to see them off. It was only a few minutes' walk to the walls, and Jason, even from his vantage point, could see that an advance party had already descended into the city and opened the gates.

As they marched in, Jason noticed a change in sound. Where, up to that moment, crowds of excited Chinese had created a true hum, now all was silent within the city walls. Of the life of the streets—vendors, acupressurists, haircutters, and beggars—none were present. As they marched he noticed an occasional eye watching them from windows covered by cloth, but even that was rare. The entire city seemed to be holding its collective breath. After almost a week of waiting, the foreigners, those who had lobbed so many shells into the city, were now entering. Remembering the stories from the Hong Kong wharves, Jason wondered if the residents assumed they would all be killed. He wondered what thoughts must be passing behind the silent walls. After a time, the column started to slow. He had not questioned the march to that point. Only then did it occur to him that he hadn't known their destination. Now it was obvious. They had arrived at the official yamen. A few minor mandarins stood nervously near the gate, obviously waiting. Parkes spoke quietly to them and then a more limited group prepared to enter as the rest of the troops arranged themselves in the vicinity of the yamen.

"Jason, come on. Follow closely. Don't say a word," Hedrick whispered.

Passing into the outer courtyard of the yamen, Jason and the others looked in amazement at the beauty of the official residence. Everyone was quite polite. Jason, too far to the rear to hear what was being said, sensed that the Chinese had forgone any thought of resistance. Noting the same thing, the allied officers visibly calmed, especially as the door to the inner chambers opened and an elaborately dressed mandarin in full regalia entered the room.

"It must be Viceroy Ye!" Hedrick whispered excitedly.

"I guess so," Jason responded, somewhat irritated at Hedrick's interruption. So much was happening. What could they be saying? he wondered to himself. Parkes was conferring with the official. The mandarin appeared calm and yet extraordinarily controlled.

For a second, Jason had the impression he was seeing a play. In fact, it reminded him of the Chinese touring companies that occasionally performed for the locals in Kowloon. Then even at his distance, he could see that Parkes looked confused and was hurriedly whispering something to the officer near him. A quick stir of action followed as several lesser officers and enlisted men left the chamber. Parkes again turned to the official and engaged him in further conversation. Jason continued to watch, catching only the occasional pleasantry from the official and Parke's reply.

Suddenly, a loud roar went up and then laughter from the rear of the crowd closer to the door. Parkes turned with anticipation, ending his conversation abruptly.

"You were right, sir. We found this bugger crawling out the back. And he is certainly no coolie. Look at the fine fingernails!" a beaming British lieutenant yelled forward through the crowd.

It was immediately obvious what had happened. Even as the fellow was dragged rudely forward, Jason could see the horrified faces of the officials. The escape of the real viceroy had been a failure. The foreigners had not fallen for their scheme, and now the viceroy himself was a prisoner. The earlier mood of cooperation had vanished. Parkes shouted rudely to his presumed host, and the real Viceroy Ye was marched off with two burly soldiers at his side. Jason had only a moment to exit the yamen and see the unhappy mandarin, now looking far smaller than his reputation, being marched off.

As the viceroy's escort departed, a score of heavily armed troops fell in behind them. It was not clear how the Cantonese would react to the capture of their chief official. But nothing happened. The streets remained empty as the foreign soldiers marched. Jason, now forgotten by Hedrick in the excitement, slowly turned to follow them, wondering what fate lay in store for the once-great viceroy who had so angered the British with his refusal to allow the foreigners entrance into the city.

Over the next week, Jason was as busy as ever working with the coolie gangs. The city itself began to come alive again within days. Chinese and foreigners wandered about freely. The deserted streets of the previous week were now full of excited Cantonese, many of them attempting to sell goods to the allied soldiers who remained stationed around the city.

"What they're going to do is use the local governor, Po-Kuei, to administer the place. We'll control him." Jason listened closely as Hedrick outlined plans for a new allied commission that was being formed to oversee the city's occupation.

"There will be Colonel Halloway and one of the Frog Captains, an officer named Chesney. And Mr. Parkes, the consul, will play a part as well."

"But how can they govern? Parkes is the only one who even speaks Chinese?" Jason asked seeing his chance.

"That's the beauty of the scheme. The buggers will govern themselves, and we'll only have to watch them. It's all arranged. We'll set up Po-Kuei in the yamen and just control access to him. They say the governor was the viceroy's enemy anyway. And he's willing to cooperate. You're right, though, about the language problem. But Parkes is around, and there will be need for you." Jason listened enthusiastically. He had been uncertain of the future. Now it was even more clear that he'd have work with the new occupation forces.

"I heard this morning they're even going to set up a Sino-Foreign police unit of sorts, maybe a score of us, and another bunch of Chinamen to patrol. If I can get the assignment, I'll make sure you're with us."

"I'd like that. I have an idea about some Chinese who could help also." He said no more, having never mentioned his friend to Hedrick. It seemed likely that Wu would prefer such an assignment to the backbreaking labor of the coolies.

"Fine. That's your department. I'll talk to my colonel and you can work with the buggers." Hedrick walked off excited by the plans.

Jason, who had been supping from a bowl of rice soup, more precisely hot water with a few grains of rice floating in it, sat back contentedly. He wasn't surprised about the decision to establish the Sino-Foreign police units. One of the more amusing aspects of that first week had been the passing of large military patrols through Guangzhou's streets. Once the initial fear of such groups had passed, another phenomenon had developed. As soon as word was spread of troops arriving in a quarter, huge numbers of Chinese would gather in the streets abandoning their stalls while waiting to see the curious-looking foreigners. But almost as soon as such conditions had begun, the local beggars and thieves had seen their opportunity. As the crowds gathered, they had gone to work, pickpockets, burglars, and the like rifling through the people's goods even as the latter ogled the strange foreign soldiers.

Jason, fluent as he was in Chinese, had understood sooner than the Western military officers what was going on. A less disruptive way to patrol had to be found. The proposal for the Sino-Foreign units was clearly a result. They would be smaller, more familiar and less likely to provoke such activities. Jason only hoped that Hedrick would be able to carry out his plans.

During the following weeks, Jason came to understand that aside from the occupation itself, many factors were contributing to local tensions. The Chinese were very angry with the continuing pillage by the allied troops, French, English, and their Indian allies. Until the allied officials ostentatiously flogged a few foot soldiers in public for theft, it seemed unlikely that the lukewarm cooperation of the Cantonese would continue. More serious, but less spoken of during those few weeks were concerns about the disappearance of the local Chinese. The coolie merchants had increased their activities during the hostilities, and Jason, who often listened to conversation in the noodle shops, heard of young men, sometimes even examination students, who had been carried off by the Americans and others involved in the trade. Jason wondered how long the allies could keep control over the city with such tensions so close to the surface. Later in the month, when many of the allied assault troops were withdrawn to carry out the campaigns further to the north, he was all the more alarmed, for by then he had become actively involved in the police administration of the city.

Hedrick's plan worked out completely. Over the next weeks, the new allied commissioners arranged for the establishment of Sino-Foreign police forces to patrol the streets. Each day small contingents of mixed units, led respectively by a minor mandarin and allied officer, set out to patrol. Once the initial surprise at seeing the two races cooperating passed, they turned out, as expected, to be far less disruptive to life in the city. For Jason it was a plan particularly suited to his talents. Hedrick had been assigned to direct one of the contingents and arranged that Jason serve as his personal assistant. The plan worked well, and Hedrick soon became the envy of the other unit officers who were stuck relying on the pidgin English language skills available among a few of the Chinese. Because of Jason's presence, Hedrick's unit was especially favored among the allied officials who directed the allied commission. The young men often found themselves at the center of developments within the city.

As for the inhabitants of Guangzhou itself, they had hardly forgotten their decade-long antipathy to the foreigners. As the first month of occupation grew to a close, one could easily sense the tension beneath the surface. At one point, it was even rumored that the military commanders had toyed with the idea of renewing the bombardment simply to discourage the Cantonese from contemplating resistance. Nevertheless, as the initial shock of occupation passed, Guangzhou did spring to life again. The blockade was lifted, the streets filled with activity. Given the limited number of allied soldiers, and the fact that the Chinese administration under governor Po-Kuei continued despite allied supervision, it was almost possible to imagine the city much as before. The actual fact of occupation was hardly that visible.

For Jason the days settled into a routine. He awoke early and sometimes spent time visiting Wu, with whom he'd become close. Wu had turned out to be the one unexpected turn in his own pleasure at developments, for the young scholar had refused his enthusiastic offer to join the mixed police units.

"I know you wish me well," Wu had explained, "but I can't take part. Too many people would see me. I have seen the way the people study the faces of those who walk the streets with the foreigners. My village is too close. I could be recognized."

"But your family doesn't even know you're alive. Surely this is better than the work of coolies," Jason implored, eager to help and aware that Wu's knowledge and intelligence could prove helpful.

"Not know I'm alive! I hope they think I'm dead or at least carried off in one of the ships that kidnap our people for labor across the sea. No, coolie work is enough for me. I can accept that but not the shame of having them know I'm alive after I dishonoring them in the exams."

They had the same conversation often that spring, but each time Wu refused. The dishonor was too great. Being recognized and publicly disgraced would be too much. Jason continued to worry about him. The young man's appearance seemed to worsen all the time, and he was often very depressed. There was something about his friend, Jason often thought, that was terribly self-destructive.

Still Jason's own life with the police unit was certainly satisfying. Most of each day was spent walking slowly through the city, occasionally stopping to break up a public disorder or perhaps helping one of the local merchants capture a thief who had dared rifle though the goods laid out on display. When they were not on patrol, Jason helped supervise the establishment of small shelters the commissioners had decreed be erected at various strategic points throughout the city. Initially established as temporary police stations, they had slowly been fortified over the course of several weeks. Jason, even as he helped with the work, wondered if they would be sufficient if the inhabitants ever made a concerted effort to force them from the city. He and Hedrick, out of reach of the other members of the patrol, often discussed the situation.

"But don't you see what's happening? We lose more troops all the time. They think that because Guangzhou's quiet, they can send more and more soldiers north. But just look at the situation. The Cantonese see almost no soldiers anymore. Their own officials administer them and yet the place is supposed to be occupied. And they're supposed to listen to the commission's proclamations."

"But the buggers know we can always send for more soldiers if they resist us. And besides we're worth any ten of them!" Hedrick added enthusiastically.

"Hedrick, maybe you're right, but that doesn't change a thing. So what if we can strike back. That won't help the two of us if the locals decide this occupation is a sham. Lord Elgin's ability to get revenge won't help your chances of ever seeing Dover again."

Hedrick had not responded. But later, during his turn at supervising the police shelters, Jason was glad to see him use his influence to have stronger barriers erected and more ammunition stored. By the end of that summer, they would both have reason to be glad about Jason's foresight.

Much of the spring passed uneventfully. Nevertheless, Jason, more aware than most of the street talk, was concerned. By early April, he told Hedrick of rumors that the new viceroy, designated by Beijing and living north of the city, was calling for resistance. It was increasingly certain that the Cantonese, shocked into submission by the previous winter's assault, were slowly, with the encouragement of the province's mandarin officials, considering an effort to drive out the foreigners.

Jason, who had previously been comfortable walking the city streets at night, now felt it impossible to continue. Even his patrols with Hedrick were tense. There was no doubt in his mind that the two hundred or so allied soldiers, most of them English, would be no match for an aroused population if it came to that. One could hardly depend on the Cantonese who shared their marches. In fact, word had come during late April that an assassination attempt had been made against one of the allied sentries, and tensions between the Indian soldiers and the Chinese who harbored a special hatred for them were even worse.

Jason heard about many incidents and was certain that others existed. Hedrick had even told him privately that a number of Indian troops had simply been carried off at night by the Cantonese. As yet though, no European had been so assaulted. By June the situation was growing more difficult. Word had come that the new viceroy, Huang Zonghan, had put out a circular reminding the Cantonese of their past patriotism and the necessity of resisting the warlike English. On the eighteenth, Dr. Turnbull, the chief surgeon himself, was killed as he attempted to aid several soldiers ambushed by the locals. Jason, who had spoken only the week before with the tall and stately Turnbull, was especially upset by the sight of the doctor's decapitated body. It had only been the memory of Turnbull's habitual clothing, as if he'd still been strolling in London, that reminded Jason of the dead man's powerful presence. His head had not been found, perhaps carried off for display on a pole somewhere as an inspiration for those considering further resistance.

The allied commissioners, normally busy with their efforts supervising the governor's activities, understood the necessity to seriously warn the foreign community. A proclamation was issued that Jason's patrol had been required to post throughout the city.

Moreover, the English consul warned the Western merchants in the strongest terms of the necessity of protecting themselves against, as he put it, the treacherous and stealthy attacks so consistent to the idea of the Chinese.

For Jason, the increasing tensions made his days more and more difficult. Part of each morning was spent continuing the effort to strengthen their police station as if the small fortified enclosure could have been so described. And then finishing that task, he would go off with Hedrick and the others to march through the city. What made the situation especially difficult was that the fairly easy fellowship that had developed between the mixed-race police teams was now straining to the breaking point. How their Chinese colleagues would react in a crisis was on the minds of every Westerner; English, French, and the few Americans like Jason who worked with them. For Jason, it was particularly frustrating that he could no longer safely slip away to meet with Wu, for the visits had become very important to him not just for the companionship they offered but the lessons Wu had finally agreed to offer. To gain the silver taels Jason was able to exchange for the Mexican dollars he earned, Wu had finally agreed to teach Jason to write Chinese. He now understood that his future lay in China, and knowledge of the spoken language would simply not be enough to establish himself. Wu, of course, had not been eager to begin the effort.

"But don't you want to be able to provide the proper services when your parents die? As a coolie you will never be able to pay for the feasts, for the burial and the proper rites. No matter that they think you're dead. You will still need to try to help your relatives when the time comes." Jason had not spent most of his life in China for nothing.

Wu had studied him closely, almost amused at Jason's ability to touch upon the one issue for which the chance to earn money could not be refused. Wu might not be in contact with his family, but to be without funds when they died would be even worse than his previous failures. The argument accepted, they had begun in earnest only weeks after the occupation had begun. In the first months, at least through April, Jason had little difficulty slipping away to the depressing hovel where Wu slept. But now as tensions arose, that had become impossible. Even the fifteen-minute walk alone through the winding streets of Guangzhou was far too dangerous and certainly so during those twilight hours when he had previously made his trek.

The incidents grew more and more common. One night word came that arsonists had torched a French ship in the harbor. That was followed by a French assault on one of the quarters near the city walls. The French had had their revenge, but the tensions hardly lessened. The allies had decided to terminate the junk traffic in the river near the city walls. Every day more and more Chinese left the city. Gone was the reasonably tranquil atmosphere that had prevailed in the weeks following the city's initial capture. Each evening after their patrol, Hedrick and Jason sat quietly listening to the sounds of gunfire as they huddled in the police station they had so carefully fortified. Few Westerners had died, but the ranks of the Indian soldiers were being devastated. The Chinese were carrying them off at a rate of more than one a day to a fate Jason was afraid to even contemplate.

One evening toward the end of July, he could feel, as Hedrick and he marched together, that something was up. He wasn't sure what he sensed, but he was certain that something was different.

"What is it, Hedrick? You've hardly said a word since you came back from the tribunal this morning. What did they tell you?"

Hedrick gestured to him to step aside and whispered quietly, "The commanders think the buggers are going to attack again tonight and in more force. At least that's the word coming in. They say the imperial commissioner wants to make sure Beijing knows he's loyal enough."

"Can't Po-Kuei control the city?" Jason asked.

52

"You know as well as I that the old boy has no prestige left. Everyone who sees him passes through that cordon of allied officers set up in the outer yamen to watch him. I heard he even tried to sneak away a few days ago. They caught the old bugger though. I don't know what he expected. I should think his own people would slice him up or something worse for working with us."

Jason didn't respond. He hadn't known that the cooperative governor had tried to escape. The conversation was interrupted by their arrival at the East-gate station they had slept in for so many months. It wasn't much of a shelter, really more of a fortified enclosure with little more space than necessary to store their goods and to sleep. Hedrick was watching with more than his usual concern not just the surrounding buildings but the contingent of Chinese who had marched alongside them for so long. Jason had gotten to know a few of them and respected several. But Hedrick certainly felt otherwise. His suspicions had never lessened, and now as Jason made arrangements for the platoon to reassemble in the morning, he seemed visibly to relax as they walked off to their respective homes. Watching them Jason noticed they scattered more quickly than usual. He wasn't sure why. He thought he'd heard the same street talk they had been hearing throughout the day's patrols. But now something made him sure he'd missed something important. But one couldn't be sure. It was probably no more than his imagination.

It was still light, and as Hedrick began to write out his reports, Jason set out on the short walk that had become his daily chore. No more than a hundred yards from their station, a small vegetable shop stood open till dusk each evening. He'd become quite familiar with the shop's owner, Lao Wang as the old man was known. Now as he proceeded toward the stall, he felt something was wrong; nothing he could put his finger on but certainly something. As he approached he realized that Lao Wang was looking at him without the usual anticipation of an impending sale. The old man was quite familiar with the needs of the twenty police who slept in the station and was dependent on their purchases. But tonight he appeared very different looking, very nervous, Jason thought to himself. The young American slowly lowered his hand toward the pistol he'd begun to carry in recent weeks.

Arriving in front of the stand, he began to order the usual melons from Wang when he spotted the sandaled feet of a man hiding within the confines of the shop. Jason started to put his hand on the butt of his gun when, to his surprise, Wu stepped partly from the shadows and motioned to him silently to enter.

"Say nothing," Wu began as he indicated that Jason should remain silent. "It is dangerous for me to be here. Friend, tonight there is likely to be an attack. Make sure your people are secure."

With that Wu turned abruptly and went deeper into the bowels of the building. Jason had said nothing the entire time. Then turning he realized that old Wang wanted him to proceed with the sale as if nothing had happened. Quickly completing the transaction, Jason marched the hundred yards as quickly as possible while trying not to appear as if anything untoward had happened. The station was close enough to the East gate that he could see the walls. They seemed empty, but Jason wondered who might be watching him from them or, for that matter, from the many buildings he passed in the short walk.

"Hedrick!" Jason called out as soon as he was safely inside the shelter. He quickly explained what he'd heard. There was now little doubt that the report from headquarters was no false alarm.

"But how do you know about it so suddenly?" Hedrick asked, not having realized that Jason had departed for the moment. Quickly explaining, Jason summarized his friendship with Wu and the report. Having done so, it was clear that his concern that the friendship would not be appreciated was confirmed. Hedrick looked uneasy, even suspiciously at Jason himself.

"You can't trust these buggers; I'm surprised you'd befriend one at all."

"Well, I do trust him, and I think we had best get prepared. There's hardly time to retreat to the yamen," he added, seeing twilight fade into darkness out in the city streets. Feeling for the first time Hedrick's disapproval, Jason confirmed for himself his often-felt appreciation that he was not one of the regular soldiers who worked under the English lieutenant. The latter had often spoken of his disdain for these lower-class English and Irishmen who filled the ranks, and that same sort of disdain now seemed to be directed toward Jason. One might work with such Asiatic barbarians, Hedrick would have agreed, but the thought of actually befriending one was unheard of.

The explosion cut short any further conversation. Something had been hurled against the shelter's walls, exploding with a deafening roar. Part of the defensive wall collapsed, and Hedrick, Jason, and several enlisted men spent the next few seconds frantically pushing sandbags into the gaping hole. For Jason, unable to hear a thing, it was almost dreamlike. One second he and Hedrick had been talking and the next, his head ringing, he could barely see or hear; so loud was the explosion and the dust it raised. Several of the soldiers screaming loudly had thrust their rifles through the gun portholes they'd so carefully prepared and began to fire widely.

"Stop!" Hedrick screamed. "Wait for a moment. Jones, do you see anyone out there?"

"Not a bloody thing, Lieutenant," the man cried back.

"Then wait. There'll be plenty of time to hit them later, when they've exposed themselves."

Listening to Hedrick give orders, Jason was somewhat relieved. He certainly sounded competent. He only wished they'd not spoken so often during the months they'd worked together. Too often Hedrick had spoken of his disappointment at missing the Crimean campaign. With the exception of the previous winter's assault, Hedrick had never been in combat. And the capture of the city was alongside thousands of allied soldiers, a full flotilla of warships, the vast majority of whom had long departed, Jason thought nervously to himself. Now they were a mere twenty hiding behind a shelter against, who knew? Perhaps an aroused city of a million!

He knew that there were other stations, but they were all too far away to matter. Jason understood that each small substation would be alone for the night, able to resist or not. He sat looking at his own pistol purchased several weeks before from an English merchant. Did the others understand how little he knew of using it?

As they sat in the shelter, few spoke above a whisper. Each of them, several of whom Jason had come to know fairly well in the previous weeks, was engrossed in his own thoughts. Occasionally from the distance, sometimes from the area of other police shelters, they heard the sound of gunfire and the fainter sound of men swearing, swearing in a host of European languages as well as Chinese. But for them, after the initial explosion, all had been calm. Was that it? One shell and then had the Chinese or Manchus, gone off to assault other shelters, perhaps those less well fortified.

At least two hours passed, for Jason most of the time was spent thinking of his father. He'd not had word. He wondered if his father had any idea where he was. A sense of guilt crept over him. Certainly the reverend had wanted only the best for him. And dying in an improvised police shelter in Guangzhou seemed unlikely to be what the older man had had in mind. He wondered if his mother had been alive, whether he would have been as willing to abandon the family hopes. He took out a few pieces of scratch paper and some writing materials he'd long stored there.

July 21, 1858
Dear Father:

But he got no further, for it had begun. The sound was deafening as bullet after bullet slammed in the shelter walls, and the Chinese-style cannon, better at discharging scrap metal than anything else, was released at them. Hedrick had leaped to the gun slits, his rifle discharging at the screaming figures who vaguely appeared in the darkness. Jason himself pulled the revolver from his pocket and found a place to fire from. To his surprise, he was both terrified and, to an extent, at ease. At least the waiting was over.

"Damn!" The bullet had whizzed just past his face and hit one of the Irish soldiers in the elbow. Several of his fellows frantically put a tourniquet around the wound, while the rest of them kept firing into the darkness. For Jason, the screaming calls for their death, the groans of the wounded soldiers, were more upsetting than the bullets themselves, for most of the latter merely thudded ineffectually against the outer sandbags of their shelter. He had found a corner for himself, somewhat away from the riflemen, and trying not to waste shells, he squeezed off a few careful shots. Occasionally he could even pinpoint a target in the dark, but that was infrequent. He wondered if the others were doing as he was, merely firing at the areas where the loudest shouts emerged from. To the front and a bit to the left, only partially within view of Jason's sight, a fire had started. It burned brightly, and Jason wondered if it would spread to the shelter itself. Only with effort, by dint of the fire itself, was he able to make out that within the branches of wood, there seemed to be a burning human form, probably a soldier killed trying to set them afire. Even as the firefight went on and Jason ineffectually fired into the dark, his principal preoccupation was with the extended arm of the fallen soldier.

The sleeve had not yet caught fire, and the arm extended, as it was from the rest of the flames, seemed curiously relaxed, as if the man had merely fallen asleep. Jason wondered if he'd had a family and for an instant realized he'd probably have felt more comfortable with the dead Chinese than with the young soldiers who surrounded him in the shelter.

The assault seemed to last for hours, though later Jason judged it to have continued for no more than forty-five minutes. Especially frightening had been the waves of Chinese who had literally flung themselves against the shelter. It had happened so quickly; one minute they were firing into the dark, and then figures had emerged, screaming at the top of their lungs, running toward them. But it had mattered little. The shelter held, and after a few more waves of attackers, relative calm again prevailed. For Jason, it was finally a moment to look back into the depths of the shelter. The wounded man looked far more tranquil. His friends had drugged him with opium. Gone were the earlier whimpers of pain that Jason had been so aware of. Looking outside, he noted a few glimmers of light beginning to lessen the darkness. Dawn was breaking, and now for the first time, he could clearly see the carnage in front of him. Scores of Chinese lay dead on the ground. The buildings opposite the shelter were riddled with bullets. Not a living thing moved. The brave soldier who had tried so valiantly to assault the shelter with his torch had been completely consumed by the flames. Jason could barely make out the form he'd studied so carefully during the long night. Staring into the carnage, he wondered for himself if the square could ever come alive again as he knew it. As he reflected, he could hear the sounds of his fellows beginning to stir behind him. They had survived the night.

CHAPTER 5

REVEREND BRANDT

Over the next several months, the relative tranquility of the previous winter slowly returned. Jason found that the daily patrols through the crowded streets of Guangzhou revealed few surprises. His initial enthusiasm for the work had already begun to wane. Jason's principal interests during the late spring were his language studies, both of Chinese and French. He had found a young French officer, Prosper Giquel, himself only a few years older than Jason, who was willing to trade Chinese conversational practice for French lessons. Giquel, who already knew English and often served as a translator between the English and French officers, was an excellent student, and though they had little time together, Jason grew to like the young Frenchman a lot. More important to Jason himself was the time he spent with Wu. With his Chinese friend, Jason spent a lot of time practicing the many characters Wu assigned him to study each day.

His Chinese friend claimed he was progressing extraordinarily well, and Jason liked to think Wu was doing more than flattering him. Jason had even managed to obtain a limited number of learning aids from one of the English missionaries who often walked the streets seeking converts. Happily, he'd never seen this one at his father's table.

So engrossed was he in his thoughts one afternoon that Jason failed to notice the tall, modestly dressed figure who had seated himself near the police station's outer wall. As they approached, Jason, caught up in his expectations of his evening rendezvous with Wu, failed until the last second to focus on the figure now rising from his seated position.

"Hello, son," Reverend Brandt said quietly as he gestured toward the patrol.

"Go ahead, Jason. He's been here all afternoon waiting for you." So Hedrick had known of his father's arrival. A warning would have been appreciated, he thought to himself.

"He told the captain he wanted to surprise you," Hedrick commented, as if reading his thoughts.

"Hello, Father. I am glad to see you," Jason mumbled, feeling terribly awkward. The reverend himself seemed unable to get past the salutation that had begun their conversation.

"Jason, you're through for the day." Hedrick waved him off, and the two men, father and son, walked off toward one of the city gates.

"I've not heard a word since that note you left last winter."

"I'm sorry, Father. I did start to write, but there was nothing to say." Nothing you would have understood, he added privately to himself.

"Commander Blake was good enough to keep me informed of your doings."

They had known all along! That answered a few questions. He had long been surprised that his father had not followed him waiting for the chance to ship him off to Oberlin.

"So tell me what has happened these last months. I have only the vaguest outline from the tribunal officials."

The story required no immediate confrontation, and Jason eagerly recounted the events of the last year. His father listened neither with interest nor disdain. As Jason spoke he wished that at least the older man could sound proud of his son's accomplishments and ability to be accepted here as a valuable asset to the allied commission. Jason recounted with enthusiasm the several times he had been called before the allied commissioners and asked during their morning sessions to offer his opinions on the mood in the streets. His observations had obviously been appreciated. At least Hedrick had been kind enough to give him that impression from time to time.

"Now I expect you have had your fill of this life—a common soldier. You'll be wanting to leave for Boston after your little adventure. Perhaps all this will even have been worthwhile. Make a man of you and all that. I've had word that the authorities at Oberlin have retained your scholarship until you arrive. So at most nothing more than a year's been lost. I'm told you can even make the second term if you hurry." Even as he spoke, it was obvious that the older Brandt was praying his son would be caught up in the momentum of his words. Then, having said his piece, he stopped. It was clear Jason would have to respond.

"Father, I'm glad to see you. I really am. Do you have a place to stay?" he asked, stalling.

"That's not important now. Well, are you coming with me or not?" His voice was growing harsh, angry, as Jason had so often seen it in the years since his mother's death.

"No." He was surprised how easy it was to say. The months in Guangzhou had given him more courage than he had realized. The older man seemed to start. He'd expected reticence, excuses, but an outright refusal and one so easily offered was unexpected. The reverend appeared unable to respond for the moment. Jason, really looking at him now for the first time, noticed how much he'd aged, how much grayer his hair had become.

"No. You mean not this year, not yet."

"No. I mean probably never. This is my home. Maybe not the police shelter over there. That's just for now. But I want to make my home here. In Ohio, I've nothing to offer, but here I can make my way. There will be plenty of fortune to be made by those who really know China."

"And you really know these heathens?" his father asked bitterly.

"Better than most, and I'm learning more each day. I think I could become somebody here. Maybe not as rich as the Matheson family...but somebody important." He'd not yet formulated such thoughts even to himself, and now hearing his own words, he hoped his father could understand.

"I can appreciate doing the Lord's work, spreading the gospel to these heathens. I've devoted my life to it. But to just choose these people to live among—these heathens with their devil worship ways and the like...Jason, I—we—wanted more for you."

The reference to his mother hurt. It almost made him waver in his determination, as he knew his father had meant it to. However, after faltering, he again held his ground.

"Father, I'm staying. Maybe you cannot understand. But I hope someday you will be proud of me. I'd really like your blessing."

"So you'll defy your father—a boy of seventeen!" The older man was getting wound up; his raised voice started to attract the attention of others on the streets. Jason wondered if they understood that the tall stern man was his father...his father who was so angered by his disobedience. For a flashing moment, he was glad they didn't know their relationship. Defying one's father in public would hardly make it easier to work with the locals. But no scene ensued. To Jason's relief his father seemed almost to deflate.

"Can I walk you to where you're staying?"

"I suppose so. They tell me it's not safe at night."

"It's been much better lately. The only real attacks have been against coolie merchants. The locals are understandably outraged by the kidnapping of their kin. But that's a problem beyond the walls. We'll be safe in this area."

He walked behind, studying his father's steps, deliberate steps as if he were carrying a great burden.

"Father, the money I took—I still have it. You can take it with you." He offered as they arrived near the merchant factories, actually warehouses where his father had apparently taken a room.

"You keep it. Maybe you'll need it sooner than you think," his father commented bitterly as he turned to enter the building. It was clear that Jason was not to follow him in.

Standing there looking at the door, he wished his father had been able to wish him well. The pain was deep, especially as he wondered if he were doing the right thing, wondered if at least his mother might have understood. She had always been more pleased by his developing language skills, skills far beyond those his father had managed for his own preaching. She had sometimes even bragged about him to the few Western women she had socialized with in Hong Kong. But now she was dead, and Jason was standing there as twilight set in staring at an unadorned wooden door, wondering if his father would even send him a message before he departed with the next morning's boats. The walk back to the police shelter took an eternity. It was too late to meet with Wu, and he was hardly in the mood to study anyway. Besides Wu would realize something was wrong, and the thought of explaining that he had again defied his father was not an attractive one. Even Wu had never faced down his own father.

The next morning Jason was especially tense. He knew Hedrick was watching him closely, perhaps concerned about the results of the previous evening's encounter. It was obvious, though, that the young lieutenant did not intend to ask. They marched a long way through the city that morning. No problems disturbed the march, and Jason tried to absorb himself watching the locals carry on their lives. The many opium dens they passed reeked as they always did, a sickly sweet smell with which Jason had become familiar, and always nearby the emaciated individuals, more skeleton than human, who inhabited their doorways. More interesting were the medical practitioners with their long needles used for treatment and the many fortune-tellers who stood calling out their skills at selecting marriage dates and other events of importance on the Chinese calendar. Still, on that morning even Guangzhou, usually so seductive in its street scenes, was unable to keep his attention.

"Hedrick, when does the first ship leave for Hong Kong?" he asked as innocently as possibly.

"It left at dawn. He was on it."

Hedrick's bluntness caught him by surprise. Why was he so concerned about Jason's private life?

"I am sorry, Jason. The tribunal asked me to keep them informed. Your father has written them several times. I think he expected you to go back with him once you'd had some time here."

"It's all right, but surely the tribunal has better things to do with their time," Jason responded, still irritated that his private business was so well known.

"You shouldn't be put off. The tribunal has been quite helpful to your father, but at the same time they appreciate having you here with us. You know perfectly well that Mr. Parkes, Mr. Hart, and the few students of Chinese that the French have been able to muster are hardly enough to keep this occupation going. Even that frog Giquel you've been teaching is nowhere near ready to really help. They really do appreciate your being here. I rather wish sometimes they appreciated my presence as much as yours."

They continued on through the same streets they always passed. Jason, upset as he was by the unpleasantness of the previous evening's encounter and longing to have had another opportunity to explain his feelings, was nevertheless pleased with Hedrick's comments. If his hopes for really establishing himself in China were to come to fruition, he needed just the sort of reputation Hedrick implied he was developing. Forcing himself to put aside thoughts of his father, who was by then probably halfway back to Hong Kong,

Jason looked forward to that evening's lesson with Wu. Wu played an important part in his plans.

By twilight, they had carried out their assigned rounds, delayed only shortly by a rather nasty argument between a new consular official and one of the local fruit merchants. The patrol had come upon the scuffle as they rounded one of the innumerable narrow corners of the walled city. As Jason slipped into his accustomed role as interpreter, Hedrick worked out a settlement. Once again, as so often in the past, Jason had to stand neutrally aside as the argument was settled in favor of the young English official.

"In Calcutta I'd have the coolie's head for talking to me so!" screamed the excited and still-somewhat-baby-faced Englishman. Hedrick, although not encouraging the fellow's anger, quietly arranged a settlement of the bill that would satisfy him. To Jason, it was all too familiar and his own role increasingly uncomfortable. From what he could see, the pink-faced English brat—and that is what he seemed to Jason after so many months in the police force—was in the wrong. But to say so was to earn more of Hedrick's suspicions. Jason knew that the latter had never quite trusted him since he'd understood Jason's close feelings for the locals. No, until he was ready, Jason understood that he would have to remain in the good graces of the occupation forces.

Happily, there was still plenty of light as they finished, and Jason headed off as quickly as possible, not even stopping to eat in order to visit Wu's quarters just outside the city gates. When he arrived, the entire crew was gambling as usual, and even Wu, which was considerably more unusual, was taking part. Jason recognized most of those sitting around the circle on the floor save a fellow in his thirties, a man of powerful build, and given the look of him, probably a northerner or a Hakka, one of the local minorities who lived near Guangzhou. As Jason entered, Wu motioned to him to crouch beside him. Something was clearly going on.

The newcomer glanced up at him for no more than a second. He'd obviously seen foreigners before. The man was very tall. His arms showed many scars, most of them faded bullet wounds and as well as a few newer ones, possibly rope burns, around his wrists. As the men played their usual card game, Jason wondered what was going on. The conversation, about food and women, the price of opium, and the occasional joke, despite his presence, about the foreign soldiers seemed no more than the usual fare. But here, Wu was taking part and not off in the half-dreamlike state he usually occupied. He was obviously very interested in the man. Only slowly, from half references and occasional jokes among the coolies, did Jason come to understand the man was different. No more educated than the others, still his appearance marked him as different, and Jason was now sure he was indeed a Hakka. But that couldn't be it. Wu's intense interest was hardly aroused by the not-particularly-unusual presence of a Hakka. Jason tried to remember what he knew of them. That they did not bind the feet of their women was known, and upon reflection, he recalled his father saying that they were a bit more open to the missionary teachings than the other Cantonese.

"So what would that long-haired rebel think? You who claim to have been an officer of the Tian Wang?" one of the coolies asked, somewhat sarcastically. Then spitting, he added, "How can people abandon their ancestors, forget the ancients for the foreign religion? It's no better *li* than that of a dog!"

The last was said with more aggression than sarcasm, and Jason for a second feared that a fight would erupt. So that was it. He was one of the followers of the Heavenly Kingdom! Jason was amazed. Here in Guangzhou, a follower of the rebel emperor who claimed to be Jesus's little brother and who had torn half of China apart in a civil war! But how could it be? How could the man, whom Jason realized now was not wearing his hair in the style of the queue, evade the Qing officials long enough to survive a trip to Guangzhou?

"You're wrong. You understand nothing. The Tian Wang, the Heavenly King, is the brother of our Lord. Don't you see? Everyone knows he was raised to heaven for forty days and there taught the truth. In Nanjing they understand. If the Heavenly King were in power, the foreigners would not rule you like slaves."

"So why are you here? As a traitor to the Qing? Not that it matters. The emperor's far away, and his officials"—the man spat—"are no better than the foreigners who rule through their dog, the governor."

The tall rebel turned back toward his cards, apparently deep in thought, casually taking the opium pipe one of the others had offered him. The game continued. Jason remained silent the entire time, not taking part but sitting close to the seated group and occasionally commenting about the results of the game with Wu. The latter, playing for the first time that Jason recalled, nevertheless played reasonably well, obviously spending most of his energy trying to establish a rapport with the newcomer.

Well into the night, the game broke up, and Jason, Wu, and the newcomer settled quietly in one corner of the crowded room. Normally, Jason would have been long gone, his sleeping hours spent in the police shelter with Hedrick and the others. But Guangzhou had been quiet recently. He no longer felt nervous in the streets as he had during the summer, and the chance to talk to a Taiping rebel was too much of a temptation.

"Did you ever actually see your famous Tian Wang, the Heavenly King?" Wu asked as they made themselves comfortable.

"No. We heard many stories about him. And every day we studied his writings. He had great dreams, you know. Heaven taught him the truth. One day we shall rule all of China."

The man had obviously not abandoned his leader. What could he be doing here in Guangzhou? Jason thought to himself. Only slowly during the course of the night did the Taiping soldier reveal his purpose, and then only under persistent questioning from Wu, who was more excited than Jason about meeting him. The rebel's father had died, his sister had been sold as a concubine, and the man had returned to bring part of his spoils to the family to save the land.

"You understand, we have no private property. The officers control everything and give us what we need. It's a good system, but my family needs help. I had some silver taels from our struggles in Zhejiang and came home to help them. Our lord, the Tian Wang, teaches us many new things, but a son is still a son."

It had been very difficult to contact his mother. In the area around his home, his departure for the Taiping camp was a common rumor, only somewhat lessened by his father's long claim that his son had been kidnapped by the foreign coolie merchants.

"That was only a story to hide the shame of having a long hair for a son. But it almost became truth a few days ago when I was taken by such men. But not for long!" he added with pride. Jason now remembered the marks of the rope on the man's wrist that had been so obvious earlier in the evening when the light had been better. So they were operating even nearer the city than usual. There would be hell to pay at the tribunal. The commissioners, although acknowledging that such labor needed to be recruited, understood that the kidnappings made the possibility of an uprising more likely each day. The locals might accept the foreign control of the city but not the constant decimation of their families as more and more respectable men, not just coolies, were carried off.

"But finally, I managed to sneak into our compound. Only Mother received me well, but she was very frightened, and my grandfather feared the officials would come looking for me. I left the money and now return to Nanjing to the Heavenly Kingdom."

He had managed an incredible trip, across half of China, through Qing lines, the lowliest of which would have executed him as a long-haired rebel on the spot. Jason wondered if he would make it back. He had many more questions, for among the missionaries, he had even heard one of his father's friends say that the Tian Wang had studied with him before embarking on his blasphemous campaigns. Certainly, as Reverend Brandt had explained, claiming to be the little brother of the Lord was hardly the sort of "Christianity" the missionaries were trying to introduce. Still, Jason had heard of the great rebellion all his life. Nevertheless, the hour was late. Even the powerfully built rebel looked exhausted, and Jason found himself drifting off. The last thing he remembered hearing that night was Wu's continuing questions about the Heavenly Kingdom.

"Was it true that women fought as well? Did they really have their own civil service examinations?" the rebel, though not the brightest individual Jason had ever met, made an effort wherever he could to satisfy Wu's curiosity. After a while, though, Jason could not keep his eyes open and drifted off.

When he awoke, Wu was still asleep. The rebel was gone, and Jason, hurriedly gathering his things, left quietly. It would not do to be late for the morning's patrol.

CHAPTER 6

COOLIE MERCHANTS

During the weeks that followed his father's departure, Jason often reflected on their conversation. Certainly, he doubted he would ever return to America for college. On the other hand, the older man had been right about his current position. There was little future with the Sino-Foreign police units. The occupation wouldn't last forever, and even a police career elsewhere on the coast failed to attract him. He'd tried to discuss his feelings about the future with Wu, but that had proved impossible. For Wu, there was no future.

"I used to worry about such things—dreaming about coming home and building a big pavilion to celebrate becoming a jinshi, the highest Confucian exam rank. But that was a very long time ago. Now all I think about my family is how ashamed they must be."

When he spoke that way, it was difficult to respond. Wu often acted as if he were already dead. Still he proved a good teacher, and his intelligence made Jason's efforts to learn particularly fruitful. Recognizing the limits of their friendship, Jason nevertheless made every effort to spend as much time with the fallen young gentry as possible.

But one evening Jason arrived at the coolie quarters Wu had occupied for so many months only to discover his friend was gone.

"The scholar hasn't come in yet. One of the regulars mumbled, hardly looking up from the game. Sitting down to await Wu, Jason leaned against the walls and watched the game. There was little conversation save reference to the bets and a feeble effort by one of them, a lively fellow to retell a Taoist tale he'd heard presented by a professional storyteller in a local teahouse. The man had none of the talents of those who earned their living by such tales, but the story was a mildly interesting one of magic and intrigue that caught Jason's attention for a time.

Only with something of a start did he realize that hours had passed without Wu's arrival. Concerned, though knowing Wu did not always come back each evening, Jason left the room while the game continued actively. He'd return the next evening to try again. At least there would be more time to practice the strokes of those characters Wu had demonstrated during their last session.

He spent the next day impatiently carrying out his duties with the police units, but they had become awfully tedious. The excitement, albeit at times pure terror of the previous summer, was now gone. And with it much of what he had found interesting about the position. Most of the day was spent acting as sort an informal liaison between irate Chinese grocers and delinquent foreign customers. He was beginning to feel that he might just as well have been in Ohio studying for a real career. As night fell he hurried off in search of Wu. Surely, his old friend would have returned. But Wu hadn't. Though it was something of an effort to get it out of them, the regulars finally told Jason that Wu had never returned, and after some pushing, he found out that the young man had set off the previous day to travel near where coolie merchants had recently been spotted. Now, alarmed lest his friend had been taken, Jason set off at a run through the narrow passages of the city. Only slightly aware of the curious faces that followed his unseemly progress,

Jason quickly made his way toward the area, several miles beyond the city walls where Wu was said to have been headed.

It all turned out to be easier than expected. The locals, though somewhat nervous at his approach, easily indicated where the foreign ship lay at anchor, and as the well-lit moon shone down, Jason approached along the shore. For the next hour, he watched the ship from which only a faint hum of voices could be heard. Well into the second hour, the ship seemed to stir. From time to time, foreigners, perhaps Americans, he couldn't tell, leaned over the railing, obviously waiting for something. A bit later, a small boat pulled up alongside the ship. With help a Chinese was dragged from the smaller boat and hauled aboard.

A conversation of sorts seemed to be taking place. Jason thought he heard the sound of dickering between the foreigners and their Chinese accomplices. For a moment he thought he heard them agree to a figure of twelve dollars, but the wooden hull of the ship creaked at that moment and it was difficult to tell. Suddenly, though, it was more obvious. The voices had risen in anger.

"What do you mean he doesn't accept? Deal with it, you black-eyed heathen," a rough voice spit out.

A thin Chinese, obviously a captive, was dragged back into the boat and a beating began. After a time, the yelling stopped. Again, the charade began anew. This time the hapless fellow "agreed" to accompany the foreigners as a laborer. The wind had died down, and their conversation was now easier to follow.

Jason didn't know why, but he was sure Wu was aboard and that he was going to get him off. But that would mean waiting till everyone aboard was asleep. Crawling deeper into the woods that bordered the river, Jason lay down to nap. By midnight, it seemed likely that he could begin the effort to climb aboard unnoticed.

He awoke with a start. How long had he slept? He sensed dawn was coming. There was now little time to spare. Jason started cautiously toward the water, not knowing how well they kept the watch.

From what he understood, it was likely that Wu and the other prisoners would be kept below decks. He'd read enough of the depositions taken from freed coolies that he felt he understood the usual operations well enough. And lately, there had even been opportunities, as the commissioners had worked to suppress the illegal trade, to interview a number of men taken from the ships.

Jason relaxed a bit as he spied in the moonlight a sleeping figure, obviously a lookout. With luck, he wouldn't be spotted as he crawled. But how would he approach the ship? It was at least twenty meters into the river. Slipping off his boots, he left them and his pistol on the shore. Only the knife was likely to be helpful. Then Jason quietly entered the water. The current wasn't very strong, and he effortlessly swam toward the ship. A moment later, hoisting himself aboard, he prayed he'd been quiet enough. He had. All remained silent save the occasional creaking of the ship's timbers in the current.

Luck was with him. The ship must have been exceptionally full, perhaps about to sail. A number of Chinese lay on the deck sound asleep, with only the snoring guard supposedly watching over them. None stirred. Wu could not possibly have arrived long before and thus Jason retained hope that he would be there among them. If he proved to be below, Jason had no idea how he would even find him. Luckily, his hunch was correct. Wu lay among them, yet as always somewhat to the side. His old friend's aloofness and isolation for once had made things easier.

"You, how are you here?" Wu asked him as he awoke at Jason's touch.

"Shush, not now; we have got to get you off this ship," Jason whispered. "They will take you as a slave to South America."

"South America." Wu sighed, clearly wondering about such a place, and then said, "I care not; it is my fate."

It wasn't going to be easy. His friend's depression was going to make it more difficult to save him.

"Listen to me; you're coming with me. These men are dogs. They will beat you and work you like a slave. You don't deserve that, and I won't let it happen."

"Ho there."

It happened so fast. Jason had not even noticed the approach of the sentry and then, at his touch, his knife at the man's throat. He'd done it. He'd killed a man. Oh God, to really kill a man there, bleeding on the deck in front of him! He felt as in a trance, watching the deck moisten with the man's blood, not even noticing how hard the foreigner—he remembered thinking he might have been an American—hit the ground. It was all happening so slowly—even the sound of stirring, people waking.

"They'll kill you," Wu was whispering with an energy Jason had never seen him reveal.

"Jason, we must go. He's dead!" But Jason had frozen, staring at the man.

"I've killed him. Oh God, I have killed him, maybe even one of my own people!" The thought of his father further paralyzed him until the snap of Wu's hand against his face caught his attention. In seconds Wu yanked him toward the railing and then Jason, recovering himself, dived overboard with Wu.

They could hear yelling behind them, yelling in English, Portuguese, and Cantonese. Three minutes later they were ashore. Jason grabbed his goods and set off running as fast as he could. For a moment he considered tossing the gun aside and then reconsidering gripped it with an intention to use it if necessary. There had been no choice. Even Wu understood what had occurred. They ran for at least a mile, several *li* as Wu described such distances.

At first they had heard cries from the ship and feared they would be followed, but that never happened. Perhaps the kidnappers were just as frightened. It was not, after all, unusual for coolie merchants to be attacked by local crowds. After a time both recognized that they were safe. Finally halting, the two friends dropped to the ground, holding their sides, and without quite understanding why, they began first to smile and then laugh. Even Jason felt uncontrollably relaxed. It had worked. He'd saved his friend, and Wu himself appeared almost reborn, so calm did he look.

Much later Jason wondered why they had never thought to return to Guangzhou. After all, no one had seen Jason's face or would be likely to remember Wu. They certainly could have renewed their former lives. But Jason realized later that they had without discussion both come to the same conclusion. They would leave, travel into the interior toward the north. It had simply been understood as they sat there on the ground resting. Jason had a fleeting thought of somehow contacting his father and then dropped it. There would be no point. Jason still carried with him the Mexican dollars he'd carried since Hong Kong and a few he'd earned in Guangzhou. They would need little more. Jason wasn't sure what he expected to find, but he vaguely thought of seeking out the Taiping Heavenly Kingdom. He'd long wondered about their society. To his surprise Wu quickly agreed to the idea.

"They say they are made up of the lowest sort—poor, Hakka, and the like—that not one true gentry stands with them. But still I too would like to know more of their people."

Over the next weeks, it became clear as they traveled that they were nearing an area where battles had recently taken place between the imperial forces and the long hairs. The peasants spoke often of the struggles, and one afternoon as they walked out onto an open plain, they realized they had come upon a fresh battlefield. Bodies were strewn about everywhere, most of them naked, having been stripped by scavenging peasants after the battle. Were it not for the distinctively different hairstyle of the Taiping soldiers, it would have been impossible to distinguish the imperial troops from those of the Heavenly King. As they hurried through the battlefield, trying to avoid being overcome by the smell, Jason felt Wu tugging at his sleeve. They had come upon another group, these having fallen more methodically—all beheaded, their corpses lying a few feet from the pile of heads.

"They must have been prisoners," Wu whispered, though, to no one, but Jason was in sight. "I've heard they execute all prisoners like this. It is a terrible and wondrous thing to challenge the emperor's hold on the Mandate of Heaven, to deny his control over China."

Jason didn't know what he meant, but it was hardly the place to talk further. The smell was overwhelming, and the prisoners seemed to have died quite recently. The stench was unbearable. Jason was sure he would faint if they didn't move on. They both stumbled along for the combination of the corpses, and the heat of the sun was beginning to affect Wu as well. Once away from the bodies and finally again in a more wooded area, they stopped to rest.

"I have been thinking that we need to disguise you. Those peasants have watched you everywhere we've gone. The foreign devils are not supposed to travel away from the coast."

Jason knew he was right. They had already attempted to disguise him somewhat by using a peasant hat with a particularly deep brim to cover the brownish locks beneath them and keep his face in shadows. But more would be required. Jason remembered hearing that the French had originally joined the Guangzhou assault because of the murder of one of their priests in the interior. To be taken for a priest. Now that was a funny thought, and to die for it. He wondered what his father would think of that. As they discussed it, both realized that making Jason look as Chinese as possible was important for both their sakes. It would hardly do for Wu to be seen traveling with a foreign devil, the very people who had carried off the great Viceroy Ye. They decided to wait until nightfall and then begin traveling again. Later, passing through a village, they had little trouble purchasing enough Chinese clothing to allow Jason to pass at least at a distance. As he put on the clothes and the new hat, Jason reflected on how bothered he had once been at his relatively diminutive height. For an American his five feet four inches were relatively small, but it might save his life now.

The next few days were uneventful; that is until quite unexpectedly they arrived in a clearing full of soldiers and peasants. Considerable yelling was going on, as some sort of makeshift tribunal was being established. Glancing at each other, as if in unison wondering if Jason's disguise were good enough, they both stopped at the edge of the crowd and tried to see what was happening. It was a trial, or at least an interrogation they realized as soon as they had edged forward enough to understand what was going on. On the ground, groveling before the magistrate were three long-haired Taipings, obviously captured by imperial soldiers. The men were frightened and being questioned closely. When an answer dissatisfied the magistrate, his assistant's staff acted quickly by striking the offender sharply. One man was already bleeding from a deep cut on his cheek. After no more than a few minutes of conversation, the men were abruptly led off to the execution.

"What injustice!" they yelled and then no more, as they died, executed a few hundred feet away. Jason wanted to pull away when suddenly Wu grabbed him and pointed. Another group was being led forward. There among them, looking as tense as one could imagine, stood the Taiping soldier they had met in Guangzhou. So he had gone so far only to end up like this. Jason felt he had to do something. He started to step forward, but Wu's touch stopped him. There was nothing to be done.

The man was dragged forward and abruptly thrown to the ground before the magistrate. In a moment two others, these no more than children, were brought forward. Both Jason and Wu strained to hear the interrogation. They were accused of being rebel deserters. From the limited amount that Jason could gather it was obvious that many former rebels were pillaging the territory.

For the moment the magistrate seemed to concentrate on the younger of the two boys. An authoritarian lecture seemed to be given. A good sign, Jason thought. Perhaps there was a possibility of mercy. He was right. The young boy was led off without any sort of sentence being passed. In another moment a similar conversation took place with the other youngster. He too in turn was marched away. Finally, the magistrate turned his attention to their acquaintance. Jason suddenly realized he'd never heard the rebel's name during that long night in Guangzhou. Now the tone was quite different. His hair, unlike the others, still clearly showed the marks of an ex-Taiping. The hair had been cut, but no queue, not even the phony one the young man had sported in Guangzhou, was evident.

The magistrate shouted that he had dishonored his family, shown disrespect for the emperor and himself. That the Tian Wang, as the Taiping king was known, was a piece of dog meat whom imperial soldiers would one day destroy. Growing excited, he cried that Confucius himself had been insulted by the Taipings and that, despite their hopes, the Western Christians would not be able to help them against the Dragon Throne.

The fellow appeared not to hear. It was obvious he was exhausted, quite probably drained from torture. His eyes viewed out through lids already puffy from a recent beating. It was clear to Jason that the magistrate's speech, unlike before, was now more directed toward the crowd than his hapless prisoner. After another moment, sentence was pronounced: immediate death. He was stripped to his loincloth, his arms tied behind his back. Abruptly the soldiers carried him away from the magistrate, but the man jerked himself away from his captors and plunged into the crowd. Not having had a chance to move, Jason found himself directly in front of the terrified rebel. For a second their eyes met, and a look of recognition flashed across the man's eyes. For one frightening moment, Jason realized that one of the imperial soldiers, who'd quickly retaken the prisoner, had seen the look. Jason expected to be abruptly stopped. His disguise would hardly last a moment under direct interrogation, but fortunately a shout from the magistrate distracted the soldier. The officer was calling out additional orders. Jason took his chance to retreat further away from the crowd.

Five minutes later it was all over. The body lay on the ground and the head had already been posted to a pole, perhaps five feet high. A placard reminded the people the fate of those who followed the Taipings. Within ten minutes the imperial soldiers and their officers had departed, and Jason, Wu, and a few locals stood around, almost alone with the pole. The eyes were still open, revealing a look of horror. For Jason, it was time to move on and as quickly as possible. He hardly needed to convince Wu. The two set off without a word.

It was many hours before they were able to speak freely again and then on almost every subject except the execution. Over the next several days, they traveled almost exclusively at night, hoping to avoid other travelers and imperial troops. Eventually, though, Jason became convinced that his disguise would only make him seem all the more suspicious to the magistrates and concluded that it was probably best to travel somewhat more openly.

Wu was able to purchase a large number of Chinese copper coins with some of Jason's Mexican dollars, and with the money they began to stay quietly in village inns as they traveled. Staying within the villages did allow them the opportunity to hear the local gossip and even occasional discussion of troop movements.

Most prominent, though, in at least two villages they passed were stories of a local scandal that was dominating conversation. A young girl was said to have deserted her husband and family to run off with a lover. Considerable energy was spent discussing the case and how the woman would be dealt with should she be found. So exciting had the story become that Jason, despite his obviously foreign appearance, was hardly a concern.

Later one afternoon, several miles beyond the village where the scandal had begun, Jason and Wu found themselves drawn unexpectedly into the drama. For as they walked along a river they hoped to ford, they found a half-drowned young woman, almost certainly the runaway.

"What do we have here?" Jason said aloud, having spotted her before Wu. For there she was, alive, only partially conscious, obviously washed ashore—perhaps having tried to kill herself. Working together, they carried her away from the riverbank into a set of nearby trees. To Jason's surprise Wu, although cooperating, seemed disgusted with Jason's efforts to pull her to safety.

"She should be left to die," he mumbled, staring at the unconscious figure. "It's obvious she has dishonored herself and her family."

"You don't know what happened to her. Perhaps she was abducted," Jason replied.

"Then all the more reason that we leave her. If she was dishonored by some scoundrel, her honor is just as soiled. In fact, she was right to attempt to kill herself. We shouldn't interfere."

"Well, I don't know why you're being so hard, but I'm going to help her if I can." No more words passed between them. It was obvious that Wu, displeased though he was, would say no more.

After a time, the young girl opened her eyes. She glanced at both of them and then, hardly even focusing on Jason's foreign appearance, dropped off to sleep again. While they waited for her to fully wake, a camp was set up, and Jason and Wu discussed the situation. For Jason, all thought of moving on had vanished. Here was someone more in need of help than they, and he at least was not inclined to abandon her. Besides, he thought to himself, there was something really beautiful about her.

CHAPTER 7

BLACK JADE

"It is obvious that you understand nothing of *li*, of appropriate behavior as taught by Master Confucius."

What Jason did understand was that Wu was furious with his insistence on caring for the still-unconscious girl. For more than an hour, as they had sought firewood and built a makeshift shelter, Wu had not spoken more than a few necessary words to him.

Later they sat watching the fire in silence, listening to the sounds of her deeply troubled sleep.

"You heard what the villagers said. This woman has run off from her husband, abandoned her family—slept like some dog with her lover. Even her own family wouldn't take her back. A woman has no greater responsibility than to honor her in-laws and husband. This worthless one has insulted both. We should have pushed her further into the stream. Do your people allow such behavior from their women?" Wu asked sharply and then spit in the direction of the sleeping form.

"I suppose not. But we don't know what happened to her. It's not for us to judge." As Jason spoke he remembered images from his father's sermons about the stoning of adulterous wives. Was he doing the right thing by helping her? Wu was obviously angry with him. He was certain his father would hardly be impressed either.

"Can a Chinese woman ever just leave her husband?" Jason finally asked after a few moments. He knew it was possible, though rare at home.

"Of course not. What a thought! Does a dog have the right to abandon its master? Divorce is possible. They say the ancients did it more commonly than today. A man can divorce a woman if she sins against him, or especially insults his parents. In fact, they can force it if that is the case. And if a wretch brings disharmony upon the household by arguing with a concubine, it's possible as well," Wu commented, getting into a recitation from one of his study efforts.

"Learned master"—the voice surprised them. It was warm yet sarcastic—"you have forgotten something. If the wretched one can't deliver a child to the husband, she can be sent home as well, if she has a home."

Her voice was curiously strong and certain for a Chinese woman, especially one apparently so recently unconscious. They both turned toward her in surprise.

"Did you save me?" she asked, her eyes directly staring at Jason, seemingly not surprised that he understood her.

"Hardly; you were already lying near the shore. Were you pushed in?" he asked, noticing that she was ignoring Wu.

"No. And I won't thank you for stopping my revenge. That woman would have been tormented forever," she said bitterly.

Jason had no idea what she was talking about. He turned to look at Wu, who was watching her closely.

"So you planned to commit suicide. To dishonor yourself and become a ghost. And who would you have tormented ghost that never was?" Wu's eyes remained steeled against the woman. Jason was realizing the situation had gotten a lot more complex than he had recognized.

"How could one like you understand? You speak the language of a scholar, though what you're doing here with this barbarian, dressed like a coolie, I can't imagine."

Jason had spent almost his entire life in Hong Kong. He had never heard even one Chinese woman speak as she did, so full of anger and defiance. Even those few he'd seen abandon their family to accept the missionary teachings remained almost as passive as their more traditional sisters. Wu had noticed as well.

"So they threw you out for your insolent tongue," he commented. Turning to Jason he lectured, almost as if the woman not there.

"There are many reasons for refusing a wife. If they are as beautiful as this one"—his words hardly sounded complimentary—"they can attract lovers who would dishonor the family. If they possess an evil tongue, as no woman should; they are even more dangerous. Such a woman understands nothing of the harmony of a household. This one's parents-in-law chose poorly indeed."

Jason sat frozen. He'd spent months practically begging Wu to teach him all he could of Chinese ways, but now the lecture was more designed to insult their "guest" than anything else. He was extremely uncomfortable. Wu neither seemed to notice nor care.

"Jason, she tried to kill herself. To become a ghost, so she could, no doubt, further torment her family more in death than she did in life."

With a humph, Wu got up and moved his sitting place farther from the fire. He'd actually not gone more than a few feet, but the meaning of the gesture was obvious.

"There is something to what he says. But he understands nothing." As she spoke, the anger softened a bit. For a moment, Jason sensed considerable private pain. Whatever it was, it was clear she was not about to discuss it.

"We have food, and you can stay with us for a bit if you need help," he offered, watching Wu's back as he spoke.

"Thank you; I've eaten. But maybe I can sit here awhile." Wu "humphed" again from his seat in exile but said nothing.

Jason proceeded to prepare the vegetables they had purchased that morning and set a few in front of each of them. She ate with relish, hardly trying to hide how hungry she obviously was. After a time, she turned to him.

"I have heard of the barbarians on the coast. Those that fight with terrible weapons and worship as the long-haired rebels do. Are you one?" She looked right into his eyes as he spoke. Jason could not get over the tone of her voice. No Chinese woman had ever spoken so directly to him. She was unlike anyone he had ever encountered.

"Yes, I suppose I am, but I don't know much about your rebels." At the mention of the Taipings, Wu's back stiffened. It was obvious he feared Jason would stupidly reveal their intentions.

"My family is from America, *Mai Guo*, the beautiful country. But we live in Hong Kong." She looked puzzled. "It's near Guangzhou." She seemed to recognize the name.

"Guangzhou, I have heard the men speak of it. It is a great city. Is it beautiful and full of markets?"

"It is."

For the next half hour, he told her of Guangzhou. Her curiosity was enormous, and Jason was proud of his knowledge. At several points, Wu appeared almost ready to correct him or to add some detail, but the young scholar held himself back. He approved of nothing about the young woman, even of her interest in the city he himself loved so much.

As night fell, Jason helped her prepare bedding and then retired to the area Wu had set up for them.

"That woman will bring bad luck. I'm sure of it. She has too much Yang, too much of the male element in her for anyone's good."

Jason listened but said nothing. He knew he could travel without Wu, but the young's man company had become important to him. In fact, especially since Wu, excited by their decision to seek out the rebels, had begun to overcome his depression. But despite Jason's feelings for Wu, he knew they could not leave her behind.

Not so much for her own safety, though he certainly wondered what would become of her, but for him as well. Jason felt an attraction to her he couldn't explain even to himself, an attraction quite different from what he'd once felt for the daughter of one of his father's ministerial colleagues. Black Jade, as she was called, was the most interesting woman he had ever met. His only thought was how to convince her to accompany them.

As dawn rose, Jason found himself awake, watching the two sleeping forms. Wu slept deeply beside him, and Black Jade about ten feet away. Her face was toward him. She was, as Wu had commented the day before, truly beautiful. Jason wondered, how true it was, as Wu had said, that families would hesitate to arrange a marriage with such a beauty. He studied her sleeping form, for now, unlike when she was awake, she appeared quite vulnerable. He looked at her feet. How incredibly tiny they were, the stained lotus shoes she wore still fitting tightly to them! How odd, he thought to himself. He'd not noticed them before, though as he now realized she had walked little from the time they had first found her. The curious gait, he'd seen so often before, had hardly been apparent.

But now, as she lay sleeping before him, he studied the foot. The right one was now protruding from under the blanket. He could stare at it as he had never been able to really look at a bound foot. He remembered how often he'd heard his father, and even more often the missionary wives, speak of the horrors of foot-binding. How could the Chinese so deform a child's foot? he wondered. How little he really knew of these people. More and more he realized that he knew nothing of China. No more than snippets of the lives of Hong Kong coolies and a bit of street life from Guangzhou. He was almost embarrassed by his recent sense of accomplishment regarding Chinese ways. Maybe his father was right; these people were heathens, or at least too different for a Westerner like Jason to make his home among them.

"You stare at my feet. It's not polite, you know." Her voice roused him from his thoughts and her comment caught him off guard.

"They seem," he hesitated, "far smaller than the feet of our women," he stammered out.

"I wish my former mother-in-law could hear you. She felt they were horribly large. In her eyes, my feet were as ugly as a thing can be. Once as I approached her room, she said aloud to my husband's brother, 'Look at this! The person isn't even here yet, and her big feet have already arrived.'" Black Jade's voice was calm, without a trace of pain.

"We have a saying. 'A pretty face is nothing, but small bound feet mean true character.' So I was doubly nothing. My feet showed little character and were ugly to boot. I used to hate them, to wish they were as small as the neighbor's girls. But, at least I always understood one thing, whatever my mother did wrong in binding them, at least, my feet are much stronger. I can walk much further than most women, and from that I always thought something positive might come."

Jason said nothing more, for Wu had woken and was already rising to prepare a fire for tea.

"We must leave soon," Wu said to no one in particular. For a moment Jason felt a sensation of panic. It would be easy enough from sheer momentum to simply walk off after a few pleasantries. He had to say something.

"What do you do now?" he asked abruptly, his voice showing more interest than he would have preferred.

"I don't know. You two destroyed my plans for becoming a ghost, you or perhaps fate—maybe just the Kitchen God playing with me. But in any case, that no longer seems like such a good idea. The spirit world might not be as nice as I'd like."

"We march north. You could come with us for a time. From what we heard in the village, they would not treat you well if you're found."

From behind him Wu laughed. "Women who betray their husbands shouldn't be treated well at all."

"Scholar who isn't. I told you there was no betrayal." Then turning again toward Jason, she said, "Perhaps you are correct. There is little for me here. I will travel with you for a time if you will allow it."

"I would be very pleased."

"And your friend, his honorable scholar/coolie person, does he allow it as well?"

Jason turned to Wu.

The latter merely shrugged his shoulders. "If that is to be, we must move as quickly as possible. There are too many imperial soldiers nearby."

Jason leaped to his feet, offering Wu the largest smile he'd ever cast in the young Chinese's direction. Wu replied with a look of disgust and continued his packing.

Over the next several days, they traveled with little inconvenience. Although Black Jade was unable to march at the pace they had earlier maintained, she was nevertheless still able to walk well. By morning of the second day, she had taken over most of the basic cooking and washing responsibilities and spent much of the rest of her time asking Jason about America. Aside from her interest in the world beyond China, which he found unusual for a Chinese, the conversation turned out to be particularly helpful. For Wu, his own curiosity aroused, became interested as well, thus allowing some common ground between the young man and the woman he so obviously disapproved of. If Wu rarely addressed her directly, they were both nevertheless interested in Jason's tales. The young American found himself carrying on a two-way conversation among the three of them.

More awkward was Jason's realization of just how little he really knew of America. He remembered it not at all from his early toddler years and relied mostly on comments his father and his reverend's associates had related over the years. And, of course, there were the many magazines and newspapers that had circulated among the Hong Kong community.

To his surprise, he found that Wu was both interested and appalled by Jason's tales of husband-wife relations in America. That men and women might socialize with each other or that young women were allowed to venture past their homes after marriage for social visits was appalling to the young man.

"They actually bring their wives to formal social occasions. How unseemly!" The idea of young women venturing forth unsupervised to visit other woman friends shocked him greatly.

"A woman should stay in the family compound. No good can come from such liberty. The family's honor depends on it," he pronounced with satisfaction. As he spoke his eyes rested on Black Jade.

For her part, she frequently asked questions, about marriage arrangements and bridal gifts, but commented little on what she heard. Jason could tell nevertheless that she was listening with interest.

"And does the woman stay with the husband's family?" she asked after reflection.

"Not always, though it certainly does happen often." She seemed a bit disappointed at his answer, though hardly surprised.

"Does the new bride get along with the mother-in-law?" she asked with interest.

For Jason's part, as he tried to answer, he wished he knew more of American family life.

He knew his own parents had lived with his father's family for a time before departing for China but little more.

"Well, I doubt they get along well," she announced definitively after hearing his comments. "There is always something that makes it impossible."

Jason, unsure what else he could add, turned the conversation to other things. Wu had asked about the American emperor and

Jason was caught up trying to explain the US government as he understood it. Wu listened skeptically.

"How can such disorder bring about harmonious government? If you let anyone lead, how can you be sure they are properly trained…wise and capable of good example and leadership?" Jason, while feeling he should defend American democracy, was unsure of the answer. Marching alongside rice paddies, much of the remaining afternoon was spent discussing what brought about good government. As it grew dark, they were little closer to resolving the issue. Black Jade said nothing. She was clearly thinking about his comments on Western family life, though if she had anything more to say on the subject, she was keeping it to herself.

On the evening of the fourth day after she had joined them, Black Jade finally began to tell her story. It had begun as another one of their many conversations about China and the West when she simply started to talk. At first offering little more than the few tidbits of her past she had shared for days, but then, almost as if some hidden reservoir had been opened, she began.

"My family is not without distinction. Perhaps I should say my father's family, for they say a girl knows not her true family until she marries. We had a distant relative who once passed the civil service exams and became a great official, a *Futai* I think. Do you know much of our government?"

"A little; I know of the civil service examination system." Jason could feel Wu wince behind him. "But where was your relative, a governor of what province?"

"I don't know. It was long ago. Perhaps my father knew, but he is long dead and hardly talked to me before he died."

"When did you leave your parents' home?" he asked.

"Maybe two years ago; I was fifteen. I remember being very excited."

So she was almost his age, Jason thought, and them remembering the Chinese habit of counting a child a year old at birth, he guessed he was about a year older.

"My father died last year. He'd been sick for a long time and was hardly of much worth even before that."

Wu bolted forward. "You should never speak that way of your father," he snapped, appalled.

"Maybe not, but it is true. He had taken up the smoking habit and hardly ever did more than come home to look for funds. My mother had to work with the silk weavers just to bring millet to us."

Wu relaxed a bit, for even Jason knew how much Wu had been shocked by the excessive opium smoking of the coolies he had worked with. Wu had always prided himself on his self-discipline and his rejection of opium.

They sat for a few more minutes watching the fire, while Jason waited, hoping she would begin again.

"My mother had a terrible time arranging a marriage. The marriage brokers always complained that I had a bad reputation for speaking disharmoniously and huge feet to boot. Maybe I do speak less softly than is appropriate, but I did look forward to marriage. When word came that a family in the next village was interested, I was terribly pleased. It was the family of Xu—said to be very highly spoken of—at least that is what the marriage broker told us. I longed to live in a family of my own. My brother now controlled our compound, and though he was kind, it is well known that a daughter is truly no child at all. Even an unfilial son will still bring water to aging parents, but a girl is raised for some other family. I was always told that and wanted my own home. But I wish my mother had warned me. A daughter at home may not be a real child, but a daughter-in-law who brings forth no children isn't even human." She said the last sentence with more bitterness than Jason had seen before.

So that was it. Now he remembered the comment several days before, when she had corrected Wu about divorce in China. So she was barren. He didn't have time to reflect further, for she went on with her story.

"My mother had accepted a good bride-price from the Xu family, and they came for me one day from their village. I was supposed to be frightened, but I really wasn't. I wanted the marriage, and the broker's talk of the young man made him seem kind. Of course, I acted very shy and sat silently on the pony as I was brought into the village. The marriage was like many others I'd seen before. I stood with my husband as one of his relatives read a long list of his ancestors. I kowtowed deeply to each name and anticipated with pleasure our married life together. Even my mother-in-law seemed kind enough, though she eyed me suspiciously.

"That first night we were never alone, as the neighbors and my husband's friends kept visiting us, but after that our married life went reasonably well. He wanted many sons, and I was sure I would provide them, for had not everyone told me even while I was still in split pants that I was exceptionally healthy. Even as a child when my feet were bound, I was less ill than many of the other girls. Some of them took on terrible fevers and even died. But despite all the pain, I'd remained healthy. Surely *Guanyin*, the goddess, would grant me healthy sons. I even accepted living there with so many strangers and his distant but correct mother. It was obvious she was exceptionally close to her second son, my husband, but still she seemed willing to accept me. But it was not to be." Her voice trailed off, and she appeared terribly strained.

"You don't have to talk if you don't want to," Jason said after some time. Although he said nothing, even Wu had been listening intensively.

Regaining her usual composure, she went on. "No, I owe you the story. You have been kind to me, though thinking I was something other than I am. No. I shall tell you my story, though it is a story few would find surprising. By the middle of the second year, I had not born a child, and although my husband had said little, his mother began to turn on me. Among us, the mother-in-law is empress over a daughter-in-law. I understood that. My mother had told me enough stories of her own youth. But this woman had begun to hate me. I was sure that she was talking against me to my husband, who himself became less open. My huge feet, at least huge to them, now became an issue as they had not been, and my occasional effort to speak my mind was unacceptable. Once I heard her threatening to force a divorce. If only I had a son! I kept thinking, but fate would not allow it.

"I was desperate, I had to have a son to open the door, to allow for future generations, but fate was cruel. My mother-in-law tormented me constantly. All I heard was that the most unfilial act possible was failure to have sons. She kept reminding my husband that beautiful women bring tragedy. He never answered her, but I could tell he listened. One night when it was very late, I crept out. I had hardly ever left our courtyard except when the itinerant merchants came by and then only with a servant. But the moon was out and I had a good idea where the temple of Guanyin, the goddess of fertility, lay. I was lost for a few minutes. At one point, some of my husband's kinsmen almost saw me, but I hid myself in the shadows.

"The temple was deserted, and as I entered, I hoped the goddess would understand. I stayed, and threw fortune bones, though I couldn't read their meaning. For weeks after that, I waited, but nothing. Still, the goddess had to listen eventually. I took to stealing out, sometimes several times a night, to pray at the temple. I never saw anyone. I remained sure the goddess would grant me a way to open the door to future generations. And something might have happened if the household had not changed.

"One day, maybe six new moons ago, just after the Dragon Boat Festival, my husband returned with a concubine. No one said anything to me. I stood there in shock as she was introduced. Such a young thing, even younger than I, with feet so small they would have pleased a court lady. My mother-in-law was beaming. I could tell she was secretly pleased that I looked so distressed.

"Could you not protest?" Jason asked.

"What was there to protest? Concubines are common and, in a house without sons, almost essential. Besides, to protest was to give further cause for hating me. Creating disharmony in the household would have been more unacceptable behavior." Her voice was resigned.

"The situation became intolerable. Constant Beauty, for that is her name, treated me with none of the respect due the first wife. I knew she was contemptuous, and when, almost before three moons passed, she was pregnant, it became impossible. She laughed at me as I worked alongside her under the mother-in-law's direction. I was given the worst jobs, the worst food. My husband said nothing. Once, when I tried to talk of it, he refused to listen. At night, when I heard him moving in the dark toward her quarters, I almost died. But at least, it gave me more time to steal away to the temple. For if he spent little time with me, still there was a chance, and only the goddess could help." Her story ended as she sat quietly, contemplating the fire.

"So that was why you tried to kill yourself?" Jason asked after a time.

"No, what really occurred was less planned. Something happened at the compound one night. I still don't know why, but they were all aroused, and my absence was noted. I heard the commotion as I walked home. Hearing voices, I hid myself. They knew I was gone, and the servants were looking for me. But their conversation, for I could hear it easily, was unexpected. They assumed—actually they said the old woman, my husband's mother, had declared I had been stealing out for months…that I had a lover somewhere. That the sages had forewarned about beautiful women for a reason.

"They walked past before I could hear more. My story about the temple would never have been believed. At first I started walking, a bit each night, but I had no food and within days I was starving. It was then that I determined to kill myself. I wanted to punish the woman, as she had me, to return as a ghost to haunt her. The idea was a sudden inspiration. I threw myself into the river. But you know the rest." She ended her story without any more ado. If she expected them to comment, it was not apparent. Jason just looked at her, feeling at a loss. It was obvious she could never return.

"Could you return to your own mother?" he asked after a time.

"That would be impossible. I am not of their family and have shamed them. No one would want me. I would only be a burden on my brother," she answered matter-of-factly.

Jason looked over to Wu, who had been listening intently. What were the young man's thoughts? he wondered.

CHAPTER 8

CAPTURE

They continued to travel together over the next weeks, and although Wu appeared somewhat less disapproving of her presence, he nevertheless remained disdainful. Jason, assuming Wu had become somewhat more sympathetic having heard her story, hoped the tension would eventually fade completely. Finally, Wu himself brought the subject up directly as Black Jade busied herself elsewhere.

"If you wish it, she can remain with us. I suppose we who travel toward the Taiping camps can hardly be considered faithful followers of the Master either."

"Don't you think we should tell her where we're going? It could be more dangerous than if she went back to her husband's home," Jason said.

"You may be right. Perhaps she should know. But it is extremely dangerous. If a word is said to the peasants we meet along the roads, we could all be dead. They would turn us in at the first opportunity. The peasants have reason to hate the long-haired rebels. They have destroyed Confucian and Buddhist shrines almost everywhere and even smashed ancestral tablets. Think long on it before you say anything."

Jason considered his words for several days. There was little reason to say anything immediately, since Black Jade had never asked. She seemed content for the moment to be rid of her hated mother-in-law and accepting of their daily trudge toward the north. One evening he decided to tell her. They had seen fewer and fewer imperial patrols in recent days, and the countryside itself was more denuded of population. It was increasingly obvious they were approaching the frontier between the imperials and those held by the Taipings.

"You should be told where we are traveling," he finally blurted out one evening as she stirred the rice pot.

"I already know. You are traitors, traveling to the long hairs," she answered calmly.

"Then you might wish to turn back, for it is, as you say, precisely toward their camps that we are traveling," he warned.

"Not at all. This one may be a lowly female, but we hear talk. The long hairs treat their women well. They don't bind the feet, and it is said they even let women fight for their foreign god. The washwomen say the Heavenly King's sister leads them. No. If you are going there, I want to see this strange place as well."

Wu had listened to their conversation without saying a word. Jason turned toward him as Wu shrugged. The young man looked surprised. He was clearly more able to accept his own curiosity than Black Jade's. Jason thought her unwillingness to accept the status of a woman as taught by Confucius bothered Wu. Nevertheless, Wu was willing to allow her to continue with them.

"So it is settled. Good, for we may soon be meeting them. I have seen many signs of their presence, and the peasants, those few we meet, clearly act as if they are near," said Wu.

"Why are you so sure of that?" Jason asked.

"Temples have been destroyed, yet the peasants speak of them with reverence, no doubt fearing their return. Friend, I think we will see them quite soon."

Much sooner than Jason had expected, Wu's prediction was fulfilled. The next day, the three of them were riding along on the two slow mules they had finally managed to purchase when they saw a peasant approaching them. The man, unusually articulate, spoke for a few minutes with Wu, while Jason, as was his habit, stayed out of the way for fear his Western features would attract attention. Finally, after the man ambled off, Wu turned to both of them.

"I think we have arrived," Wu announced. "That was no peasant but some sort of scout. He was far too intelligent to be anything else."

"What did he ask?"

"He tried to sell me an egg from his basket but was much more interested in asking about our party. I told him we were taking my sister back to her village after a visit, but I don't think he believed me, certainly not if he looked at your face under the shadow of that hat."

Wu was correct. Less than a half hour later, as they continued their march, a group of horsemen came into view. The riders rode very quickly toward them. One could see even at that distance that they were neither Chinese nor Manchu bannermen. Their clothing was less formal, and their hair lacked the distinctive queue that Wu and other Chinese wore.

"Do not do anything. We could be cut down immediately," Wu whispered.

"Maybe Confucius will save us," Jason whispered, trying to be funny but merely sounding nervous, as he waited for the horsemen to reach them.

"I doubt the Master would bother—a failed student, a foreigner, and barren woman traveling to meet rebels. Perhaps it would be better to ask your God for aid."

Before Jason could reply, the horsemen were upon them. Reining in their horses as the animals' nostrils flared, they jumped to the ground. To Jason's shock, he was thrown roughly to the ground, his face pushed into the dirt. From the corner of his eye, he could see that neither Wu nor Black Jade had fared better. After a second, his hands painfully tied together, he was pulled to a half-kneeling position as a young man, roughly his own age, stared at him with a combination of curiosity and contempt. Jason felt sweat rising on his brow, part of it running into his eyes, stinging him. It appeared unlikely that the Taipings were pleased by their arrival.

"Who are you, a foreign spy or merely an opium dealer?" The voice was harsh and sneering. "Or do you not understand the speech of the Heavenly Kingdom?"

"This humble one does understand," Jason replied. He tried to turn his head toward the speaker but was stopped by a sharp blow to his back.

"Keep your eyes to the ground. Again, who are you?"

"We are here to learn more of the Heavenly Kingdom and of the ways of the Elder and Younger Brother," Jason said, grateful for that evening in Guangzhou talking to the young rebel.

"Be careful, dog, when you talk of the great Tian Wang, the younger brother of Christ. Speak before we grow weary." The soldier's voice was frightening.

"It is as I said; we are here to learn of your ways to approach the truth."

Nothing more was said and he was roughly pushed to the ground again. The pain in his back was excruciating, and the midday sun, which a few moments before had been tolerable, was now burning against his cheek with ferocity.

One of the soldiers approached the leader. "The Han over there is a gentry. I'm sure of it. He speaks like an official."

"Great, they are as unimpressed with Wu as with me," Jason thought, perversely amused. Beyond his vision he could hear his friend trying to explain their presence, using terms similar to those he had employed. But it was obvious that Wu's speech itself irritated them. For the first time since meeting Wu, Jason was glad he'd learned his own Chinese on the wharves of Hong Kong. At least he didn't remind these angry young men of the Confucian gentry they apparently despised.

Trying, despite the heavy boot on his back, to look about, Jason finally located Black Jade lying prostrate on the ground a few feet to his left. No one seemed to be holding her, and she lay as they had thrown her. For that at least he was grateful.

After about ten minutes, the foot on his back was removed, but as he tried to find a more comfortable position, the voice from behind barked again.

"Move and you're dead. You, opium dealer, and your gentry friend." The voice was harsh and in a dialect Jason had difficulty understanding. He strained to become used to its unfamiliar tones. It was likely that his life might depend on understanding as quickly as possible.

To his surprise the soldiers, about twenty of them, were beginning to prepare camp. They apparently felt secure in the area and were planning to spend the night. Straining to see behind him, he noted his tormentor, a young man perhaps no more than twenty, now sitting on a rock watching him closely. A very sharp sword, not unlike the one he'd seen used weeks before to behead the Taipings, lay at his side.

The heat was becoming unbearable. But no effort was made to relieve his discomfort. To his right, Wu lay on the ground in a similarly prone position. Jason wondered if he were as uncomfortable as he was.

Much of the afternoon passed that way. The Taiping soldiers took their meal and began to gamble at some distance from him. After a time, another soldier replaced his own guard, but not a word was said. Jason needed to relieve himself and after a time, fearing a blow if he asked, quietly urinated on the ground where he lay. Would they ever offer them water? he wondered. By late afternoon the heat was intolerable, and Jason was contemplating some effort to demand attention. If it allowed for some comfort, perhaps a little water, fine; if not, it didn't matter; he could no longer lie there. As he started to rise, he heard a gasp from the soldier behind him and the sound of the sword being unsheathing. At that moment, though, the noise of arriving horses brought all the soldiers to their feet. Whoever they had been waiting for had obviously arrived.

The horseman, clearly an important officer, was accompanied by about ten additional riders, perhaps part of his guard. The commander, for he was quite obviously of high rank judging from the reactions of Jason's captors, reined in the horse as they arrived and jumped to the ground.

The man was about thirty and quite athletic looking. Holding himself somewhat aloof, he listened to the brief report offered by the soldier who had initially interrogated them.

Jason could hear nothing of the conversation. His emotions swayed from fear to relief that at last the waiting appeared to be over. Turning to the three, the officer finally gave them a long look and then, taking some water from one of his subordinates, drank deeply and then proceeded to a makeshift table that had been set up.

It looked like another tribunal, a mirror image of the one they had only weeks before seen, sentence Taipings to death. Only now it was their turn, Black Jade, Wu, and himself standing in the dock. Although he had already half risen, Jason was abruptly pulled to a standing position. When he attempted to walk forward, his shoulder was rudely pulled backward. Wu was to go first.

His friend had only a slight moment to glance at him before being led forward and then thrown brutally to the ground before the seated officer.

"Who are you?" the voice growled. "A stinking gentry come to spy—tell the truth or you will die here!"

"My name is Wu, from a village near Guangzhou. I am not a spy, only someone interested in learning more about the Heavenly Kingdom of Great Peace."

"That's a lie. Confucian gentry have no interest in the truth. You turn the peasants against us, and serve the dog Manchus!"

Jason was as nervous as he could imagine. There seemed little likelihood that any of them would leave the place alive. What would happen to Black Jade? She had merely come with them lacking alternatives. Was she to die as well? He tried to turn toward her, but a blow to his head sent him spinning to the ground. As he struggled to stand again, his mouth filled with blood from a wound on his lip. A small trickle of blood ran down his neck.

"I am not a gentry; at least I have passed no more than the lowest of the exams. I speak the truth when I say I am interested in the teachings of your Master the Heavenly King."

One of the officers whispered something into the commander's ear and the two smiled among themselves. Finally turning back toward Wu, he began again.

"Then you are a servant to the opium dealer there. Another poison on us, Confucius and the opium dealers. We execute opium smokers and dealers here."

"I can only answer that I know nothing of such things. I do not deal in opium, nor does my foreign friend."

With a gesture Wu was abruptly jerked upward and moved to the side. It was not clear whether a decision had been made. In another second Jason was on the ground before the makeshift tribunal.

"And you, opium dealer, if you understand me. Prepare to die, for we will not allow opium here," the man barked.

As Wu had done, Jason attempted to explain in his most polite Chinese that he did not deal in opium or any illegal activity; that he too had come to learn about the Heavenly Kingdom. Ignoring Jason, the officer turned to his colleague. "He speaks the language of the Hong Kong masses and very well indeed. That is unusual."

"We noted it as well. That is why we sent you the message. He is an unusual foreigner."

"Why do you speak Chinese so well?" he asked, turning back toward Jason. "Tell me who your father is and of your family."

Jason began to tell of his father's role as a missionary. It was the truth, but knowing what he did about Chinese attitudes toward the missionaries, he wondered if the story would finish him off faster than admitting to selling opium.

"Do you know the missionary Roberts?" the officer asked, now looking for the first time to be actually interested in the prisoners.

Roberts, Jason wondered to himself. Did he know such a man? It seemed important and then remembering, he said, "Issachar Roberts, I remember him well. He is a friend of my family, a close friend of my father, though I've not seen him for a long time."

As he spoke he could see that something significant had occurred. The officer's visage took on a warmer appearance. "What does the man look like?" he asked after a moment.

"It's hard to recall. He left Hong Kong some time ago; I was much younger. Wait..." An image came to mind of the harsh wind-blown reddish face of the older missionary. Then another thought, something he heard his father's friends speak of.

"Wasn't Reverend Roberts a teacher, I mean a teacher of your Heavenly King?" Yes, he was sure of it; a letter had arrived years before from Nanjing, written by the Heavenly King himself. His father's friends had often spoken of it.

"Yes, you must be of Hong Kong, and my soldiers found no trace of opium on you. What of your gentry friend? Who is he?"

"He is as he says, a young man like myself, interested in learning about the Heavenly Kingdom of Great Peace, the *Taiping Tianguo*."

"And the woman?"

"Merely a companion."

It was the first time anyone had mentioned Black Jade's presence. The answer seemed enough.

"Well, son of a missionary, you will have your way. You can see the Heavenly Capital. If Roberts accepts you, you can learn of our ways."

With that the officer rose abruptly, and gave orders to his associates. Everything had changed. They were given two horses and set off alongside the others. Wu rode his own horse, which, to Jason's surprise, he seemed to ride well. They were off to Nanjing to see the Taipings they had long sought. To Jason's private relief, there was someone there he even knew slightly. For the rest of that morning, as Black Jade sat behind him, her arms wrapped tightly around his chest, Jason tried to concentrate on remembering everything he could about the old minister who had from time to time visited his parents.

CHAPTER 9

WITH THE TAIPINGS

O ver the next weeks, for it was still a considerable distance to Nanjing, the three travelers were left largely to themselves. Each day the Taiping soldiers provided them with food and mounts, but beyond that little else. Jason would have enjoyed speaking more with the soldiers, but few seemed willing to talk. Perhaps, he speculated, his status remained ambiguous enough to require caution. Jason was particularly interested in talking with the senior officer who had originally asked about Roberts. But the man was busy most of the time and seemed not to have given them much thought after their original conversation. Only once did Jason get the chance to approach him.

"Sir, is the Reverend Roberts actually in Nanjing now?" Jason asked as if by chance, though he'd long looked for an opening.

The officer looked at him very closely, as if he'd forgotten who Jason was.

"I am not sure. Roberts is very well known among us. The Tian Wang has often spoken of his old teacher. Though we follow the Heavenly Master, we are still Chinese, and among us one's former teachers are very honored. But no, I don't think Roberts is in Nanjing yet. We have heard that he has long tried to visit it. I let you accompany us because I believed that he will soon arrive. As the son of his friend, you will no doubt be warmly received by him." With that the man turned to an approaching soldier who had business with him.

So that was it, Jason thought to himself. Roberts is so well thought of among Taipings that the officer hopes to win the support of the potentially influential missionary by doing him the favor of bringing Jason back to Nanjing.

"What did he tell you?" Wu asked excitedly as soon as Jason had returned to their cooking fire. Black Jade sat near equally interested.

"It is as we thought. Roberts is very well respected and thus we are under his indirect protection. At least for the moment," he added after reflection.

"But who is Roberts? You must remember more than you've said. Will he know you?" Black Jade asked concerned, remembering how tenuous their reprieve from execution had been.

"It's as I have told you. He and his wife lived in Guangzhou, not Hong Kong. So my family didn't see him often. I do remember they visited us several times, the last only a couple of years ago. I think he'd been back to America. He's from the southern part of the United States. I don't know very much. He's maybe fifty. All I really remember is that he was a fiery man, much more emotional and louder than my father. In fact, as I think about it, I vaguely recall that my father found him ill mannered. Though I'm sure he admired his missionary work. There was some trouble with the group back in America that sponsored him, but I don't know exactly what."

"Well, I hope he remembers you. Knowing the Tian Wang's teacher could be very important," Black Jade commented.

"Are you nervous about going to Nanjing?" Jason asked.

"It's hard to be nervous when you have already tried to kill yourself. But I do want to go there. I have heard impossible stories about the women there. I want to see if it can be so."

"What do you mean?" Jason asked, his curiosity aroused.

"They are said to do unheard-of-things there," Wu cut in. "It is rumored that they let women wander shamelessly in the streets... that they live apart from their families and that some attain high rank, even as soldiers. It is impossible to believe. I doubt it can be so."

"That is as I have heard, but even more, that they teach that women are equal and that foot-binding is wrong. I would like to see such a place," she added, with a considerably different tone to her voice.

"I've never heard of such things. Can Taiping ways be so different from the rest of China?" Jason asked Wu after a time.

"For me, I think it impossible. The ways of the Master have always served even those who destroy empires. Did not the Manchus follow the Master as the Ming had done?"

"Maybe they did, but the Taipings are different. They follow the foreign religion, the ways of Jason's people, and such things are done among them. We will see," she added.

Although Wu was slowly getting used to her, he was obviously put off. He said nothing, but it was clear he still found her behavior difficult to accept. Nevertheless, he had been willing to travel with her, and for that Jason was grateful. The next morning, after a breakfast made primarily of small bits of sweet potato floating in hot water, Jason and Black Jade assumed their usual positions on the horse.

"I don't know how to ask this, but if the Taipings are against women with bound feet, do you think you will be accepted?" asked Jason.

"That is something I have thought about. But they are still Chinese, and most women among them must still have lotus feet. It should not be a great difficulty."

"What would happen if you unbound them? I see you at night forcing the binding cloths around your feet. Could you stop doing that?" he asked, unsure of the subject. He knew enough of foot-binding to know that it was a very private matter. To his relief her natural outspokenness allowed the conversation to continue without offense.

"For most women, for my own sisters, beautiful tiny feet are a source of extreme pride. But for me, who suffered so as a small child only to have my feet remain too large, I would gladly stop. But could I? I don't know; the pain of binding them stopped long ago, but even now, if the binders are too loose, some of that pain starts to return. Would they return to a more natural form? I don't know. I only know the pain would probably be terrible."

"Have you ever heard of a woman who tried it?"

"Occasionally one hears things, that it is terrible to let them out, but who knows, maybe the stories are lies to frighten. Everyone knows men love tiny feet."

Her comments reminded him of his New England-bred mother, as tough and outspoken a woman as he had ever met. More and more he was coming to understand how little chance Black Jade had had to be accepted into a traditional Chinese household. The inability to bear children had probably been only one of the tensions. Would the Taiping's Heavenly Kingdom provide a more hospitable atmosphere for her? he wondered.

Over the next weeks, he continued to spend as much time as possible listening to the conversations of the Taiping soldiers. Their dialects were often difficult to understand, yet Jason was certain he'd need to improve his skills. Nevertheless, he found himself thinking constantly of Black Jade, not as a friend but as something much more. Sometimes as they rode, he imagined that the grip she held on him meant more than mere security. Did she feel anything for him? he wondered. In the almost two years since he'd left Hong Kong during the entire time working in Guangzhou and in the many months since, he'd never had any real interest in a woman, but now that had changed. Again, to his irritation, the image of his father came to mind. The older minister was upset enough about his leaving Hong Kong; what would he think of Jason's new thoughts?

As the days passed, they found themselves more and more often traveling by boat toward Nanjing. The soldiers accompanying them changed often, and only a few of those who had originally imprisoned them continued with the group. It was pure luck that had brought them into the hands of the officer who had originally decided to send them on to Nanjing. As for his subordinates, although they were more willing to talk given the intimacy of boat travel, few of them were very knowledgeable about the capital itself. Among the common soldiers, most had never even been to Nanjing.

After a time, primarily by eavesdropping on their conversations, Jason was able to establish that among them, at least two groups predominated. The Guangxi people, apparently longtime followers of the Tian Wang, and many Cantonese. The former was far more difficult for Jason to understand despite considerable effort. The Cantonese were less pious than many of their Guangxi brethren. It was clear from their mumbling that despite the official attitude of the officers, they were quite familiar with opium. Although he never saw any opium among them, their easy jokes regarding the substance made it apparent that the famous Taiping abhorrence of the stuff was perhaps more ambiguous than he'd heard.

Some of the men were quite bombastic, and one, caught up one evening in telling tales of his military prowess, had almost completely disrobed in order to impress them with the many wounds across his body.

One day, though, tensions again surfaced. From whispered conversations it was clear they were approaching an area only recently captured by the rebels. As they neared another settlement, the sounds of gunfire could still be heard, and to Jason, Wu, and Black

Jade's horror, the river heretofore empty suddenly seemed filled with bodies. Most of them were recently dead, almost all were, as was obvious from their bald heads, Buddhist monks slaughtered at some nearby monastery.

Watching Wu carefully, for he knew how basically traditional the young man was, Jason put his arm on his shoulder.

"It could be dangerous to ask any questions," he whispered into the young scholar's ear.

"It is obvious anyway. They were merely monks, unfilial followers of the Buddha," Wu said calmly.

The comment surprised Jason and again reminded him of how little he really understood his friend. That the gentry hated and despised the missionaries he'd known all his life, but that the Confucians had so little sympathy for Buddhists was less familiar.

Black Jade, though, was more visibly upset. Her eyes remained rigidly fixed on the water, saying nothing. Jason watching her could see that her eyes moistened.

If Wu's attitude had at first been harder than expected, he quickly changed. For no more than a few minutes after arriving in the area, they pulled along shore as their escorts jumped out to gather provisions and consult with their countrymen. For the moment the three of them were alone on the riverbank waiting to see what would happen next.

Suddenly Wu set off at a fast pace toward the center of the village. He'd seen something.

"Stay here!" Jason yelled at Black Jade as he set off after his friend. It would not do for the local Taipings to see an unfamiliar woman running about. Realizing she had followed him anyway, he turned back toward her.

"Listen, we need to stay with the group on the boat; you saw what happened when we were mere strangers among them."

"We stay together. It's too late to change that. Look, we'll lose him."

They set off at a run trying to catch him. After a moment he was in view again. There was no problem now. He had stopped at the door of a Confucian temple or what had been one. All the figures were destroyed, the altar pulled down. The smell of urine emerged from the broken figurines.

Wu said not a word as they walked back toward the boats. Jason could feel a coldness coming from him that he'd not seen before. Climbing back into the boats, for it was obvious no one had even noticed their absence, the three sat in silence. Was Wu still as interested in seeing the Taiping's world as he had once been? Jason wondered to himself. Thinking of the smashed ancestral tablets that had been strewn across the floor of the temple, he marveled at how different these Taipings were from any Chinese he'd ever known.

"Are you regretting our decision to go to Nanjing?" Jason whispered into Wu's ear after the boats had pushed off, apparently their business having been taken care of.

"No. Well, perhaps a bit, but there is still nothing left for me in my father's home. The life of a coolie is worse than this." His voice remained resolute, determined to pull on.

"Besides," he added a moment later, "I don't think we could leave anyway. We would hardly last long in the region. Either the Taipings would kill us or some gentry militia would determine our fate."

He was right, Jason thought to himself, and then before he could continue, he felt an unfamiliar presence moving near them. To his surprise Liu, the commanding officer of the detachment, came over to them. Seating himself near Black Jade, at whom he glanced closely but did not address, he turned to the two young men.

"You will see more of the same as we near the Heavenly Kingdom. Understand we only destroy those who resist us, as that village had. The local gentry often arouse the people against our soldiers. When people accept our rule, they are allowed to live peacefully. The Qing generals, especially those dogs of the Manchu, Zeng, Li, and Zuo, always kill every one of our captured people…all of them whether they resist or not. Understand, we can be merciful and our troops controlled. There have been times when our soldiers have been told that their feet would be cut off if they even tried to steal from a private home."

And then almost with a sigh, he said, "But that was long ago. Sometimes now things happen that we would never have been allowed in the early years." His voice trailed off, perhaps in thought.

It was the first time he had spent more than a few seconds with them since that initial interview. For the first time, Jason thought, the man actually looked interested in talking with them.

"Have you served the Heavenly King long?" Jason asked carefully.

The man looked at him closely, seeming for a moment to be suspicious, wondering how frank he could be. It was a look Jason would eventually find common in Nanjing.

"For a very long time—almost since the beginning. I even served under the great Prince Feng Yunshan in the early years. He was one of the greatest Wangs of the Heavenly King. My family is from Guangdong, as is the Tian Wang, and we early on followed him. I was very young but found his tales beautiful. His stories of the Great Lord, of Jesus, his elder brother, and his teachings moved me—that we shouldn't smoke tobacco or opium that we should share. Many who followed were shunned by their families, but my sister and I joined together. The Tian Wang preached against prostitution, against foot-binding, against concubines, and she decided to join even in defiance of our family. Today my sister is a great figure in the imperial palace," he said with pride.

"Have you yourself ever served in the Heavenly Palace?" Wu asked with enthusiasm.

Surveying Wu, for the officer was clearly less than enthusiastic about Wu's obvious gentry manners, he finally answered.

"I have been there but only at the formal audiences. Except for the Tian Wang and his own family, only women serve the Heavenly King within the palace. But I know more than most about what goes on there."

So his sister keeps him informed, Jason thought to himself, though the man said nothing further.

"Are there many Westerners among you?" Jason asked.

"From time to time, they come. Since last year, when our forces broke out of the imperialist encirclement and began our new offensives, many have come. Most of them are missionaries." Then turning to Jason once again, he asked, "How well do you really know Reverend Roberts?" The answer was obviously important to the man. "Don't be afraid to be honest."

"He often visited my family. He and my father are good friends, both Americans, and he has stayed often at our home. I think he will remember me, though when I saw him last, I was more of a child." The answer seemed to satisfy the man, and after a moment he moved off, not though before turning toward Black Jade.

"Are you trying to unbind your feet?"

"Yes," she said quietly, much to Jason's surprise.

"Be warned. I have seen women try it. It rarely works well and always brings great pain," he said quietly.

"But are women of the Heavenly Kingdom not expected to have unbound feet?" she asked.

"Yes. But among us, large and tiny feet are both common. Our movement is young." With that he moved off a bit, but not before whispering something in her ear.

Jason was astonished. The officer was certainly more aware of them than he had realized.

He turned to question her, but it was clear she did not wish to discuss the matter further.

For the rest of the afternoon, as they continued to travel along the river, little conversation took place. It was still very hot despite the fact that fall was finally starting to arrive. Jason guessed it might be about September on the Western calendar. He'd heard that the Taipings had even devised a new calendar to accompany their new Heavenly Kingdom. But more than heat made conversation difficult, for the countryside they were passing through was largely devastated by fighting.

Very few buildings still stood in the villages they passed, and no more than an occasional peasant could be spotted. The intensity of the fighting was horrendous. The region had probably, he guessed to himself, passed many times between the Taipings and the imperial soldiers.

Later that evening, after they had all settled along the shore and the bulk of the Taiping soldiers, to the officer's noticeable displeasure, had formed a large gambling circle, the man returned to the three friends. To Jason's surprise, Liu carried a flask and handed it to Black Jade, who poured it into one of the cooking bowls.

"It's cold water from an underground spring," he said. "I've been there many times." She discreetly put her still-bound feet in the pot. It was obvious that the cold water was meant to ease the pain that had resulted from the loosened bindings. At least if she were going to try to do it, Jason was grateful that the officer knew something of the process. Nevertheless, he found himself irritated as well.

"So, young scholar, tell me the truth. Why are you really here?" Liu asked, turning toward Wu. His voice carried none of the anger of the original interrogation, now long weeks behind them.

"It's as I have told you before. I merely wished to know more of your people and the ways of the God-worshipers." Wu was recognizably uncomfortable.

"Young scholar, I have no desire to harm you. Too few gentry have been willing to listen to the truth of the Tian Wang. But I am not stupid. Tell me the truth." His voice, although restrained, made it clear the time for stalling had ended.

As he watched Wu's face, Jason could see how nervous his friend was. In the corner of his eye, he saw Black Jade lean forward from her sitting space.

"Well," Wu started with considerable difficulty. Once he began, the whole story—the exams, the horrible mistake—came out in measured tones of pain. Wu was still terribly hurt, disappointed, and ashamed. When he finished he stared at the ground, as if spent. To Jason's surprise the officer said nothing at first. He seemed deep in thought and then a smile breaking on his face was followed by a tremendous bellow of laughter. The man found the story hilarious. Wu was dumbfounded. He'd expected almost any reaction except that.

"I'm sorry, scholar," Liu finally said, catching his breath. "I have no desire to hurt you. But here, insulting the emperor's ancestors is hardly the horror you think it is. Among us you may find it a badge of honor." With that he continued to chuckle to himself as he got up. The three friends stared at each other in complete shock, and then as Wu himself started to laugh, the group broke out in peals of merriment. Jason had never seen Wu look so relaxed.

CHAPTER 10

NANJING, THE
HEAVENLY CAPITAL

I t was just over a week later when the last two boats, for the group had grown smaller, arrived at the Heavenly Capital. They paddled into the creek that passed from the Yangtze up to Nanjing and disembarked at a small walled city located there. Liu was well known to the officers in charge. Little time was spent in formalities. Neither Jason or Wu nor Black Jade were asked a thing. Within minutes horses appeared to take them the short distance to the city. Upon arriving at Nanjing, the only delay was finding a passable gate, for at the first they tried, no one seemed able to receive them. Some time passed as they searched for a gate to let them in.

"It was not always so," Liu said, turning to Jason. "I remember when the Heavenly Capital was as well run as any in the empire and our soldiers all devoted God-worshipers."

He then turned and consulted with his assistant. Although Liu was from the south, he was clearly comfortable with the northern dialect, which was still beyond Jason's skills. Not understanding made him more nervous than he had expected to feel.

Nothing though could have prepared him for the scene within the walls of Nanjing. In almost two years at Guangzhou, a city itself severely bombarded, he had never seen anything like it. Literally half the buildings were torn down; devastated ruins with broken pottery and burned timbers were everywhere. As they passed through the streets, the small group became terribly quiet, surveying the devastation. Some buildings seemed to have been destroyed more systematically, perhaps for fuel during the winters.

"You should understand," Liu began, "we have been almost completely encircled by the imperial forces more than once. The city has experienced great sufferings."

From behind, for Black Jade had continued to ride with him, he felt a strong nudge in the shoulder blades.

"Look, it is unheard of. The stories were true."

Turning in the direction she pointed, Jason spotted a group of women walking freely through the streets, reasonably well-dressed women, obviously from respected households. There were several groups of them, some walking alongside young men and others on horseback. As the group passed, he could feel Black Jade straining to see their feet. Just as they'd heard, the feet were unbound and their behavior in public more open than any of them had ever seen. Glancing to his side, he noticed Liu watching her intently. The man seemed pleased, especially at Black Jade's obvious delight.

After a time, they arrived at a small compound. Liu dismounted, and motioned to them to relax while he went inside.

"This place is even more curious than I had imagined. It looks Chinese, as Chinese as people from the north can look, but the feel of the place is so different. Did you see the women?" Wu asked with a tone of wonderment.

"We did, and the devastation as well. It's hard to think such a place can really defeat the Manchu emperor," Jason commented.

"But did we not hear of their great victories on the coast, in Guangxi and elsewhere?" Black Jade asked defensively. She already wanted to make their cause her own. But before either of them could answer, Liu had returned.

"The young scholar and Black Jade will stay here. They will be well taken care of. I promise that. Meanwhile, we two will visit Roberts. They say he arrived only a few days ago and that he himself awaits the summons of the Tian Wang, his former student."

It was apparent that Black Jade and Wu were apprehensive about separating from their foreign friend. But there was little to do. If Liu had long before dropped his authoritarian tone, it was nevertheless obvious that their fate still remained in his hands.

"We will see each other soon," Jason said as he hurried to mount alongside Liu. With that they rode off. The American could feel his spine tense. He'd come to realize how well known the Tian Wang's old teacher was among the Taipings. Liu's interest in bringing him to Roberts was clearly designed to gain the influential foreigner's gratitude. Given the situation it would hardly do for Roberts not to receive him well. But would the man even remember him? Had the man even noticed him as child?

No more than twenty minutes later, at a compound considerably larger and better maintained than most, Jason later learned it was that of the Heavenly King's cousin, Hong Rengan, they dismounted. Several servants appeared at the gate, and after a consultation with them, the two were led into the courtyard and eventually settled in a sitting room. Within minutes Roberts walked in. Jason, fearful at not been recognized, stepped forward.

"Reverend Roberts, it's Jason Brandt, Abraham Brandt's son."

"Of course, but you—here! This is indeed a surprise."

Jason breathed a sigh of relief. From his left he could tell Liu was satisfied.

"Let me introduce, Commander Liu; it was he who helped me travel overland to see you." Roberts turned to the officer, bowed graciously, and switched into Chinese.

"I am most pleased that you have brought my young friend here. His father and I are old friends. I knew his mother well; may her soul rest in peace, as did my wife. Please sit down. I myself am merely a guest here. But I believe I can offer you tea." Turning to a servant who stood near the door, the request was made.

"You may have just arrived, Mr. Roberts, but we of the Taipings have long known of your work and that of our other foreign brethren. Among those of us who have followed the Tian Wang since the early years, his old teacher is most well thought of. I have heard the Heavenly King himself speak of his study with you at Guangzhou."

"You are most kind, but I am no more than a humble servant of the Lord, whom we both serve."

"If I might ask, have you seen the Heavenly King yet?" Liu asked after a moment.

"No. Not yet. I only arrived a day or so ago, but I expect to see him shortly, if only to offer my support. There is much work here for the Lord, and I wish merely to teach of Jesus."

"I think the Heavenly King will be pleased with your intentions. Many of us, perhaps even the Tian Wang, have noticed a decline in the religious conviction of our people. That is something all of us must work to arrest."

The tea was brought, and after sipping it quietly, Roberts told Jason he wanted him to stay there as his guest. Liu was obviously pleased. The Taiping officer had concluded bringing them to Nanjing had been worthwhile. The powerful foreigner was grateful and that might one day be helpful. After a moment he took his leave with a promise to visit Jason again soon.

Roberts, the soul of politeness, accompanied the officer to the gate of the compound and then, still without saying a word to Jason, quietly returned and closed the doors to the room. Once alone, he turned angrily toward Jason and barked in English.

"What are you doing here? Your father is almost dead with worry! He's not heard from you in almost a year! He told me everything—of your impiety—that childish decision to run off to Guangzhou. I can't imagine what your mother would think. May her soul rest in peace!"

Then to Jason's surprise, Roberts abruptly spit with expertise into a nearby vase. Going on, he said, "I've had two letters from Abraham in the last six months. He doesn't know if you're alive or dead. He begged me to keep a watch for you in Shanghai. And that police unit you joined—what a waste for the son of Abraham Brandt! And then to abandon Guangzhou for God knows what! So what are you doing here?"

Jason could hardly believe the outburst. His throat felt incredibly dry. It was as if Roberts had shed his disguise to become his own avenging father.

"It's, ah, hard to explain; you wouldn't understand. I couldn't return to America, to college." Then feeling his own anger rising, he said, "I may not have been sure what I felt back in Hong Kong, but that was almost two years ago. I have become an adult. China is my home. Maybe someday I could be a preacher like you or my father, but only here in China, and not for a long time. I love my father. But I can't live as he would have me live. It was wrong not telling him when I left Guangzhou. But it really wasn't possible. This is the first time I've seen another Westerner in almost a year, let alone found a way to send a message."

Roberts stared at him quietly for a long time and then said, "So you've come up country. That must have been an incredible trip. Tell me about it."

As Roberts's interest was sparked, his tone changed. Now less fatherly, treating him somewhat more equally, he listened quietly as Jason described the trip, the months of walking, the endless boat trips, and the horses they had had available near the end. He spoke at length of Wu, almost nothing of Black Jade, fearing misunderstanding. He was glad that Roberts never asked about the initial reason for leaving Guangzhou. Happily, Roberts's questions were mostly of the countryside, how receptive to foreigners the people had been, how open they might be to the presence of missionaries. Roberts also wanted to know if they'd encountered any Catholic priests.

His interest was professional, and Jason was pleased with the chance to share his knowledge. It was clear his understanding of the interior exceeded even that of the experienced gray-haired missionary. However, though Roberts's curiosity was satisfied, Jason felt he was looking at him again with the original look of irritation.

"If you want, sir, I am sure I can find another place to stay. I don't want to be a burden to you."

"Nonsense, boy; everything I said is true. But still you're certainly welcome to stay here with me. I owe that to your father. Besides, maybe you can be a help in my work. I might even make a God-fearing man out of you here in the Heavenly Capital. Though from what I have seen so far, it's difficult to be confident."

Jason wasn't sure if he was talking about the Taiping religiosity or his own but thought better of asking. At least he had a place to stay, and as soon as he determined that his friends were settled in, he'd be able to relax completely.

"Now go, clean yourself up and return when you're presentable," the old man barked out after a moment.

"You are most kind, sir. Am I not keeping you from your work?"

"Saint's alive. I've no work for the moment; I just got here. I'm waiting for my call to see the so-called Heavenly King, and for the master of this place, Prince Gan, to arrive. He told me he'd not be here for at least a week after my own arrival. Now go wash up."

The servants were as attentive as any he'd ever seen. They saw to it that his filthy clothes were taken away. Plenty of water was made available for washing and an incredibly soft silk gown laid out for him when he was ready. The room, if not large, was more comfortable than any he'd ever seen and the decorations, mostly of birds, incredibly well done. He was half tempted to take a nap but then thought better of it. Roberts was interested in talking and there might not be as good a time later.

"There! Now you look like a presentable Chinaman." Roberts laughed as he came in. "Sit down; have some melon and more tea. I can tell you it's hard to find either these days."

Roberts started talking…of his boyhood in South Carolina and then of his work in Mississippi. As he spoke, Jason realized that some of the stories were familiar, that he'd heard them around his own family table years before. Roberts's youth working among lepers in Macao was particularly terrifying as the older man described with relish the ravages of that horrible disease. Later, his tales of battling the various missionary societies that sponsored him were told with humor and anger. Roberts was a man of strong conviction and fiery temper.

"But what of the Tian Wang?" Jason asked after a time.

"Ah, that's another story. In truth, I did not at first remember him. It was a long time ago, almost thirteen years. He came to the Guangzhou mission about five years after the end of the Opium War. He was very pious and spoke of fascinating visions. He was there for several months, working with me, a couple hours a day on the Bible, prayers, and so forth. Then he went off. I heard nothing of him for years. I'd really quite forgotten him, didn't think a thing of the man, even after news of the rebellion arrived in Guangzhou. That it was anything more than the usual Chinese rebellion, secret societies and all, all of them devil-worshipers, didn't occur to me. That is until—I was in Hong Kong; I might even have been staying with your parents—I found out that my old student was running the entire thing. Good Lord, was I surprised and determined then and there to visit his society of God-worshipers, as they were called!"

"Was he baptized?"

At that the older man took a long breath.

"No. That is one of the more curious elements to the whole story. Just as we were about to baptize him, he implied that he required some financial support to go along with it. Well, as you know, that showed a considerable lack of faith, and we terminated our plans."

"So you think he was insincere?"

"No. Maybe just a bit naïve. Found out later one of his fellows, forget the man's name now, put him up to it. Knew I'd not abide by it and wanted Hong, for that's his family name, thrown out. I suppose Hong's visions aroused the man's jealousy. But that was long ago; it's all forgotten. Hong even wrote once asking me to visit."

"I'd have liked to sooner. But it was impossible. The Manchus controlled the lines toward Nanjing. My wife was ill; I even had to return to the States for a while. It was impossible to get here until recently, when the Taipings began again to advance toward Shanghai. Now one can travel fairly freely, or at least I could have given my association with their Heavenly King."

With that their conversation ended. Roberts was approached by one of the household servants and something whispered into his ear.

"This is it, boy. Prince Gan, our host, has returned. I expect to see him shortly. Perhaps before I explain my extension of his hospitality to you, I'd better meet him alone."

"Do you expect to see the Tian Wang soon?" Jason asked.

"I'd certainly like to, but there's that issue of the Kowtow— seems the Heavenly Kingdom's more pagan than many'd like to believe. Still insists that every foreigner who sees him fall to his knees as if he were our Lord himself. Well, I'll be damned if I'll do that, not even after waiting all these years."

"But would the Tian Wang make you, his old teacher, do it? The Chinese revere their teachers so much."

"That's my hope. He'll understand I'm here doing the Lord's work as I once taught him and that this nonsense can be done away with. But now, I really need to go."

With that he hurried off. As Jason sat there thinking about the day's events, he was terribly excited. Here he was here at the center of the most exciting developments in China, maybe even a chance to meet the Tian Wang himself if he were lucky. As he sat musing over the possibilities, he was more and more aware of the commotion going on in other parts of the compound. It was obvious that Prince Gan, cousin of the Heavenly King, the master of the house, had returned.

He knew little of the man save the few comments Liu had mentioned during their travels. It was said that he was very intelligent and more worldly than the Heavenly King. Liu had even mentioned that although he now held positions of great responsibility among the Taipings, he'd only recently joined the movement. Meeting him would be worthwhile in itself.

Nevertheless, his own standing in the household was precarious at best, and Jason returned to the room he'd been assigned. The rest of the afternoon was spent looking over Taiping literature, which lay in shelves around the room. The material, far simpler than most of the Chinese literature Wu had provided during the two years of their friendship, was full of Taiping prayers and other liturgical works. Some of it was quite familiar, material he'd studied his entire life, but other parts of the work, the stories of the Tian Wang's visions from God and his relationship with Jesus, would certainly have shocked his father. As he read, Jason wondered how familiar Reverend Roberts was with the basics of Taiping thought.

After a time, growing bored, he considered venturing out into the streets of Nanjing but decided against it. The sentries at the gate of the compound had no orders regarding him, and it might later prove impossible to return. Creating an awkward situation for Roberts was hardly what he had in mind, especially on his first day in Nanjing. He went back to the Taiping material and continued to study it. Whatever Roberts might think of the material, he knew that he himself was little bothered by the tracts. His own questioning of the basic ideas of Christianity was so far advanced that such heresy, as he was sure his father would pronounce the material, hardly moved him. He felt a little guilty but nevertheless understood that the more he read of the Taipings, the more worthwhile his own stay among them might be. If only he were sure just what his own goals actually were.

A bit later, a servant arrived and quietly placed a package on the sleeping couch. Without a word, the man then withdrew. It was from Roberts. Jason opened it eagerly. There folded neatly were several months' worth of *North China Daily News*. How thoughtful of the old missionary to think of him! Taking up the earliest of the newspapers, an edition from the previous summer, Jason eagerly devoured the English-language Shanghai newspaper. So involved was he that at first he didn't even notice when another servant arrived to inform him that he was expected at dinner in a few minutes. Jason was to dine with Roberts and Prince Gan himself. With enthusiasm, he prepared as well as possible. It would not do to make a poor impression. Much might be riding on it.

CHAPTER 11

ROBERTS AND PRINCE GAN

The older servant led him down a long hallway toward the dining room where Roberts and Prince Gan sat. As they approached, he could hear sounds of laughter. After opening the door, the servant indicated that he should wait for an invitation to enter. After a second, Prince Gan, an elegant man of about fifty, dressed in beautiful silken robes called to him.

"Come in. Please sit. Forgive my lack of English, but your language skills precede you. Here, sit down near me. Dinner is about to begin—'supper,' as I believe Americans call it." He pronounced the English word with care—it was obviously part of a very limited knowledge of English.

"The good Reverend Roberts and I were just discussing how much we have in common."

When Jason looked puzzled, Prince Gan began to explain.

"It is quite true. We two were both involved almost at the beginning of our movement. My cousin and I studied with the good reverend when you were no more than a boy. In fact, I for a time studied as well in Hong Kong. I believe I even remember your father."

At that, Jason was amazed.

"No, it is true; he knew me by another name. Could hardly advertise my ties to the leader of the great rebellion. But I did serve among the missionaries for a long time. On occasion I even dealt with your father, though I doubt he would remember me."

"So you studied with the Western missionaries longer than your cousin?" Jason asked, becoming more comfortable. He was increasingly aware that this man was much more familiar with Westerners than he expected. He spoke with an air not only of learning, as Liu did, but also appeared quite familiar with foreigners and their different ways. As the evening wore on, Jason would find to his embarrassment that the man's knowledge of the West far exceeded his own.

"Yes, I have spent much more time with you 'barbarians' than my cousin. And that is another comparison between the good reverend and myself. Each of us knew the Tian Wang long before anyone had ever heard of the long-haired rebels. Yet after the rebellion broke out, neither could get to the Heavenly Capital. Both of us spent years in the port cities. It was not until last year that I was able to finally travel to Nanjing. And of course as you know, the Reverend Roberts has only just arrived."

There was something about the man that made Jason feel immediately comfortable.

"But you are one of the major leaders of the Taipings. Would that not be difficult after such a long absence? Would you be truly trusted?" Jason asked.

Prince Gan looked at him closely. "Your question shows that you are wise beyond your years. Just as Roberts and Commander Liu have told me."

So he and Liu had already spoken. He wondered if now were the point when he might inquire about his friends and then thought better of it.

"As your question implies," Prince Gan went on, "it was not easy for one gone for so long to have influence. But my cousin, with whom I had been very close, was glad to see me. There was a time when our movement had great energy and leadership. But times have changed. The Tian Wang prefers religious subjects to those of practical administration, and many of our best leaders were killed in an unfortunate power struggle some years ago. So I might say simply that I arrived at the right moment. Still, my influence is still quite limited. The Tian Wang is ultimately in charge, and we have many powerful commanders in the field; the Loyal King Li is probably the best known among your people."

"Prince Gan is a truly great gentleman," Roberts added. "He has studied far longer among us than the Tian Wang and understands the need to bring their movement closer to the true faith. There is entirely too much idolatry even in this place."

"That is true; our movement's knowledge of the Heavenly Father is limited. But still, the Great One obviously guided the hand of the Tian Wang, or we would not have traveled so far."

"But my God, man, ancestor worship is still rampant among you. The common people still burn their prayers to send them to heaven, and some of the stories of the Tian Wang are as heretical as any the Mormons of America ever claimed. I need scarcely add that it is rumored that your people practice polygamy, an abomination in the eyes of the Lord, as are other heresies obvious to the most casual visitor.

"Yes, of course, even here in China, we know how your people treat heretics such as the Mormons. Nevertheless, much of what you say is true. That is partly why I have encouraged missionaries to come among us—to teach us more of the Lord. But I should add that there is still much to the revelations of my cousin. Many among us would add that your truths come from a period as long ago as the Han Dynasty. Our own revelations from the Heavenly Father are far more recent."

It was a standoff. Each had made their point and seemed satisfied. For the moment, the three ate quietly.

"Why do the Western powers so distrust your movement?" Jason asked after a few minutes.

"They often claim, as does the good Reverend Roberts, to find unacceptable contradictions among those of the God-worshipers. For me, the same contradictions exist among foreigners. How else can you explain that the foreign armies have in recent memory both attacked the Manchu capital at Beijing while resisting our own attempts to defeat the imperial forces near Shanghai! How can they fight both for and against the imperial armies? It makes no sense. How can you people claim it is difficult to understand the Chinese when your own people act so?"

Jason, who had only that afternoon learned of the fall of Beijing in what was rapidly becoming the last stages of the struggle begun in Guangzhou so long before, looked to Roberts for an answer.

"Prince Gan, I am not a soldier and hardly a diplomat. The ways of such people are beyond me. I do understand that your movement is not well thought-of among the foreigners," Roberts commented, speaking with more diplomacy than Jason expected.

"But surely the Taipings, themselves Christians, would be more attractive partners for the French and English. After all, their people so often proclaim the desire to end heathenism in China," Jason commented.

"Would that it was so simple. I am afraid the world of diplomacy is more complicated than that. The Tian Wang has treated the foreigners no differently than the Manchu emperor. Am I not myself, his old teacher, being pressured to do the kowtow merely to see my former student?"

Their Chinese host said nothing as Roberts went on.

"As for the missionaries, the talk of the Tian Wang being the little brother of Christ smacks of a heresy more frightening than the presence of paganism."

"Is that how you really feel?" Prince Gan asked after a moment.

"For myself, no. But I know the talk. I believe you have done wonders to lessen idolatry among your people. If the Taiping teachings are not what we would like, how could they be otherwise without the proper instruction? Am I not here myself exactly for that reason—to help your people move closer toward the truth? And, I confess, hearing your own concerns and knowing your influence, I am more optimistic than ever."

"I am honored to hear you say that. For I too doubt our goals are that far apart. But for now, given that this is a time of war, it is hard to make progress. Even to get the common people to stop burning their prayers sheets after recitation is almost impossible. But with your help, and I am beginning to believe the help of young Mr. Brandt, much can be accomplished." Finishing his sentence, he turned back toward Jason.

"I am pleased to hear you say that I could be of help," Jason began. "But I am not fully mature enough to serve as a missionary." He spoke, hoping that his words had not conveyed the wrong message.

"No. Perhaps not, but there is much else to do—to serve both Reverend Roberts and myself. I think we can keep you properly busy."

Jason turned to Roberts, who was clearly pleased with the developments. Then while he still felt comfortable speaking, he said, "If I could, sir, I arrived with two friends. Might I inquire about their whereabouts?"

"Don't fear; Commander Liu has taken care of both of them. The female is to be assigned to the women's camp, a residence for widows and others who have lost their husbands. She will be well treated there. As for the almost literati, the honorable Wu, I may take him into my own service. We have too few people familiar with the examination system. I could use him in my own efforts to create a Taiping civil service system."

For the next few minutes, Prince Gan discoursed on what was certainly a favorite topic, his hope to reorganize the selection process for officials, with examinations covering both traditional classical topics as well as points of Taiping and Western Christian practice.

Before the dinner ended, Jason was able to obtain passes to visit each of his friends and then took his leave, guessing that the two older men would have more they wished to discuss alone.

The next morning, after a light meal taken alone in his room, he set out with the sheet of paper Prince Gan had written out the previous evening. Talking with the sentries who guarded the front gate of the compound, he determined that the women's camp was closer than Wu's lodging. Still, it took considerable time, and he had to stop for directions many times, but he was eventually able to locate the protected compound where Black Jade was being housed.

Part of the delay, aside from the common problem of navigating through so many narrow alleys, was one of language. Many of those whom he encountered spoke nothing but the northern dialect, which was still quite foreign to his ears. As he walked, finally establishing his bearings, he determined that his first goal would be to work on his comprehension of the Nanjing dialect. He knew he'd made considerable progress as they had traveled north. Nevertheless, it would be a long time before he was as comfortable with these people as he had felt with the southerners.

Finally, before the women's compound, he showed his pass to the young sentry who stood guard over the entrance, but she was unfortunately illiterate. At least she was from the south and understood his explanation. Neither she nor any others he met later seemed particularly surprised by his presence. The Taipings, if in most ways like ordinary Chinese, were nevertheless more familiar with the foreign barbarians, or, as he'd heard them called, "the foreign brethren."

After a few minutes, a male officer appeared, and after glancing at the pass, and especially the seal of Prince Gan, he ushered Jason into a small waiting room and had him served tea. No more than ten minutes later, she arrived.

"You're here!" she exclaimed even before he'd spotted her. Jason had an impulse to embrace her and then held himself back. He wondered if she'd noticed.

"Can we take a walk?" he asked.

"Certainly." She walked out the door and again into the streets. They said not a word for a few moments and then each eagerly told their story.

"They have been most kind to me. The women here are all very understanding, even when I told them what had happened. And best of all, they are helping me unbind my feet. It is said that one as young as I am, and one whose feet were never as small as they might have been, should be able to do so without excessive difficulty."

"How long does it take?" he asked.

"I don't know. A long time, perhaps many months, but how I would like to see my mother-in-law's face—to have her find me actually trying to unbind them!"

"But the pain. Does it not hurt greatly?"

"Yes. Last night, I cried with pain, but the others massaged my feet, and again, as on the trail, an aid of Commander Liu arrived with very cold water. It must be from a very icy underground spring, far colder than before, and it made the pain much more bearable. The women said having access to such cold water to soak my feet was very helpful. Isn't it lucky we met such a kind man?"

He nodded in agreement but found himself less than appreciative of the officer's continuing solicitude.

Hoping to change the subject, he asked whether she could stay at the women's facility.

"It is reserved for widows and others like myself without husbands. The sister of the Tian Wang founded the camp, a great woman, a warrior herself they say. I believe I can stay as long as I like. Already they have begun to teach me of the Heavenly Father and of the Tian Wang's great voyage to heaven to study there. Did you know he was with the Heavenly Father for forty days?"

Jason nodded, seeing how excited she was at being accepted, perhaps more enthusiastic than he had ever seen her. It was hard not to feel happy for her.

"And you? Is it true you are staying with Prince Gan himself? The officer who admitted you told me so!"

"It is. Roberts remembered me better than I could have hoped." He smiled to himself as he spoke.

"And Prince Gan—is he as learned as they say here among the women?"

"I only spoke to him last evening for a time. But he seemed quite learned. He even said he remembered my father from his time in Hong Kong."

"Do you think you might see the Tian Wang himself? The women here say that Old Roberts is much revered by the Heavenly King. That the Tian Wang has long awaited the arrival of his old teacher."

"I think Roberts will soon be summoned." There seemed little point in explaining the issue of the kowtow. "But whether I'll be allowed to go is hardly decided. If I do, I will certainly tell you all about it."

"And what of scholar Wu? Has he fared well?"

"I'm surprised you even ask. He was hardly very kind to you."

"That is so. But he is a good man. Much of what he said was true, even if I could do little about the situation. Even now as I feel almost happy among these people, I wonder if my own mother has been humiliated by news of my supposed disappearance with a lover."

"And are you feeling so charitable about your former mother-in-law as well?" he asked, teasing.

Laughing, she jabbed him in the ribs, a gesture of affection he'd never felt from her or from any other woman for that matter. For the rest of the hour or so they spent together, he felt enormously energized.

Later in the day, sometime after the sun had passed its high point, she steered them back toward the compound.

"It is best if I return for now. You will come again?" she asked, looking at him warmly.

He nodded.

"And maybe even the three of us, Commander Liu as well, can spend some time together exploring the city. He once promised he would show us."

With that, she turned and reentered the compound.

Damn, he thought to himself and walked off.

CHAPTER 12

EXPLORING NANJING

O ver the next several days, Jason explored the city and made repeated efforts to visit the compound where Wu was staying. Each time, although the sentries were friendly enough, he could learn nothing. The young scholar, while known to the guards, was invariably out when he called.

On the third day after their arrival, as he made one more effort to locate his friend, a runner from Prince Gan's yamen hurriedly ran up to him.

"Young brethren," he said when he'd caught his breath, "your presence is urgently requested by Reverend Roberts. Please accompany me back immediately." There was nothing to do but turn around and return. What it might be he couldn't imagine. Less than a half hour later, he was back. Roberts and the Taiping Prime Minister were having a heated conversation. As he entered the room, Prince Gan turned to leave and then stopped at the door.

"Remember, Reverend Roberts, he has changed a great deal. Yet he reveres his former teacher and honors you greatly. Do not forget that no other missionary brethren have been so treated." With that he walked out, leaving them alone.

"Good. You have arrived. This is a very special day. The Tian Wang has relented. I'm to see him without doing the kowtow. We leave shortly for the audience. This may be the beginning of our great work for the Lord."

"But why has he agreed? I thought all foreigners and his own people had to recognize his sovereignty to see him," Jason asked, amazed by the concession.

"Why has he agreed? I haven't the foggiest idea. The man's probably crazy anyway. He has claimed all week in our correspondence that he is truly the Son of God, that God has a male form and a female helpmate, that he has actually seen him! All the usual sacrilege and more. Who knows the mind of such a man? But he has relented, and that's what matters. They are open to learning more of the truth of our Savior, and that's the chief thing!"

"How long do you think you will be able to see him for?"

"How long how long indeed? But that's not why you're here anyway. We are both going."

Jason was dumbfounded. He himself was to see the Tian Wang! Roberts was clearly pleased with the effect of the news. "Me…it's a great honor."

"Hogwash! I need you there. This will be very important. I want another observer, one less tied to the conversation so that all can be recorded. You have the language and I trust your observational skills. What I'll want is a separate account from you of what occurred. A great many people have waited a long time to meet with the Tian Wang, and the papers will be very interested. Too many of our brethren, and I include your father among them, see the Taipings as merely new Chinese idolatries, only this time borderline heretics as well. Our work can change that, how the West sees them and the Heavenly Kingdom itself. This is a very special opportunity. Now go get dressed. Prince Gan has agreed to your presence, and appropriate clothing has been prepared."

Rushing to his room, Jason found several female servants waiting eagerly to prepare him for the audience. Quickly he was washed and fitted into appropriately formal Chinese dress, clothing as magnificent as any he had ever seen or certainly worn. Less than a half hour later, he had returned to the courtyard of the yamen where Roberts, in equally if not more elaborate garb, was pacing nervously.

"Good, we can go. Now listen carefully. I'm told all of the visitors will do the kowtow as will the entire entourage. It has been agreed that we would not do so. You should follow my lead exactly. They know I'll not bow to any but God and perhaps a few women. But I hardly told them that." The old man laughed loudly for a second and then caught his breath as he watched the sedan chairs being brought forward toward them.

"It's important that you not say a thing. But even more important, that you note everything going on—every word of the conversation. We'll compare notes later before the reports are sent off to Shanghai. This is it!" They were quickly loaded into the sedan chairs and set off toward the southern part of the city.

A short time later, the company slowed. Jason leaned out the window to discover that they were approaching a very impressive walled complex.

"Is that their new imperial city?" he asked.

"It is indeed; it's said to be modeled after the one in Beijing. But I'm told it's really the former Qing Viceroy's compound they've modified."

"And are they as secretive as those in the Forbidden City?"

"As much so if not more. Almost no men are allowed inside save for special audiences. Only women guard the inner sanctum of the compound, or so I'm told. And from what I've heard, it's the devil's work that too often goes on in there." And then almost as an afterthought, he said, "But then, that's what we're here for. You heard Prince Gan. They recognize their knowledge of the

136

Lord is limited. That's what matters now. That's what makes this so important."

With that Roberts grew quiet. He was obviously deep in thought. Perhaps wondering about the man he'd taught so many years before, now an adult worshipped as a God by perhaps millions.

Jason, for his part, was able to study the thick walls as they passed within the compound and to admire the ornate stonework and gardens that abounded. After a moment, the sedan chairs stopped and the curtains were dramatically opened by a Taiping officer.

Slowly but with clear enthusiasm, Roberts stepped down, as did Jason, a second later. Quietly they were led in the direction of one of the larger buildings.

A few moments later, they were ushered into a beautiful audience hall. The room was resplendent with the symbols of imperial China and the presence of the emperors. Between themselves and the throne, where Jason assumed the Tian Wang would shortly appear, there stood two long rows, one on each side, of Taiping officers, presumably the many Taiping assistant kings or wangs he'd heard about. Himself dramatically garbed and now standing near the throne stood Prince Gan, their host. The man gave no indication that he had noticed them and seemed intent on giving orders to a young man who stood at his side.

Jason, remembering his instructions, tried to memorize as much of the room as possible, noting the form of the decorations and the faces of those who stood quietly at attention waiting for the audience. To his surprise, Commander Liu stood there obviously waiting for Jason to notice him. They both nodded imperceptibly. Despite Black Jade's comments about the man, he still felt relieved to see a familiar face. As for Liu, Jason thought he perceived a smile of satisfaction on the officer. It was now even more apparent that the trouble he'd taken to bring the three travelers to Nanjing was worthwhile.

After a few seconds more, the room took on a special level of tension. Nothing had been said, but all somehow sensed that the Heavenly King would soon arrive.

"Now remember, follow my lead; there's to be no bowing and scraping. None of that kowtow stuff they demand of inferiors."

Jason nodded, hoping it had, as Roberts thought, been arranged. It seemed like a bad place to show disrespect. The swords of the soldiers looked as sharp as any metal he'd ever seen. But there was no time for further reflection, for a second later the doors at the right front opened up and a large middle-aged man in incredibly beautiful flowing yellow robes filled with dragon engravings walked in followed by a young man, probably the Tian Wang's son, Jason thought to himself.

The entire room dropped to the floor at his entrance, save Roberts who stood defiantly and Jason a foot behind feeling terribly awkward. The Tian Wang surveyed the room, looking first at his soldiers and then at the two foreigners. For a quick second, Jason thought he spied a subtle smile on the man's face, a look perhaps of amusement.

"Let us all pray to the Heavenly Father," he announced with drama and dropped himself to the floor, turning toward an obviously Christian shrine Jason had not previously noticed.

Roberts froze, even from somewhat behind him; Jason could tell the man was dumbfounded. It was not turning out as he had expected. Then realizing his former student had outmaneuvered him, the old missionary slowly dropped to his knees. Not a word was said, but Jason was now certain he could see a look of amusement on the monarch's face. For the next few minutes, the Tian Wang led the group through a series of prayers Jason's own father might have offered back in Hong Kong. They were as traditional as any Westerner might have offered. Jason realized they were probably part of the liturgy Roberts himself had taught the Tian Wang.

When the prayer was over, all of them rose.

"Do you remember me, old Master?" the Tian Wang began.

"In truth, I do not. I remember a young man with great interest in learning of our Lord. But here as you have become, a great king in His court, it is truly difficult."

The Tian Wang looked pleased.

"It has been a long time since we requested your presence, but you, like our cousin," he nodded toward Prince Gan, "were not for a long time able to visit us."

"That is true. It has been many years since I first heard of your great kingdom and received your letter to visit. But only recently with the advances of the great Wang Li was I able to pass through the imperial forces to come here to the Heavenly Capital. My hope now is to teach the ways of the Lord as I once taught you, so that His glory might be better known throughout your kingdom."

"That is truly a great goal. We have, as well, high hopes for your presence to add to my own teachings and to help us with the foreigners who don't understand our community. They fail to understand how much we have in common, we the children of the same Heavenly Father."

"That is true, but many have heard unusual things of your people. Things many find difficult to accept. But I think they simply fail to understand you."

The Tian Wang smiled slightly.

"And what sort of things have they heard?"

"Well, the curious stories of revelations from God…the visits to heaven have been questioned." Roberts was obviously a bit nervous but determined to give no ground when challenged.

"Those stories are quite true, as true now as when I first told you of them in Guangzhou. And now, after so many victories, surely it is the Heavenly Father who has guided the hand of my armies. Would we be here were the Heavenly Father not our chief shield?"

"You honor me greatly, but you know I cannot accept such things, and here in your Heavenly Capital, I can only teach as I taught you so long ago."

"Old Roberts. That will be quite enough for now. You had not the honor to learn from the Heavenly Father and the Heavenly Elder Brother, Jesus himself, as I did. It is, of course, difficult for you to understand. But that matters little now. You are to be greatly honored among us. I have given orders that you shall want for nothing while you stay with us. And we will be pleased if you can continue to teach of the Heavenly Father."

"That is my only role and desire." For a second Jason thought the old man was going to say more, perhaps challenge the Tian Wang's last comments, but then the man checked himself.

"And now, we take our leave; you and your young assistant are invited to dine with my officers to celebrate the arrival of the one so long awaited."

And with that, the Tian Wang turned and, followed by his young son, abruptly left the room. At his departure the room visibly relaxed. The forty or so officers began to converse quietly among themselves, and arrangements were made to have a banquet served in another room.

"Jason, I'm sorry you will miss the food, but you have another task. I want you to return to your quarters and write down everything that has happened. When I get back after the meal, we can compare notes. Now go."

With that Roberts went off, following the lead of Prince Gan and several other officers. As Jason himself turned to leave, Liu approached him.

"It is good to see that all is going well for you. I'm told you have tried to see our young scholar friend. I'm sorry that has not been possible. He was on an assignment for Prince Gan. But he should be available soon. I think he will be here in the next several days." With that Liu himself walked off, and Jason, accompanied by a servant, a young woman of about seventeen, left for the front gate. All the way home, he reviewed in his mind what he'd seen, especially the appearance of the Taiping emperor, his fine whiskers and powerful voice. He wanted to get every detail down as soon as possible.

It was almost three days before he had a chance to again set out looking for Wu. This time it was relatively easy. He now had access to a horse from Prince Gan's stable and already knew the way well. Fortunately, as he neared the compound, Wu himself came in sight and hailed him.

"Jason, here friend, 'Foreign brethren,'" he added, smiling. "I'm sorry I've missed you. Everything has been so busy since we saw each other last." With those last words, Wu jumped down from his own horse and greeted Jason with more warmth than he'd ever felt from the young scholar. The separation had made more obvious how close they had become in the two years they had known each other.

"Come, have tea with me. I know a teahouse nearby. They have fine rice cakes, almost like home, and even storytellers."

They walked in silence for more than a hundred yards and then Wu turned into a small back alley. Stopping for a moment, Wu hired a waif to watch the horses and then entered the small house. It was not very large, but the clientele was lively and had more energy than Jason had come to expect in the streets of Nanjing. His foreign face was noted as he walked in, but nothing was said. Jason now knew that many missionaries and foreign mercenaries had lived and worked among the Taipings. His presence would attract no undue interest, he thought to himself. They could talk in peace.

"So tell me. Are you working for Liu and Prince Gan?"

"Yes. But first, you have more to tell. Is it true you saw the Tian Wang himself? It is a great honor! He hardly shows himself to his own people anymore. What was he like?"

For the next few minutes, Jason told Wu everything he could. His several hours' effort at writing up the visit for Roberts now had him in good stead, and he was well able to satisfy Wu's considerable curiosity. After a time, he finally finished the tale.

"But enough, tell me what you are doing?" Jason asked.

"It is indeed an exciting story, not as noteworthy as yours but, for one like myself, most gratifying. Almost as soon as we arrived, I was told Liu had a place for me and later, even more wondrous, that I might be able to serve Prince Gan himself!"

"Doing what?"

"I myself had no idea, a failed examination scholar—what could they want? I know nothing of warfare and less of their, your foreign religion, the religion of the Heavenly Father, no more than the few bits you've told me yourself."

"Well, so tell me."

"It's not completely clear yet. But I now know Prince Gan well. He is a very learned man, one interested in helping the Heavenly Kingdom to assume the Mandate of Heaven from the Manchu dogs. And he says I can help him."

"But you're not, as you say, a soldier. And how can you serve these people who reject the Master you so revere?"

"You are right, they appear to behave very differently from the teachings of the Master. They hardly understand the ways of *li*, of relations between husbands and wives, of ancestors and families, but they are not so different as they seem. There is much here that is purely Chinese, and Prince Gan wants to preserve it. He is having me play a role in reorganizing the exam system, to include not only the teachings of the Heavenly Father, but much that is part of classical teachings. And even if they seem too willing to destroy temples, the people themselves still know and understand familial virtue and proper behavior."

"So you have decided to join them permanently then?"

"I don't know the future, but they say I have a place. Too few scholar gentry have joined them. I'm told I can also be useful in convincing such people not to oppose us."

It was difficult to tell how really committed Wu felt, but Jason was sure he was tired of being an outcast hiding from his past.

"For me, it is a life I can lead," Wu began again. "It is far better than the Hong Kong wharves or going home to my family and ultimate disgrace. Here perhaps I can become someone, maybe marry, have children and sons to open the door to the next generations. It is far better than I could have hoped…much better than my terrible destiny should have allowed. But what of you? You are certainly not going to go home to your father either."

Wu's question forced him to consider the issue he'd been avoiding as usual.

"I'd rather discuss you, but you're right. We are both unfilial sons. And I'm not going back either. But what happens next, I don't know either. I want to stay here for a while at least. There is much that interests me. I think I'd like to study the Heavenly Kingdom. Maybe even write about it for the foreign newspapers."

He hadn't actually known what he was going to say, but the comment hardly surprised him. It was the culmination of the pleasure he'd felt ever since Roberts earlier that morning had expounded so energetically on his summary of the meeting with the Tian Wang. Yes, writing for the foreign press did sound rather nice.

"But can you do that? Would they let you and pay you for doing so?"

His friend's question deflated the burgeoning dream.

"Actually I don't know. But I suppose I'd better learn more about the Heavenly Kingdom before I even try."

With that they finished their tea and departed. Wu explained that he was expected at Commander Liu's yamen shortly. After agreeing to meet often, they both returned to their horses and went their separate ways.

CHAPTER 13

GOOD AND BAD NEWS

O ver the next month, Jason was as busy as he had ever been. Roberts, pleased with his report on their meeting with the Tian Wang, had assigned him the task of keeping a full record of their activities and his impressions of the Heavenly City. Roberts, who was well known among the Shanghai foreign community, had apparently promised to send regular reports to the China-coast papers, which were hungry for news of the decade-long rebellion. Moreover, Jason's own insistence on learning the Nanjing dialect kept him even busier. On most days, for his responsibilities did not require regular attendance with Roberts, he wandered the streets talking with the locals, improving his understanding of the unfamiliar dialect, and trying to answer many of Roberts's questions about actual Taiping religious behavior. How much had they truly abandoned traditional Chinese practice? Did they really follow true Christian practices as many of the officers, especially those from the south insisted on? Each day, though, it was more confusing. One minute he found himself startled by the greater freedom of women and then would be stopped short by a row of wall posters advertising rewards for runaway wives, which sounded as traditionally Chinese as anything he'd ever seen. On several consecutive

Saturdays, for the Taipings had apparently adopted the Jewish schedule for the Sabbath, he wandered about trying to find some sign of religious worship with a recognizable Christian stamp, but that often proved impossible. And yet many of those he spoke to among Prince Gan's entourage were as devoted as any he'd met among his father's friends. Evenings were spent writing up his reports and submitting them to Roberts. After a time, he found that the work pleased him more than anything he'd ever done.

Late one evening, perhaps a month after his initial arrival in Nanjing, very loud noises caught his attention. Roberts's voice was raised in the hallway. The missionary was very angry. At first, unsure whether to intervene, Jason eventually decided to quietly peer out the door, hoping to understand the nature of the commotion. Unfortunately, Roberts was closer than he'd realized.

"You there. Boy, stop hiding behind that door. Come out at once!"

Opening the door, Jason exited. "Should I ask what the trouble is?" he started. "No, perhaps it's none of my business."

"None of your business, quite rightly…No, you're not a child any longer. These heathens…they simply won't understand."

With that he turned and strode back into their sitting room. Jason, unsure, followed along.

As he entered the room, Roberts sat staring at the wall, apparently contemplating one of the painted silk birds that hung there.

"I have often been thought a fool for defending these people. A great many have said it was ridiculous to see them as more than heretics, little better, if not worse, than the imperialist pagans. Your very father once accused me of hurting the cause of our Lord simply by holding out some hope for them."

As he spoke his anger seemed to dissipate; whatever had upset him seemed to be passing. For a time, Jason, his curiosity aroused, feared he'd never find what had happened. Happily, though, the older man was in a talkative mood. Apparently, attempting to honor him as the Tian Wang's former teacher, he'd been informed that afternoon that three females had been assigned to service his physical needs.

"Three they told me. As befitting an honored official! My God, how could I have retained hope for such people and me a married man, a preacher! It smacks of Sodom and Gomorrah. To think I've attached my fate to such a place!"

"Perhaps they were doing no more than trying to honor you. It's common among the Chinese to have more than one wife."

"That's just the point, youngster. Did your father teach you nothing?"

"But is it not true the Old Testament patriarchs often had several wives?"

"Boy. I don't care what it says; it's an abomination. Maybe you're no more than the malingerer your father thinks you are!"

At that Jason turned and started for the door. It was late, but he was not going to spend another minute in the place.

"No, wait." Roberts caught his shoulder before he'd reached the door.

"I'm sorry, Jason. I spoke harshly. Your father doesn't talk that way. I was wrong to lash out at you so. Now come back in the room and sit."

Only reluctantly did Jason sit down again. The man's temper was volatile; he'd often heard that said but only just begun to believe it.

Roberts sat down opposite him, obviously seeking a different subject.

"Forget this nonsense. They don't like it, but I refused. It will all be forgotten by tomorrow. Besides, there's other matters for us to attend to. I had a letter from Shanghai, from the *North China Daily News.*"

"Did they like the last material you sent them?" Jason asked, calming.

"It's more than that. I didn't send them anything in the last dispatch."

"I thought—"

"I know what you thought, but what I really did was send them the report as you had prepared it. And I sent it under your name. And you know what those bastards said?" He was smiling broadly. "What they said was that the material was better than anything I'd ever sent in."

"I'm sure they were just being kind. They—"

"Balderdash, I don't care. I've my own work for the Lord to do. What matters is that they liked your writing and said they could use anything you send in. May even be some money in it."

Jason was stunned. He'd actually see his own writing in the paper. They liked his reports. It was almost too much to take in at once, a chance for the future.

"I'm terribly grateful," he finally stammered.

"More balderdash, boy. A month with you and it's obvious you're no more a future missionary than I'm likely to join up as one of these infernal Taiping Wangs. But here's maybe a career for you. But don't get too excited. It will be a long time before you earn your bread by your pen. That much I do know. Now go back to your room. There'll be more work for you in the morning."

Jason rose and left, his heart beating so strongly he could feel it. He'd hardly believed his dreams of writing for the newspapers, but now that might be a possibility. It seemed like the first sign since he'd left Hong Kong that he had made the right decision. There was much to think about, and he doubted he'd sleep a wink.

Over the next several days, Jason spent considerable time wandering the city, considering the sort of topics he might choose to investigate for the newspaper. From copies of foreign newspapers, Roberts and others of the foreign community had supplied him, it was obvious that superficial accounts of short-term visits to various Taiping strongholds had appeared over and over again. What he hoped to do was something special. Using his opportunity for an extended stay and his language skills, which despite limitations he knew to be far better than most foreigners in Nanjing, he sought a way to produce something he alone could do well, something more specific and substantive than had heretofore appeared in the newspapers. What that might be, though, he wasn't at all certain till one day he found himself, as so often before, near the quarter where Black Jade and the other unattached females were housed. In their many late-afternoon talks, she had often told him of Taiping treatment toward women as she was coming to understand them. Now he realized that through her and their friendship, he had the topic he needed at hand. Almost every visitor, even those convinced that in all other ways the Taipings were no different than generations of Confucianists, had remarked on the relative freedom of Taiping women, little more though than images of young Taiping women walking freely without bound feet had appeared in their accounts. Jason was sure he had the perfect opportunity to learn more about this astounding change in Chinese attitudes, a topic he was certain would attract the attention of the editors in Shanghai.

As he now turned decisively toward the women's residences, he felt himself walking with a confidence he'd not felt in weeks. Black Jade would certainly approve of the project, and he thought shyly to himself, it would give him reason to spend even more time with her.

Ten minutes later he was at the gate of the female quarters. He'd seen the attendants often enough that there was no need to explain himself. They left almost immediately to fetch her. Unfortunately, she did not arrive at once, and he paced nervously in the street before the entrance, anxiously awaiting her.

"Jason." She'd spotted him before he'd realized she had even arrived. She walked up and touched his shoulder with as light a touch as he would have thought possible. Whirling around, he faced her.

"Can we walk?"

"Of course, have you another meeting with the Heavenly King to tell me about? Here the women have heard every detail and await more."

"Well, it's not exactly that," he said, losing his enthusiasm for a moment and then regaining it.

"No. I've not seen the Tian Wang again. I'm not even sure if Old Roberts will see him soon, but there is good news."

"Wait." She turned back toward the entrance and gestured. A moment later, a young woman walked out and handed her something warm to place over her shoulders. To Jason's surprise, their relationship seemed that of a mistress and servant. He thought of asking her about it and then forgetting the distraction plunged in. For the next hour, he told her of his conversation with Roberts, of the *North China Daily News* offer and most importantly of his own hopes to do a piece on women.

"That's where you can help me enormously. Tell me about your life, at least generally with your father and then your husband; how you felt as a young girl, mostly what you used to talk about while we traveled."

She made a face, as if not pleased at the thought of reliving the memories.

"But it will be much more than that. I want you to tell me what you can of Taiping women's lives of how things are different here. Not just one person's feelings, but in general, of how they feel about not binding their feet, to wander the streets so much more freely. He went on for quite a while, though all the while wondering what she was thinking. So often, even after all the months of knowing her, she remained a mystery, her eventual reaction to a situation almost impossible to predict.

"Do you think such a work would be of interest to anyone? The lives of mere women?"

"I'm sure of it. The foreigners on the coast want to learn as much as possible about you. Why do you think so many of them come here to Nanjing? You have surely seen many of them in the streets."

"That is true. Would such a work gain the help of the foreigners and their powerful weapons of war? Colonel Liu says that we could defeat the Qing if the foreigners would not protect places like Shanghai."

Jason wasn't pleased at the mention of Liu's name but said nothing.

"There is one thing I'm sure of, and I have heard Roberts and Prince Gan speak of it often. That the foreigners could certainly find better friends in China among the God-worshipers than among those at the imperial court. Maybe, if they understood that the Taipings treat their women more as Western women are treated, they might be more sympathetic."

He had no idea whether it really mattered a whit, but still, the articles couldn't hurt matters, and it would give him a chance to impress the paper's editors and spend more time with Black Jade.

She said nothing for a time and then finally said, "I think you are right. There is little one as insignificant as I can do. But if the story of Taiping women might impress the foreigners and their powerful armies, I shall help you. When do we start?"

Over the next weeks, they spent many afternoons together, discussing both the lives of village women as she had known them earlier and among the Taipings. Sometimes she would come out of the compound filled with tales from the other women whom she'd asked questions of. Jason took notes copiously, trying to get all the information down. He wanted to be sure the article was as accurate as possible. And doing so was difficult indeed. Women were obviously freer than he'd ever seen in Confucian China, but from Black Jade and the others came stories of huge harems, serving the principal Wangs and the Heavenly King himself. It was all very difficult to document, and the few times he'd tried to gather further information on the harems, he'd gotten nowhere. So much of the information was hearsay, and he soon learned that one had to be very circumspect when asking questions about women, Taiping or not. Many Chinese found his curiosity quite inappropriate.

Nevertheless, after putting final touches to the work, he sent it off. The following weeks were terrible as he waited to hear. He'd taken the precaution of copying over the text several times and giving it to a number of different merchants and travelers who claimed to be heading for Shanghai. But one never knew when it would get to the paper or even whether it would. The imperial and Taiping lines were very fluid. It was often difficult to pass between them.

Still, in the early spring, a letter finally came. He opened it with tremendous anxiety. A letter from the editor of *North China Daily News* addressed specifically to him, not Roberts. Taking a breath, he opened it and read as follows:

Dear Mr. Brandt:
   I take this opportunity to note the arrival of your fine piece to our office and to the warm appreciation with which we received it. It is every bit if not better done than the earlier material Reverend Roberts submitted under your name and far more detailed and serious. We are certain our readers will read it with interest. Please find enclosed a draft for the sum of five pounds sterling. I look forward to receiving more material from you in the future.
Sincerely,
James Barlow

For a second it occurred to him that he'd not the foggiest idea where one would cash a bank draft in the Heavenly Capital. But that was merely a passing thought. He'd done it! They liked the work and paid him for it. Jason read the letter over and over, until he could recite it by heart. Finally rushing from his room, he sought out Roberts, but the old man was nowhere to be found. He had to tell someone. It was late in the day, but nevertheless he resolved to tell Black Jade.

Somewhat later, his horse winded, he pulled up in front of the women's quarter. To his surprise he saw her already standing near the entrance. Jumping from the horse, he ran up to her. She seemed surprised to see him but upon hearing the news was delighted. They talked at length about the piece, about other essays he was considering writing and the possibility of his having found a career for himself. Jason did not remember when he felt so happy, that was until, hearing footsteps behind him, he turned to see Colonel Liu approaching.

"Did you tell him?" the officer asked her, his face smiling broadly.

"No. But I was about to," Black Jade said.

Jason had no idea what was going on and then realizing, he wished he were anywhere in the world other than sitting there in front of the Taiping women's facility with the two of them.

"We are to be married." The man smiled at him, oblivious to how Jason himself felt about her. As for Black Jade, she appeared more aware of the awkwardness of the situation. Taking his hands, she spoke with affection.

"Jason, it was fated. If you had not saved me, I'd not have come here to the Heavenly Kingdom. I'd not have understood the true Lord, nor met the man I could be a true wife to. Colonel Liu and I owe you everything."

Two hours later, after he'd returned to his room, he could not imagine how he'd gotten through the encounter, listening to their plans for the wedding, their joy and talk of the future. Finally, having waited for the right moment, he'd managed to excuse himself and get away. How he made it home without throwing up he never knew.

CHAPTER 14

THE WEDDING

For the next several weeks, Jason was more depressed than he'd ever been. Only now did he fully realize how much Black Jade meant to him. He found it impossible to talk to anyone he really knew. His mornings were spent talking to strangers in the streets. It was much easier that way, gathering impressions and information for the series of articles he was planning for the newspaper. In the afternoons, he returned to the yamen, occasionally speaking with Roberts and then going off to his room to write. He knew Roberts had noticed the change in him, but happily, the old man had his own concerns. The missionary's efforts to proselytize among the Taipings were not as successful as Roberts had hoped. Jason was aware as well, though more vaguely, of developing tension between their host, Prince Gan, and Roberts. Happily, Hong Rengan occupied other parts of the compound, and their paths rarely crossed.

Jason was so depressed he even ignored several letters from Wu asking him to visit his quarters. From what he gathered, Wu had been steadily rising among the Taipings. His rank, authority, and influence were growing at an astonishing rate given his recent association with the Taiping movement. His letters gave the impression that he wished to tell Jason of his improving fortunes. But for the young American, spending an afternoon listening to Wu's tales of success sounded simply too depressing. Even the pleasure of finishing various pieces for the paper failed to rouse him from his lethargy.

He began to feel that the entire decision to defy his father had been wrong. What right had he, a foreigner, to pretend to have a place in China? Black Jade had understood it even as he'd been blind. He had no more right to claim China as his own than he could have expected to win Black Jade for himself.

Only gradually did his mood improve and that ironically due to the deterioration of the city's situation. Wandering the streets as often as he did, Jason became aware of the increasingly bare avenues. The commercial and civil life of the city was winding down. Increasingly, Nanjing was becoming no more than an armed camp. There was a story there and Jason gradually found that his depression lessened as he thrust himself further into the effort to record the evolution of the Heavenly Capital.

One day as he walked along, a voice from behind hailed him.

"So has the foreigner become too important to answer the letters of his friends?"

Jason whirled around, more pleased than he expected to be at the sound of Wu's voice.

"I'm sorry, old friend. That's not it. I've just been...well, busy." His voice trailed off.

"Not too busy to hear of the impending marriage of our traveling partner. You think this one, who watched you so long stare at our companion, doesn't know what you're feeling. I see your sadness and wonder at those like the foreigners who reject arranged marriages as we Chinese practice them. No, Western-style love marriages only cause pain. Look at you. You never married her at all and already she causes pain." Wu went on. "Our friend Liu may yet one day regret not having his own parents chose for him. And remember she can bring forth no sons, and that is what marriage is for."

"If you understand so much, why do you torment me so? You always disliked Black Jade, and we both know it," Jason said.

"I didn't dislike her, merely understood how much pain a beauty like her with an excess of Yang could cause a man. And look, I was right."

"Well, it's good to see you anyway," Jason responded. Then changing the subject, he said, "They tell me you have become quite important, practically another Wang."

"Hardly that, but my present life is very different from what I once knew. Different from my years of study and different as well from those months as a coolie. I may even have beaten my own unlucky destiny. I'd like to tell you more, but that is not the reason for my seeking you out. Black Jade is the reason for the visit. She came to me, not exactly correct behavior for the bride of a fellow officer, but knowing her, not particularly surprising. In any case, she says, she hopes not to presume too much, but if she hurt you with her decision, she begs to be forgiven. Let me add that I have come to know Commander Liu well since we arrived. He is a fine man. He has been with the Taipings almost since the beginning and, compared to most, is a dedicated officer without personal ambition. He could rise even higher among them, but I doubt he cares. Among everyone I have met, he is deeply respected. Black Jade has indeed chosen well, even as she fears she hurt you. So do you forgive her?"

"That's easy enough; I was the fool. There was nothing really between us; no promises made. Maybe only my own foolishness was a problem. Tell her, all is forgiven," Jason said, not believing a word of it.

"That, old friend, is not quite enough. She expects, no, asks, for once, I might add, very politely, that you, in fact both of us, attend the wedding. It's only a moon away, and your presence is very important to her. Much more than mine, I noted."

So he'd have to go through that as well. There was no way to get out of it. Having agreed, the two of them spent the afternoon walking through the deserted streets of the capital, discussing the likelihood that the Kingdom itself would be able to withstand the growing threat from the Manchu militia armies and apparently the foreign soldiers who were said to be siding with the imperialists. Just before they parted, Jason asked Wu if he had enough influence to arrange for Jason to travel with frontline troops for a few days. Lately he'd the idea that reports from the Taiping side of the lines might make especially interesting material for the editors in Shanghai. Apparently, Wu's influence was as considerable as he'd heard, for the former Confucian scholar claimed it could be easily arranged. After that they parted ways, promising to see each other more often and most immediately at the wedding.

Less than three weeks later, Jason found himself, having dressed in the finest clothes available to him in Prince Gan's compound, setting out early one evening with Wu to meet Liu and the rest of the wedding party.

"Have you ever seen a Chinese wedding?" Wu asked him as the rode toward the appointed rendezvous Liu had designated for the event.

"Not among the Taipings, but often enough in Hong Kong. I used to listen to the fortune-tellers and matchmakers speak of their work. I remember how the astrologer would argue about the right dates for the ceremony. The Westerners always found it very strange that the Chinese could marry someone they'd never met. My mother always spoke of how difficult that would be for a Western woman. Once I even attended a ceremony, watched the bride bow down to a long list of her husband's ancestors, and all that. But it will surely not be like that this time. I assume."

"I'm sure it won't," Wu commented and then added, "Actually, I've never seen a Taiping ceremony either. I'm told it's hardly like those you describe or I myself attended often in our village." And then lowering his voice somewhat, he said, "I doubt it will be what the Master would have required."

The reference to Confucius surprised Jason. He'd spent enough time around Wu since they'd arrived in Nanjing to notice how much the young man had come to accept the tenants of Taiping Christianity, and as often as possible quote them. Though at times he'd wondered how much of his friend's enthusiasm came simply from the same personality traits that had allowed him to excel at the Confucian teachings. Wu had, after all, before the catastrophe of his last set of civil service exams, been a very ambitious young man. For a moment Jason wondered if their friendship was strong enough for him to question the young scholar on the subject. But then, before he had a chance to decide, they arrived at Liu's compound.

The sun was settling and torches were only just being lit. Nevertheless, the size and majesty of the group impressed even Jason, who'd only slowly come to understand how much his former protector was respected among the Taipings, especially among those who'd been part of the movement since the early years in Guangxi. Scores of officers, dressed in their finest, either rode on horseback or were seated in sedan chairs, the curtains open to reveal the full splendor of their uniforms. Liu, conforming to Chinese custom, had gathered a full contingent of his friends to accompany him to the women's quarters, where Black Jade awaited his arrival. She would then be accompanied back to Liu's compound to await the ceremony scheduled for the next day.

As the contingent set out, Jason and Wu took up positions somewhat near the middle of the contingent. After a few minutes, even as the sounds of laughter, music, and even a few firecrackers filled the air, one of the higher officers who'd been riding toward the front of the group reigned in his horse and waited for them to catch up. Signaling to Wu, he indicated that they were to move forward in the line. It was an important honor, and Wu quite clearly was pleased by the gesture. As for Jason, struggling to keep his intellectual interest in the procedures dominant over his depression, he was less thrilled. He'd be all the closer to Black Jade when she emerged to greet them. That was hardly what he wanted. No. A place much further back, where he might not have even been able to see her, would have been much more to his liking, but there was little to do. He tried to put her out of his mind, as if that were possible, and concentrate on the spectacle itself and all that had happened since he and Wu had made the decision to proceed north toward the Taiping lines.

A short time later, the entire entourage arrived at the women's barracks. There probably every woman among them had gathered in front of the facility. A moment or so after their arrival, Black Jade, accompanied by two older women, was brought forward.

"When my cousin was married, this was the very first moment he'd ever seen his bride," Wu whispered into Jason's ear as they stood alongside each other.

She was as beautiful as ever if somewhat less recognizable, since her hair, in the usual Chinese custom, had been tightly bound backward. Her eyes were downcast, as befitting a bride even among the Taipings. For a moment Jason thought he saw her looking cautiously about and clearly not in Liu's direction. Could she have been watching for him? he thought to himself and then angrily pushed the thought aside.

Black Jade then disappeared into the sedan chair prepared for her. Again, the entourage amid considerable laughter, for the streets were narrow, and the crowd large tried clumsily to reverse itself and return to Commander Liu's compound.

For the rest of the trip, Jason concentrated on seeing everything around him, trying to sharpen his observational skills, for he knew they would be valuable if he were to continue to sell his articles. Thus far, he'd been quite successful. They had already accepted more than half a dozen of his works. He was only just beginning to feel more confident that he'd truly found a profession.

The abrupt halt of the procession brought him back to reality. It was already quite late, and as custom the wedding was expected to take place the next morning. He and Wu watched Black Jade being escorted into the compound and then prepared to direct their own horses toward their respective barracks. It was getting dark, and he was expected to return early the next morning.

Before he left, though, he stood among the other men listening to their conversation. Their words were full of praise for the brave officer and his new bride. Liu was very respected—certainly an excellent husband for Black Jade, he kept reminding himself. Just before he left, an incident took place that Jason later wondered about. Wu had disappeared for a time and then returned, seeming much happier than usual. The young scholar, despite his enthusiasm regarding the festivities, had until then retained the dour attitude Jason generally associated with Wu since their early days together in Guangzhou. But now, Wu seemed different; his eyes, although the light was bad, reflected a strange light, and the man himself appeared to be struggling to control his tongue as he spoke of their long friendship and the events that had brought them together.

Only later, after Jason took leave of his friend, did he realize what he'd only vaguely sensed. Had Wu been smoking opium? No. It seemed impossible. Despite the general Taiping ban, the stuff was easily available. But the men around Liu never touched the stuff, and Wu had always seemed about as unlikely an opium smoker as anyone he'd ever known in China. By the time Jason arrived back at his quarters, he'd convinced himself that his imagination had gotten the best of him. But still he determined to watch his friend closely the following day.

The next morning came too soon despite the fact that he'd not gotten a wink of sleep all night. There was little to do save await the arrival of the wedding party. Liu had been awarded a major honor. Prince Gan had offered the use of his own Heavenly Hall for the service rather than having Liu, like most of his compatriots, use the church facilities in his own district. As Jason exited the building and found a place to wait near the entrance, he studied the crowd, which had already begun to gather.

"Ho there, boy. Wait up for me. Seems there will be much to see."

Old Roberts's hand on his shoulder exerted a singular pressure of affection, which pleased Jason. They had not spent much time together lately. Each had been busy with his own activities and their paths, despite residence in the same section of Prince Gan's compound, rarely crossed.

"Have you seen many Taiping weddings, sir?"

"That I have; it's one of the few ways I've been able to tell whether the Heavenly Kingdom believes what it says."

Jason noted a bit of sarcasm in his voice, though he felt it best not to comment.

"I've actually had the honor of performing a few of them myself. Some of the Taipings feel it's a special sort of grace if the Tian Wang's old teacher hitches them up."

"So the ceremony is that similar to ours."

"In large measure, it really is. None of the old superstitious malarkey and most of the prayers are just as Christian as one would ever ask for."

"Are you then..." Jason's voice trailed off, realizing that Roberts would not be standing there talking to him if he'd been asked to officiate.

"Hardly, I don't even know your friends—at least no more than you've already told me, and Prince Gan and I have, *well...*"—his voice dropped to a whisper—"difficulties."

"In fact, the old boy is a lot more of a heathen than I or a lot of others have claimed," he added.

Roberts then turned to watch the procession, which was then arriving at the compound. It seemed unlikely that Roberts would say more. There was little more for Jason to do than take his place among the scores of people who had gathered for the ceremony.

As the official entourage arrived, Jason near the edge of the crowd had only a glimpse of Black Jade as she went into the hall. Staying close to Roberts, he followed the party in. Once inside they withdrew to the rear of the hall and watched the official members of the party take their places.

"What happens now? How long is the ceremony?"

"It will be quite some time. Both of them will be examined at length on their understanding of the teachings of our Lord, at least as the Taipings understand them."

"Does anyone care that she has a husband in South China? The man I told you about."

"What's a pagan wedding? Nothing. In the eyes of the Lord, this is her first wedding; no, it means nothing."

They stood there for quite some time listening. The distance was considerable. Nevertheless, Jason was able to follow part of her replies to the officiating officer's questions. She had obviously studied very hard and sounded far more knowledgeable regarding the principal tenets of Taiping Christianity than he would have imagined.

"As you can see the ceremony itself, save the lack of a ring, is quite similar to our own," Roberts whispered after the formal marriage had begun. A few minutes later, it was complete and the wedding party exited the hall. Jason strained to see Black Jade's face as she left but was unable to. The only thing he later remembered was the look Prince Gan had directed toward Roberts as he passed by. There was clearly bad blood between the two men, though Jason was unsure just how deep it went. Both of them had been good to him. It was difficult not to feel distressed about the tension. Still he thought to himself, at least it was a distraction from the marriage itself. As he left the hall, his last thought was how he might avoid talking to her during the festivities, which were sure to follow. He knew he could not congratulate her without revealing his true feelings. Happily, he was able to slip away and took a long walk through the deserted streets of Nanjing.

CHAPTER 15

TENSIONS GROW

O ver the next weeks, curious about the tension he'd seen between Roberts and Prince Gan, Jason made a special effort
to spend more time with the older man. Each morning, rather than
leaving immediately after dressing, he entered the common rooms
and waited for the older missionary's arrival. More often than not,
while waiting, he had the opportunity to talk with Huang, the
young man who over time had come to serve as Roberts's personal
servant.

Listening to Huang, Jason noted how much influence Roberts
had come to exert over the servant. Huang, whom Jason had hardly
spoken with in earlier months, had obviously abandoned Taiping
Christianity for the more orthodox tenets of his missionary master. On more than one occasion, the young man, as zealous as any
Jason had ever known among his father's friends, attempted to
engage him in theological disputes.

Moreover, Jason was more and more aware of just how loyal the
young servant was to his American master. Huang rather blatantly
spoke of his dislike for their host, Prince Gan, and of his faith in
Roberts's teaching. More than once Roberts had arrived during
their conversations, and rather than silence the man's dangerous
talk, he'd encouraged it.

"Jason," Roberts had once commented after several moments of silence, "it's time you began to think of making your own way here among the Taipings, or even away from these heathens. For I don't know how much longer I will remain."

Roberts's negative tone about the Heavenly Kingdom surprised him. Roberts, almost alone among the missionaries and others whom Jason regularly met in the capital, had always been one of the regime's principal Western supporters. The vision of the older man walking the streets in the regal yellow robes granted him by the Tian Wang was almost a given among those who knew Nanjing. Something though was obviously happening.

"Are you planning to leave—to return to Shanghai?"

"I'm not planning anything as of yet, but it is more and more obvious that these heretics, and it's hard not to see them as such, have little chance of abandoning their evil ways. They offer me no end of honors but ignore all my efforts to bring real Christian teachings to them."

Huang, the servant, who had taken a chair up at a respectful distance, nodded in agreement and satisfaction.

"But you yourself have said they have abandoned most of—"

"I know what I said," Roberts cut in. "But that doesn't explain away the ungodliness of this place"—and then lowering his voice—"and the sin going on in the palace of the Tian Wang."

"What do you mean? Their old pagan ways—" Jason started.

"Against the ways of God himself. There are thousands of concubines there," Huang added, moving closer to the table.

"Nothing is certain," Roberts began. "I'm merely telling you that a decision will have to be made. I may be leaving. From what I can see, the Taiping officials have nothing against you. Besides, your friends Wu and Liu are your protection. Still, I may not be here much longer. I can little stomach the hypocrisy found here. Some days I wish I were among the Confucianists, so I could at least start over with true pagans rather than these hypocrites."

At that the older man called for his breakfast and, once it arrived, sat eating silently, staring at the tableware deep in thought.

"Do you expect to return later today for your meal?" Huang asked Jason after a moment. Since Huang had never before asked him such a question, it was obvious the remark was meant more as a termination of the conversation than anything else. Rising from the table, Jason mumbled good-bye and left the room, leaving the two men in silence.

That afternoon was spent, like so many before, wandering the city, braving the cold, for January in central China was hardly what he'd become used to in Hong Kong. Almost by accident, he found himself in the ruined tartar quarters that had always offered a graphic example of how much the Taipings hated the Manchu peoples they had long hoped to displace. But that morning, to his surprise, he realized something was different. Devastated as the ruins were, they were actually little different from the rest of the city. Contemplating his new image of the place, he realized that not the tartar city but the rest of Nanjing had changed since his arrival more than a year before. Since his earliest days, the city had teamed with energy, not only of Taiping soldiers and officials but with the noise and sounds of a commercial life as vibrant any he'd known in South China. But slowly the Taiping leaders, the Tian Wang himself, or the others, for it was always difficult to know just how much the Heavenly King was really involved, had driven all commercial life from the city. Afraid that Manchu spies might infiltrate the city, they had increasingly tightened the rules, driving practically all from Nanjing save those directly working for the state.

As he walked, the sounds of a commotion in the distance caught his attention. He couldn't quite make out the figures who gathered in a group, but it was easy to guess the situation. The authorities had become incredibly zealous about carrying out their mandate against commercial activities within the city. In recent weeks it had not been at all uncommon for merchants, unlucky enough to be caught, to be beheaded. As he walked slowly toward the crowd, Jason assumed that to be the case once again. Having come within a few hundred yards of the assembled group, he realized his guess had been correct. Two young men were cowering on the ground, their commercial goods strewn about near them. At a signal, for the interrogation had obviously been a short one, they were both abruptly pushed to the ground, and the Taiping commanding officer condemned them to death.

It was all over in a moment. Seconds later, their heads lay separate from their bodies on the ground. He had seen such doings several times before, but now he realized for the first time how much it reminded him of the execution he and Wu had seen on the road—the execution of the Taiping they'd met so long before in Guangzhou. Thinking of the man made him realize just how long ago Guangzhou had been, how much had happened since his departure. Then suddenly he realized why he'd thought of that long-ago trip, for something about the Taiping officer caught his attention. With a start, he recognized him. It was Wu himself, his friend, now commanding Taiping troops! At the same moment, Wu spotted him. Both young men, long friends, stared at each other across the several hundred yards that separated them. Jason, although familiar with the severity of Taiping laws, nevertheless knew it was the wrong time to greet him. Hoping to avoid embarrassing Wu, and upset that his friend could so involve himself, Jason nodded subtly to signal his recognition and then turned around and started in the opposite direction, still trying to absorb this new revelation regarding Wu's growing role.

It was not though to be a quiet walk, for no more than a minute later Wu had caught up with him, dismounted from his horse, and started to walk alongside his Western friend.

"How is my friend, whom I have not seen since the wedding?" he asked.

Jason hesitated, quite unsure what to say.

"My old friend is upset about what he just saw. That is understandable. But, friend, they were scum, certainly imperialists, come to spy on the Heavenly Capital."

"Are you so sure of that? Maybe they were poor merchants just trying to fill their rice bowls."

"Our laws are well known; only true imperial spies would try to fool us. Their very presence proves they were more than simple merchants."

"Perhaps, but it's hard to forget how easily we might have been killed as opium dealers in the first hours of our meeting the Taipings."

Wu said nothing, perhaps less sure now than he'd been. Still, if he felt that way, he certainly said nothing, merely continuing to walk alongside. After a second, Jason realized that another soldier, perhaps some sort of assistant, was following at a discreet distance. Had Wu become so important that he needed protection from his oldest friend in Nanjing?

"I know you are displeased with me, but we do need to talk of other things."

Jason, nodding, turned fully around. Peripherally he noted the stranger who followed them stopped as well.

"What can you tell me of the anger between Roberts and Prince Gan?" Wu asked earnestly.

So that's it, Jason thought to himself as he searched for the right words.

"I'm not really sure. We don't speak that often, but there clearly is considerable tension."

"Has he said anything to you?"

"Not specifically, but he is quite upset, frustrated that he can't really preach here in Nanjing as he expected to."

Jason wondered to himself if it was appropriate to be speaking so to Wu. Still the questions were obvious enough and Wu, a far closer friend than Roberts had ever been.

"What of the servant Huang?"

"There is little to say. He is quite loyal to Roberts, seems as devoted Christian as Roberts and the Western missionaries define it. Why do you ask about him specifically?"

"It's all quite awkward. Prince Gan is very displeased. The servant does have something to do with it…but I'm not sure. He is a servant of Prince Gan, not Roberts. And Prince Gan has been offended in some way by him."

"Why doesn't he just arrest him? He clearly has the power to do so."

Wu began to walk again, seemingly to put some distance between them and their silent partner.

"It's not that simple. Old Roberts is not just another foreigner here. He is not even like many of the Taiping Wangs. He is, after all, the former teacher of the Tian Wang, hardly a man to anger, something even Prince Gan cannot forget despite his own close ties to the Heavenly King."

"I see what you mean. Do you expect anything dramatic to occur? How serious is it?"

"I really don't know. But it could be awkward if there is a break between the two of them. What would you do? Would you leave with him? He is, after all, your countryman."

The question surprised Jason. He had never thought about it. Finally, after a moment he began.

"I don't think I would. I didn't come with him. I'm not a missionary myself, and our ties are limited. But I suppose others might not see it that way."

Wu had obviously considered the matter at length.

"I can't tell you what to do. But I can try to help my old friend— my friend from Guangzhou and even that night on the coolie ship. I can't imagine where I'd be if you had not arrived."

Jason smiled and said nothing.

"Do you remember when you asked if I had the influence to let you accompany some of the soldiers, so you could gather material for the Western newspapers?"

"Were you able to arrange it?" Jason asked enthusiastically.

"Yes. I had to talk to Prince Gan himself, but he did give permission. He even said he thought your reports might be helpful to us with the Westerners. They are, you know, increasingly hostile."

"I had no idea Prince Gan even knew of the articles I'd written," Jason said, astonished.

"It's more than that. He is quite interested in them. Even had them translated and distributed among a number of the officers."

"Why did you never tell me that? I had no idea."

"There is plenty that you don't know, old friend," Wu said, smiling with considerable amusement. Then turning to go, he hesitated for a second to add "Send me word when you are ready to leave. I can arrange travel with a number of different groups that are leaving to join those fighting near Shanghai."

"Well, perhaps it should be as soon as possible."

Acknowledging Jason's request, Wu nodded slightly turned and rejoined his companion who had continued to retain a discreet distance some twenty paces behind. Jason watched the two men as they went back in the other direction. Wu was obviously in charge; the other man's subservient attitude was clear even at the distance. Finally, they rounded a corner and went out of sight. Jason himself walked especially slowly, for there was much to think about.

Whatever efforts Wu had made to send Jason off before a clash occurred between Roberts and Prince Gan were proven only days later to have been too late. For on the third day after their meeting, Jason, walking home late one evening planning his departure, found himself abruptly manhandled as he walked the darkened streets.

"Quiet!" an American voice commanded as Jason was literally pulled backward into the shadows. He put out his arm to strike his assailant, only to realize at the last second that it was Roberts himself.

"Good, it's luck that I saw you before that heathen caught you."

"What's going on?"

"Silence, boy. They are probably watching for us. That coolie king wants to kill me and probably you too; he's already killed my poor Huang, killed him dead!" His voice trailed off for a moment in obvious distress.

Jason sat half crouching with the old man; only a little light from the half-visible moon illuminated their meeting place. The long-impending clash had finally broken out.

"Your servant is dead? By Prince Gan's own hand?" Jason finally asked, partly wanting to know, partly to distract the older man from the dreamlike state he seemed to be falling into. Jason had always considered the man old looking, but now Roberts looked ancient and more worn than he'd ever seen, like an enraged and exhausted Old Testament prophet.

"I've been such a fool to believe there was some salvation in these heathens. How many have laughed at me…your own father I'm sure. They are nothing but pagans…worse than pagans…That coolie king thinks he's equal to our Lord himself, that he has seen the face of God, and I have, like a fool, labored to bring them to the true faith…labored to honor heretics."

He went on at great length about the terrible polygamy found among the Taiping Wangs and their heretical ways. As he spoke, Jason hoped that no Taiping spy was nearby listening to his litany, for Jason knew that among the Taipings far less deserved beheading, and he doubted Roberts's influence was that strong.

After a time, Roberts seemed to recover himself. Jason was finally able to ask what had actually occurred.

"Actually I'm really not sure what provoked it. We have been at loggerheads for some time, but only recently, he fixed on poor Huang my servant as the object of his hatred. Why, I have no idea."

Jason, aware of how vocally Huang had mouthed his master's opinions, knew he could guess what had provoked the animosity but said nothing.

"Then tonight he came himself into our private quarters, Prince Gan himself, with a sword in hand, and in a great rage killed the dear boy in front of my own eyes. I screamed at him, called him every insult I could, insults few God-fearing men even know. He turned on me and started to strike me down. I'm a strong man, but I remembered the teachings of my Lord and held back, and perhaps that saved me. I thought I was dead and only just managed to flee the place with only what I have on my back."

"What will you do now?" Jason asked.

"The only thing I can do—make for the river and try to board one of the foreign ships at anchor. If I'm lucky, I'll be gone before that devil realizes I've left."

"Is there some way I can help you?" Jason asked.

"No. I think I'll manage well. But, boy, look to yourself. Don't trust that man…I don't think he has anything against you. But know that these are heretics, worse even than their pagan brothers. Be careful. Do you give me your word?"

"Of course."

"At least I can tell your father I spoke to you of the danger, if he and I see each other again. There is no chance that I could offer him better news, news that you had decided to accompany me out of the city."

When Wu had asked the same question, he'd been unsure, but now the answer was obvious. At least for now his place was among the Taipings and among his Chinese friends who had cast in their lot with the Heavenly Kingdom. He knew he would not desert them.

Hearing his refusal Roberts hugged him, as he had never done before, and drifted off into the night. Jason wondered, as the figure became less and less distinct, if he'd ever see the fiery preacher again.

CHAPTER 16

DEPARTURE

The next several days passed quickly as Jason, having decided not to return to Prince Gan's compound, stayed at the home of one of the few remaining Western missionaries. He'd not known whether he himself was in danger, but it seemed likely that precautions were in order if Prince Gan were as angry as Roberts claimed. After all, the old man had been, or at least initially, Jason's only patron among the followers of the Heavenly King. Naturally his host, a middle-aged Englishman, pressed him to reveal what he knew of the affair, but Jason, unsure of the situation, chose not to discuss his late-night encounter with Roberts, letting it be assumed that he'd only heard the same rumors everyone else had. Happily, the awkwardness of the situation was short-lived, for on the second day after Roberts's hasty departure, an envoy from Wu arrived telling him of the imminent departure of the Taiping detachment he was scheduled to accompany.

"Can you tell me anything of the journey, at least the direction or how long the trip will be?" he asked.

"I know only that my master said to fetch you and that some of your things have been gathered from your former residence, items you were thought to need for such a journey." It was clear the man knew no more, or at least was not willing to volunteer anything else.

"How much time do I have?" He could hardly add that he'd hoped to say good-bye to Black Jade, another man's wife.

"They leave immediately, and I am ordered to take you there now." The man, while remaining polite, was becoming more insistent. There was little Jason could do. After all, he himself had requested the opportunity to travel with the troops. Besides, how much his status had changed since Roberts's departure was not at all certain. Jason realized he'd best leave with the man. After a hurried good-bye to his host, he set off. At the gate of the compound, he was relieved to be presented with an excellent-looking mount. Surely his own situation must be reasonably secure for such a fine horse to be assigned him, he reassured himself.

Less than an hour later, following alongside a small detachment of Taiping cavalry, no more than a few score soldiers and officers, Jason set out. Their Taiping banners flew energetically in the wind. He couldn't help noticing how much better his status seemed among the soldiers and officers than during his trip across country so long before. Wu had, it seemed, given these troops reason to think that he was a person of some status.

For the first several miles, few spoke to him save the especially polite greeting. Nevertheless, he felt certain, given their attitude, that his status among them had been established beforehand and that he would be treated reasonably well.

After the barrenness of Nanjing, especially in recent months, Jason was pleased with his decision to leave the city. Once out in the open, the beauty of the Chinese countryside flooded back to his eyes and he, riding silently, immensely enjoyed the view. Whatever the future might bring, and he was certainly nervous about encountering imperial Qing troops, the moment seemed worth whatever dangers lay ahead.

As the days and weeks later dragged on, Jason found considerable time on his hands. He had no duties among the soldiers, and only a few among them, save some of the officers, showed much interest in him. He knew large military movements were going on to the east, perhaps, it was rumored, even a Taiping advance on Shanghai, but it was impossible to know. Although near the front, it was even more difficult than it had been from the Heavenly Capital to know what was actually going on in the struggle between the Taipings and the forces of the Manchu Qing Dynasty. Still he had requested the opportunity to follow the troops in his new capacity as a journalist and was anxious to have something to send off when the time was right. Most evenings were spent sitting among the ordinary soldiers, watching them gamble and trying to gather information.

"Why do you think the Taiping forces have so often defeated the imperial armies?" he asked one of the brighter-looking men one evening.

"The imperials are corrupt. They can't fight without big fortifications. They move slowly. We have always just marched on. The Tian Wang tells us what God wants and the general Li leads us. They say he is respected even by those whom we conquer."

"Do you think the Tian Wang will one day rule all of China?"

"Certainly, it is his destiny. The Manchus have lost the Mandate. Even the rivers overflow to prove the point. Our armies are victorious. We're on the march now as we have not been for many years. Surely heaven will be kind and end this struggle soon enough."

From Jason's viewpoint, especially after seeing Nanjing's deterioration during his more than a year of residence, an ultimate Taiping victory was hard to envision. Still, he too had heard stories of renewed Taiping success. How could one know? For Jason at least, win or lose, the civil war, as long as it lasted, was allowing him to develop his skills as a newspaper correspondent.

Nevertheless, he often found himself drawn away from the pages of his notebook during the evenings as his thoughts drifted to his friends Wu and Black Jade. Both had, more than he, thrown in their lot with the rebellion. If the kingdom collapsed, he feared it would lead to both their deaths. The image of Black Jade, another man's wife, but the woman he loved, in danger horrified him. One quiet evening as he listened to the sounds of exhausted snoring, Jason vowed that he would sacrifice his own life if necessary when the moment came, if ever, to rescue her. At that he finally started to drift off, satisfied that at least if he couldn't have her, he would, at least, dedicate himself to her security.

For the next few weeks, as the contingent marched on, Jason was able to gather little new material for the essay he was putting together. Still he was occasionally able to detect an increased level of tension after the arrival of one of the many couriers that brought updated information.

One day something unusual occurred. He could hear the officers talking among themselves, but curiously, they seemed to be making an active effort to use dialects Jason could not understand. What could be happening that might require his being held ignorant? he wondered. For the first time since the early days of his arrival among the Taipings, he felt unsure about his personal safety. Still, appearing nervous seemed only likely to worsen the situation, so he did everything possible to carry on as usual.

After about three days, he finally had the summons he had long expected. Sitting near his campsite watching the fire that had so often occupied his attention during the long evenings, one of the younger officers approached him.

"Is there anything wrong?" Jason asked, feeling uncertain.

"Nothing of concern, foreign brethren, but we do need to talk with you."

At that Jason rose and followed the man. A few minutes later, he was escorted into the tent of the party's principal commander, a man he'd rarely spoken with but whom Jason knew, somewhat to his relief, to be an acquaintance of Commander Liu.

"Sit down. Have tea." The older man beckoned as he entered. "I trust you have been treated well among us." Jason nodded, quite unclear of the tone the meeting was likely to take.

"And your writing, has it gone well? You know that among us, men of letters are highly esteemed."

Jason answered as politely as possible, nevertheless surprised at the question, for no one had ever asked him about his work. For the next few minutes, they spoke of life in South China, of Hong Kong, Guangzhou, and for a time of Nanjing. The older officer was in no hurry to get to the point.

"And the foreigners, your brethren, do you consider that they favor and understand the cause of the Heavenly King?" There, it was out. That had to be the real reason for the interview. What did they have in mind? Jason wondered. What could have happened?

"My brethren, as you call them, the *Wai Guo*, are a very diverse group. Their feelings about the Heavenly Kingdom and its king cannot be easily categorized." Jason was choosing his words as carefully as possible, wishing he had more information about recent developments.

"But do you think they favor the Manchus or our own people?"

"I cannot tell you. Some of them, such as Reverend Roberts, have long favored your cause."

The older man looked displeased. Jason realized at once that Roberts's name was no longer the positive reference it had once been. Undaunted, for there was little choice, he began again.

"I can tell you that the foreign papers report less positively on your movement than they once did. That much I can say."

"And do your own reports make them reconsider their opposition?"

"I am only one voice among many Westerners in China. My words tell more of your kingdom…but can hardly have much influence beyond that. If I might ask though, has something happened—something I don't know about?"

The older man looked toward his officers. Then taking a sip from his tea, he sat silently for a moment before beginning again.

"We have word that the armies of the foreign kings are planning to move aggressively against our own forces near Shanghai."

Jason sat thinking about the news. Could it be possible? Had the British or French...maybe the Americans—for the older man had spoken only vaguely of foreign armies, decided to fight the Taipings so soon after their assault against the Qing Dynasty so soon after they had captured Beijing itself?

"Is the news reliable? It is hard to imagine such a thing. Much of the last five years has seen them fighting the Manchu armies along the coast and in Beijing itself. Is it possible?"

"It is a great question—one that we too wish to understand. I thought you, as a friend of the Heavenly Kingdom, might be able to understand."

Now it was Jason's turn to sip tea and reflect. The room remained quiet. All seemed willing to let him collect his thoughts.

"I can only assume, not that they are helping the Manchus but that they see your own troops as a threat to their holdings in Shanghai. Thus, for them such moves would be defensive efforts to protect their own nationals."

"And if that is so, what does it mean for us?"

"That is a more difficult question...one that you won't like. They have better ships, ships that can sail upstream without wind or paddles, weapons that can destroy the walls of your cities as no cannon you possess can."

"We have heard of such things. But are the stories true? Do the foreigners have such wonders?"

Jason nodded and then said, "I think any attempt to oppose them will be far more difficult than fighting the imperial Qing forces you have for so long struggled against."

The several men looked to each other for reaction. It seemed to Jason that they wished to speak in private. A moment later, his impression was confirmed, as the older man thanked him for his visit. The young American bowed to the group and departed.

Back in the fresh air, for it had been quite stuffy in the tent, he reflected on this new development.

Over the next several days, Jason felt, or perhaps he sometimes imagined, greater suspicion coming from his hosts. On several occasions, one or more officers asked him additional questions about the Westerners, but little else. Since they had set out from Nanjing, the officers with whom he had ridden had been generally an unresponsive group. And now they acted even more distant. He wondered if he'd been wrong to follow the Taiping soldiers into battle. It might have been better if he'd known some of the officers during his months in Nanjing. That might have helped, but unfortunately it wasn't the case. Wu, anxious to remove him temporarily from the Heavenly Capital, had obviously sought permission for him to accompany the next departing group. There was little for Jason to feel bitter about. After all, Wu had only tried to help.

Several days later, though, whatever ambivalence he felt toward the Taipings became insignificant as their group neared the areas of fighting. Everything became even more confused. From what the young American could establish, the officers had no idea where they might find the larger bands of Taipings they'd hoped to link up with.

In fact, only one among them seemed to even know the terrain, and he was obviously unsure where the military lines now lay. Unfortunately, for Jason they found out sooner than he had anticipated.

It was well after midnight when the alarm had sounded. Within seconds, the camp was filled with screaming, cursing men. Fires were breaking out around him as Jason hurriedly rose and grabbed the pistol he'd carried since his days in Guangzhou. But it was too late. Struck in the forehead, the only thing he remembered later was the blood that had blinded his eyes. A moment later, groping around trying to clear his vision, he felt himself struck again. This time a sharp pain in the left shoulder—a stabbing pain and then nothing. His last thought was of Black Jade.

CHAPTER 17

A PRISONER AGAIN

Over the next several days, Jason only vaguely understood what was going on around him. At times, he'd been partially conscious, or at least later thought he remembered hearing distinctly American voices near him, men whose New England accents reminded him of his father and who were apparently trying to communicate with Chinese soldiers. At one point, he realized that the Chinese were trying to get the Americans to take responsibility for a foreign mercenary, but he wasn't at all sure how any of it related to him.

Most of the time, he simply slept. That is, until he found himself being dragged behind a pony on a makeshift sled. The pain from his several wounds was excruciating, and he was grateful that his body, exhausted from loss of blood, kept him only partly conscious. Eventually, though, perhaps due to the rough treatment or the simple process of healing, he slowly came more and more to understand that he'd been turned over to Westerners. He had heard enough of their conversation to understand that the entire Taiping contingent, with whom he'd traveled, had been wiped out. What he eventually came to understand was that the Chinese imperial forces, mindful of the immunity the foreigners enjoyed vis-à-vis

Chinese law due to the Opium War treaties, had imposed upon a passing patrol of foreigners and asked them to take responsibility for the "mercenary," as he heard himself referred to. Knowing how much the Westerners looked askance at the thought of any foreigner, criminal or otherwise, in Chinese hands, it did not surprise him that they had accepted what was clearly a burden. For a time after he had fully come to consciousness, he remained silent. It certainly wouldn't be a bad idea to gain a better idea of who these men were before revealing himself. But his plan had not worked out.

"So you're awake?"

The question came in a matter-of-fact tone.

"Fellows! Our little mercenary is awake. Maybe we can get him up on a horse and really get going."

"I am not a mercenary."

"Makes no difference to me, boy. Imperialists claim you are. Found you with a bunch of long hairs. But that's for the Western officers to decide. We simply didn't think the heathens should hold a white man prisoner. Not good for any of us." At that the older man, certainly an American, rode off. Nothing more was said to Jason, and he himself was grateful. He was far weaker than he had at first realized and now, more conscious, was aware of the crude bandages that had been placed against his shoulder.

Somewhat later, almost to his regret, for the crude sled had at least required little from him, a horse was brought forward. Jason was clearly expected to ride. Slowly he rose from the sled, took a snort of some powerful liquor one of the men offered, and climbed into the saddle. With his mounting, the entire band, about twenty men, took off at a much faster pace. Jason, as weak as he ever remembered being, hung on for dear life. Happily, the horse was tethered to one of the others, and there was little more for him to do than cling to the animal.

The next hours passed horribly. He was incredibly weak, and the liquor rather than reviving him only made him giddy, all the less able to hang on. Nevertheless, he knew these men would have been just as happy to let him fall. Calling upon his remaining strength, he forced himself deeper into the saddle. One of his wounds had reopened since he'd mounted the horse, but there was little he could do. The wound continued to seep blood slowly into his clothes. That too would have to wait for attention.

Finally, to his relief, the column eventually arrived at a Western military compound. Jason assumed they were somewhere near Shanghai, but it was impossible to know. He was abruptly helped from the horse and led to a tent, which appeared designed to hold prisoners, although he alone occupied it. The front was guarded by an armed sentry, though the man did not seem particularly menacing. As soon as Jason's head touched the makeshift bed, he collapsed in exhaustion.

When he awoke several hours later, to his surprise, a familiar face sat opposite him.

"*Mon ami, le petit Americain, commet ca va?*" And then switching into English: "No one thought we'd ever see you again."

It took Jason a moment to place the man. Then suddenly he realized it was Prosper, Prosper Giquel, the French officer with whom he'd often worked during his months with the Guangzhou Sino-Foreign police.

"Lieutenant Giquel. How good to see you. But where am I?"

"Friend, it is good to see you as well. We were sure you were long dead, carried off by the Cantonese like so many others. At least we thought so until your articles started appearing in the English newspaper. You have had a fine adventure!"

Jason, still weak, sat up and took a long drought of the soup Giquel had brought. When he'd last seen the young French officer, the man had commanded one of the Sino-Foreign police units; in fact, he'd a position similar to that of Hedrick.

"Don't speak. You are obviously exhausted, but you are safe. I don't think your situation is critical. I've already identified you to my superiors, and they know you're a journalist, not a Taiping mercenary. And a man many of them—at least those who follow the English-language papers—have read."

"Am I to be freed soon?"

"I think it likely. But for the moment, you should rest, regain your strength. You'll have to be interrogated. But I think all will be well."

"Do they consider me an enemy? We had heard that the foreign forces were fighting alongside the imperial soldiers."

"There is some truth to that, at least near the ports. Shanghai will be defended from the Taipings. English and French soldiers are likely to advance further into the province to guarantee the security of the city. More than that, I cannot tell you, at least not now. I am pleased, though, to report to my former language instructor that I now often serve as a translator myself. My Chinese is not at your level. However, I have learned much since you so abruptly disappeared. You will have to tell me what happened one day. But for now, I must take my leave."

At that, Giquel departed. He'd never known the young Frenchman well, but the man's interest during their months in Guangzhou in learning Chinese had set him apart from most of his fellow Westerners. Jason remembered with fondness the hours he had spent working with Giquel and in turn practicing his French.

For the next several hours, all was quiet. More food was brought to him. A young officer arrived to change his bandages, but beyond that little else, at least not till about twilight when suddenly he was summoned to the senior officer's tent.

As he was hustled in, not roughly but with clear direction, Jason noticed that his saddlebags lay partially open near the officer's makeshift table. On its surface lay a pile of notes and dispatches Jason had been preparing during the expedition. The officer, an Englishman of around forty, gestured for him to be seated and then sat silently reading through the material.

After what seemed a very long time, the officer looked up.

"They're quite good, you know," he commented. "Though, of course, I already knew that. You have developed something of a following among the *Daily*'s readers. At least among those of a certain frame of mind," he added after a moment.

Jason nodded, accepting the compliment but not at all sure where the conversation was going.

"You don't seem to have changed many of your opinions since the good Reverend Roberts was driven from Nanjing. I assume you know about his departure. Or had you left before he did?"

"I was aware he'd left. We spoke briefly the night he decided to leave."

"And yet your own writings seem unaffected by the way they treated the good minister."

Jason said nothing and then after a moment, he said, "Prince Gan and Roberts are both very strong men, perhaps too strong to work together, but in truth I spent little time with Roberts during the latter part of his stay."

"Then I assume you have seen nothing of his recent writings."

Jason indicated he'd not. Another stack was brought apparently there waiting, a pile of recent issues of the paper. Now it was Jason's turn to read as the officer sat quietly. The first issues carried a few of Jason's own articles, now quite dated, but then Roberts's own byline caught his attention. The older man had written in anger regarding the Taiping. Now in print accusations he'd only occasionally whispered in Nanjing. Little of it was surprising. Much of it was true. Jason read while imagining Roberts's ability to draw himself to extreme heights of indignation.

When he put them down and said nothing, it was obvious the officer was disappointed.

"What do you say now?" he finally asked.

"There is little to say. Among the Taipings, there are good people, as well as evil. They are much like people I have known all my life."

The officer looked frustrated and then said, "I'd forgotten. You were raised among these people. The French officer."

"Prosper Giquel."

"Right. Giquel told me something of your background. Quite interesting. He says your Chinese is far superior to his own, and we rely on him."

Jason remained sitting quietly.

"Well, enough talk. You're obviously still weak. I assume you are recovering sufficiently?"

The young man nodded and then said, "Am I free to go?"

"Go? Of course. You're not a prisoner. I have no orders about you, simply couldn't have the Chinamen holding white men and Christians to boot—might give them ideas."

Jason thanked the officer for his hospitality and asked if he could accompany the convoy back to Shanghai.

"Shanghai? Of course, would hardly do to leave you here. Consider yourself our guest."

At that, Jason rose and began to pick up his materials. But the officer, losing his warmth, put his hand down on the papers.

"Don't misunderstand, young man. The stuff is quite excellent. Makes one really admire the hardy heretics you've ridden with. I learned a lot, but these are not to leave this room."

At that he picked up the lot and began to feed them into a small stove in the corner of the tent.

Jason stood there dumbfounded, unable to think of anything to say.

Finally, he said, "But if I'm free, how can you destroy my property?"

"Look, boy, I can't stop you from writing what you want once you're back in Shanghai. But as long as my men are fighting these heathens, I'll not help you build sympathy for them."

At that, with a thrust of disgust, the rest of the pile was thrown into the stove. For a second the tent lit up with their light. Jason used the moment to find his way out of the tent.

CHAPTER 18

SHANGHAI

Although Jason continued to travel with the soldiers for another three days, he never again spoke with the officer who had destroyed his papers.

"What will you do when we arrive back in Shanghai?" Giquel asked one evening as they sat before a campfire.

"I suppose most immediately I'll try to recover from the wound in my shoulder. It still hurts a lot. After that I'm not sure. I don't know anyone there. I only hope I can somehow continue to work for the *North China Daily News.*"

"Do you have any money?" Giquel asked.

"I did. At least until your officer confiscated my bags. I had some savings, money I'd brought from Guangzhou and money from the newspaper."

"You shouldn't be so hard on Captain Dew. He's an Englishman. They have certain ways we French don't like. I can tell you that because you're an American. But he was right. We are now fighting the long hairs. They threaten our positions in Shanghai. We both know your writings are very sympathetic."

At that the conversation soon drew to a close. Despite his bluntness Jason remained impressed with Giquel. He spoke Chinese far better now than when they had known each other in Guangzhou, and his English was excellent. Giquel had apparently become a very valuable trilingual translator for the various Shanghai groups—Chinese, English, and French—who were working together in the defense of the city. As the young Frenchman walked off toward his own quarters, Jason wondered if he'd see him often in Shanghai.

The next morning the entire company marched into Shanghai. For Jason, it was terribly exciting to see the city, which was fast passing Hong Kong as the principal center of Western commerce in China. He'd heard of Shanghai all his life. Shanghai boasted, unlike Hong Kong, not only Chinese and English communities but an American settlement and even a French one.

His excitement was even more pronounced when, having woken that final morning on the road, he found his saddlebags again lying at his feet. Quickly opening them, he found not only his writing implements and paper but also his hidden purse restored to him and the money intact! That it had come through his time with the imperial soldiers simply dumbfounded him. But there it all lay, enough to survive on for weeks depending on costs in Shanghai and his ability to husband his resources.

Later that morning, as he rode alongside the walled Chinese city past the river toward the Anglo settlements, he considered his next move. His hope, of course, was to continue working for the *News*. Whether they would want him was quite another matter. He no longer had the advantage of living among the Taipings, a vantage point that had surely helped his dispatches. Now he would merely be one of perhaps many—he had no idea how many—Westerners in Shanghai who could speak Chinese and perhaps write articles.

He finally realized he could not arrive at the editorial offices empty-handed. He had to have something ready to begin the relationship on the more permanent basis he'd long dreamed of. Having decided, he took his leave of Giquel and the others and set out alone on foot. Only the density of the crowds slowed his progress. He had to find a place to stay. Exhausted yet determined, his wound starting to hurt again, he had only one idea in mind. The obvious spectacle of the city itself would have to wait until his plan was accomplished. Finally, having found what he was looking for, a lodging house near the creek, which divided the British community from the American, he entered the building. Happily, his Manila dollars bought him a room, and he arranged for a meal to be sent up.

Almost six hours later, he finally allowed himself to fall asleep on the bed. He'd rewritten all his manuscripts from memory and before falling asleep concluded that the work had improved with the effort. He was sure the editors would be pleased. But that would have to wait. For now, he had to sleep, and even the sounds of Chinese talking late into the night just below his window hardly bothered him at all. He lay there dead to the world, drained yet satisfied.

The next morning, after descending the stairwell, he discovered to his astonishment that he'd slept through the entire night and the following day as well. It was longer than he'd ever slept in his life, and he knew he'd needed it. Sitting down to a meal in the lodging-house dining room, he listened casually to the conversation of the other guests. The majority seemed either sailors or unsuccessful salesmen, at least judging by their clothes. Some sat quietly munching their rolls while quite a few read, to Jason's satisfaction, copies of the *North China Daily News*. For himself, he took the opportunity, after ordering food, to go over his manuscripts. They were as good as he'd thought. He'd been nervous about looking at them in the light of day. But that hadn't proven a problem. The material flowed well. He was sure the editors would feel the same way. Where new material might come from in the future, though, was quite another matter. He hardly had the vantage point of a rebel city to exploit.

Once breakfast was over, and another few hours spent making copies, he arranged with the hotel to have the stories sent with a note to the newspaper office. He knew he could just walk in with the material but felt intuitively that he'd be better off not doing so. Then, sending off the material with a silent prayer, he started out to explore Shanghai.

It was all fascinating. He wandered at first in the area of the walled Chinese city and then back into the foreign settlements. Though many Westerners passed him on foot and in carriages, he finally concluded there couldn't be more than a few hundred of them in the entire area. On the other hand, the settlements were teeming with Chinese camped and living everywhere. These were refugees from the Taiping advance, he guessed. They were everywhere, living and dying in the streets amid the many stagnant pools of water. Piled conspicuously along the roadside at regular intervals where coffins apparently waiting for burial, and given the smell of the place, Jason assumed disease had to be rampant. Shanghai was more alive and energetic than the dying Nanjing he'd just left, but nevertheless he was sure he'd have to be just as cautious to retain his health.

On almost every street boarded together in cangues were pathetic prisoners trying to move about despite their punishing neck braces. Surely, with so much poverty, such curious punishments for theft must be common, he thought to himself, and almost every corner proved his impression correct. After hours of wandering, he really wasn't sure how many he finally made it back to his hotel. He'd thought of taking a rickshaw but, not knowing how long his funds would hold out, thought better of it. Finally, near dinnertime, he entered the rooming-house lobby and asked with trepidation if they had any messages for him.

"That we do, lad." The man's heavy Irish accent delighted Jason as much as the response. A minute later he was sitting in the lobby trying to muster the courage to open the envelope. Finally doing so he slowly unfolded the short note, which read as follows:

April 3, 1862
Dear Mr. Brandt:

   Delighted with your most recent work and that you have arrived safely. We admit to having wondered whatever became of you. Might we have the honor of receiving you here at the paper's offices tomorrow at teatime?
Yours
James Barlow
Associate Editor
North China Daily News

Despite the distractions of Shanghai, the next day dragged on interminably. Getting employment with the newspaper was as important as anything Jason had ever wanted. Long before, when he was no more than eight, Jason had understood that despite his father's best efforts, he would never follow in his footsteps, neither with a pulpit at home in Massachusetts nor one in Hong Kong. But not till the last year or so had he come to understand that only as a journalist, especially in China, could he support himself with some semblance of satisfaction.

   As he sat in front of the rooming house, casually watching the crowds carry out their daily lives, he could only speculate as to the eventual outcome of that afternoon's meeting. Finally setting out quite early, for he wanted to assure himself that he knew the exact location of the building that housed the *North China Daily News*, he was ready. Once there, certain that no chance for a late arrival was now possible, he wandered in the neighborhood until the appointed time. Finally, the hour was at hand and he started back toward the modest structure.

   Ten minutes later, he was at the door and then quickly ushered into the offices of Mr. Barlow, until then only a name on a number of checks and short letters of correspondence.

   "Come in. Come in." The greeting was even warmer than Jason had hoped for.

"Do sit down. Tea will arrive shortly. Can't say how pleased I am to meet you. You're quite the adventurer and more importantly to us an excellent writer. Here, try some of the cake. Young men like you are always hungry."

Jason was not hungry at all. He was far too nervous. But trying to be polite, he took a small portion. For a moment he thought of his mother. She would have been pleased with his demonstration of etiquette.

"Your reputation has long preceded you. The good Reverend Roberts has written me of your activities and skills, and I've come to see parts of China only through your eyes. And that's quite a compliment coming from an old editor like me. I've been in this business longer than you've been alive!"

"That's very kind of you, sir."

"It's not being kind. I'm a businessman, like almost everyone you'll meet in Shanghai. We buy and sell. I've got a product a news-paper that's got to sell. Now let's get down to basics. Do you want a job? Of course, you do, or you wouldn't be here. Well, we can use as much as you can produce. I've already spoken to the other investors. I can't offer you a regular salary at least not as yet. But say three cents a word for now. Maybe more later. Roberts tells me you can write Chinese as well as speak it. That true?"

"It's not as true as I'd like it to be, but I have learned a great deal of the written language, and I hope—"

"Good, for now that's fine. Do keep working on it. Not that I care much for the Chinaman's strange symbols. But there is talk of start-ing our own Chinese-language press. Certainly have enough cus-tomers for it, and you could help out there as well when we're ready."

At various points Jason tried to cut in to express his apprecia-tion. But to no avail. Barlow just went on laying out policies to keep in mind when writing for the paper.

"Our customers are hardly a bunch of Chinese scholars or even men of God, like I suppose your father is. These men are

191

businessmen, here to make their fortunes. And the others are some of the most uncouth white men and drifters from the rest of Asia that I've ever seen. Really a rough crowd. So watch yourself, on the streets and with your pen. Do you have a place to stay?"

Jason gave the name of the lodging house.

"I know the place well. Good place to meet people. In fact, that would be a good place to start, to get to know your readers. I'll send word over to you in a day or so regarding specific stories you're to cover."

With that Barlow, not without warmth but with precision as well, turned back toward his work. Jason, somewhat taken aback, thanked the man and left the room. In another minute he was again in the street as excited as he ever remembered being.

CHAPTER 19

A WORKING JOURNALIST

M r. Barlow, his new employer, or Jim, as Jason eventually came to call him, had been right. There was plenty of work for someone with his talents. The lodging house had worked out as well. The room was small, but he was rarely there, because Barlow kept him almost constantly in the field, covering the English and French campaigns against the Taipings. That spring he'd been especially busy. Almost every week some sort of engagement had taken place between the allied forces and the Taipings who, at least until early summer, appeared bent on capturing Shanghai. Most interesting had been the chance to report on the imperial forces led by the increasingly well-known governor, Li Hongzhang. Talking with the *Futai*'s soldiers had been especially worthwhile, because with the exception of Governor Po-Kuei's forces in Guangzhou, Jason had never had the opportunity to speak with imperial troops. The gentry who usually served as officers to Li Hongzhang were far more like his friend Wu than any of the Taiping soldiers, even officers, he'd previously met. And they were certainly different from the coolies and peasants he'd spoken with so often in the past. Sometimes they made him feel he could now better understand his friend Wu than when he'd actually traveled with him.

Unfortunately, memories of Wu had the predictable effect of forcing his thoughts toward Black Jade. He missed her a great deal. It was almost impossible not to dream of her, and she filled his daylight thoughts as well. Was she safe? He kept wondering, but he had absolutely no idea how to find out. She was especially on his mind as more and more events indicated that the Heavenly Kingdom was reaching its end.

If there was any unpleasantness at all during the almost two years that passed so quickly after his arrival in Shanghai, it was the occasional lecture he'd endured from his editor.

"Brandt!" Barlow yelled at him one afternoon as they sat together some six months after Jason's arrival in Shanghai. "How many times do I have to tell you? Your readers want to make money from the Chinamen. They don't love them! They are not in the least interested in reading your praises about the wonders of Chinese civilization. How many times do I have to warn you? They want only one thing from your pen—word that this damn civil war is almost over and that your heretic friends are on their way to hell so the interior trade can be opened up and more money made!"

Jason had always nodded and protested halfheartedly as Barlow cut out his best paragraphs, usually without any notice. Fortunately, Jason understood. Barlow had to please and not irritate his readers. At least Barlow didn't object when Jason found periodicals in the States willing to carry his expanded pieces.

By the summer of 1864, despite the confidence gained from his growing literary success, he'd even been profiled in a minor American adventure magazine Jason was increasingly worried about Black Jade. The Taiping cause, after its reinvigoration of the previous years, was again fading rapidly. City after city was falling to the avenging armies of the Qing Dynasty. The loss in human lives was staggering.

Although the English and French regulars had long since been withdrawn from direct combat, irregular forces led by European officers had emerged to complement the huge imperial militias that were now completing the destruction of the Heavenly Kingdom. Hangzhou had fallen to the forces of Governor Zuo Zongtang and his French allies the year before. By July of 1864, Nanjing itself had been captured.

While almost everyone he knew was obsessed with learning the fate of the Heavenly King—one rumor had it that he had escaped to the south to reorganize his forces—Jason himself was preoccupied with only one thought: saving Black Jade. It didn't matter that she was Commander Liu's wife. He knew he had to find her, had to save her from whatever predicament she probably now found herself in. That she might already be dead was a thought he simply refused to allow into his consciousness.

Using his contacts among the various imperial and European forces, for he'd developed a tremendous number of them over the previous two years, Jason took every opportunity to interrogate captured Taiping soldiers. Sometimes he had literally to force the prisoners from their captor's hands to have the chance to talk with them. More often, though, it was easier, for many of the Taipings were abandoning their leaders and switching sides, making it relatively easy to find them.

Finally, after weeks of effort, he found someone with the information he needed. The wizened old Taiping had known both of Liu and Wu and, to Jason's astonishment, claimed the latter was now a Taiping Wang in his own right! That the man knew nothing of Black Jade was to be expected. If she were alive, she would certainly be somewhere near. More importantly, the old soldier claimed both officers were in Huzhou, in Zhejiang, one of the few remaining Taiping cities.

There was something about the old soldier that convinced Jason he was telling the truth. From that moment the young journalist was frantic to find a way to Zhejiang and the besieged city. He had to get there before Huzhou fell. But trying to get into a Taiping city had been hard enough in the first place. With the Heavenly Kingdom now almost totally lost, it would be all the more difficult. Moreover, Barlow had balked at his going into the field again. The civil war was practically over. It wasn't at all clear how many more military dispatches the paper would run. Interests were turning to other issues, Barlow claimed. Jason, though secretly agreeing, had nevertheless argued with more vehemence than Barlow had ever seen in his young reporter.

Despite their many clashes over Jason's effort to more fairly characterize the Chinese in the paper, the young man had never become so adamant. Finally, Barlow, realizing something more was at stake than Jason let on, agreed. Jason would be allowed to travel to Zhejiang and cover what remained of the anti-Taiping campaign. That Jason, who'd specialized in the fighting closer to Shanghai, had suddenly decided to travel south to report on unfamiliar officers and units was certainly unusual, but there was nothing to be done.

Having obtained Barlow's permission, for he was sure he'd need to appear on an official assignment, Jason planned his next move. In Jiangsu, it had been relatively easy to follow the activities of Governor Li and the ragtag Sino-Foreign contingent known increasingly as the Ever Victorious Army. In fact, before his death, the band had been led by Frederick Ward, who'd hailed from Salem and who'd been more than willing to help his fellow "bay state'r" with information. Charles Gordon, the English officer who'd succeeded Ward, had been less helpful, and the man's constant religiosity proved difficult as well. Nevertheless, Jason had at least known the foreign contingent's leaders. In Zhejiang, he knew nothing of Governor Zuo Zongtang or the French officers who commanded the local Sino-French contingent.

Nevertheless, he had to do what he could. After considerable effort, especially within some of the Shanghai bars, Jason finally located a group of Westerners who were leaving shortly for

Hangzhou. Arranging to travel with them the next morning, he hoped it would then be relatively easy to go north toward Huzhou and the battlefront.

His sense of urgency was intense indeed. Nanjing had fallen weeks before. The entire imperial military effort, including limited Western help, seemed to be converging on Huzhou. With some alarm, he noted a rumor that Prince Gan himself had arrived in Huzhou. Would his old host's presence make it more complicated to enter the city? He wasn't at all sure.

The next several days spent traveling by boat dragged interminably. Normally he'd have used the time to prepare his notes for later articles, but now his goal was entirely different. He had to get into the city as soon as possible. The rebellion was, for all practical purposes, already over. He knew it was unlikely the paper would even use his material. Nevertheless, it was important he felt, to appear as no more than the busy journalist he usually was.

It was mid-August when Jason and his company arrived in Hangzhou. His companions wished him well as he set out on his own. To his delight, luck was with him. Upon asking about the Sino-French contingent, known in Hangzhou as the Ever Triumphant Army, he found that although the French officer Paul D'Aiguebelle still officially commanded it, Prosper Giquel, his old friend, had become the contingent's second officer. He could not have been more pleased. He had not spoken to Giquel since the latter's return from France, where he'd recuperated from a bullet-shattered elbow. He'd not even known Giquel had returned, let alone formally reinvolved himself with the Sino-French contingent. Nevertheless, Jason hoped that Giquel's presence would make the situation easier, though keeping his mission a secret from someone he actually knew might be more difficult. Still it had to be done. After no more than a day in Hangzhou where he found himself, despite all he'd seen in the last several years, overwhelmed by the level of devastation, he set out again.

There was no time to tarry or even to write an essay on the destruction of the city once so famous for its beauty, an essay that at any other time would have taken all his energies.

No. There was no time for such indulgence. Jason set out almost immediately with another group who'd been sent to Hangzhou for supplies. Happily, many were familiar with his reporting of the campaigns near Shanghai and delighted to be helpful. Jason was careful to get their names correct, for they were more likely to be cooperative if they hoped to be mentioned in one of his articles.

The area between Hangzhou and Huzhou was filled with rivers and small lakes, which had to be forded as they traveled north toward their first destination. There was said to be considerable fighting in the area, and Jason assumed it would therefore be the best place to begin his effort to get into Huzhou. Exhausted he pushed on encouraging his traveling companions, who were not moving fast enough for the young journalist. Most of them had fought for months, some for years, and already understood that as the Taiping resources dwindled, so too did the potential take in stolen goods. Especially interesting to Jason was the greatly increased number of former Taiping soldiers he encountered, men who'd switched sides and now fought more or less alongside the Imperial Qing troops and their allies, the mixed contingents. Some of the officers even looked familiar. He sometimes wondered whether he'd seen them during his months in Nanjing.

Finally, on the afternoon of the third day out, they arrived at the site where the Sino-French, Ever Triumphant Army, was encamped. As they rode in, emerging from a tent, with as wide a smile as Jason ever remembered, was Prosper Giquel. The man could simply not be confused with any other, for he had as broad a forehead as any Jason had ever seen.

"*Bonjour, une fois de plus.* So good to see you. Have you forgotten your French? I have been waiting for you. My spies have told me of your impending arrival, and we are most pleased. However, I am sorry to say that not many of those here read your illustrious paper.

Too few here know more than Chinese or French. But enough for now. Come in."

Giquel could not have been more gracious. Within minutes, Jason had been whisked into his tent, served a meal as fine as any available in Shanghai, and literally filled with champagne.

"So you have come to report on our little battle. I hope we don't disappoint you. This is probably the last battle of the civil war. But don't expect much. I can hardly get my superiors to advance. They are interested only in chasing the rebels from the province not ending the rebellion once and for all. The imperial military officers are certainly not officers as we understand them in Europe. And you know I say that not as my countrymen do but with genuine warmth for the Chinese, as you can understand."

Jason could only sit and appreciate his friend's candor. Giquel had always been free from most of the prejudices of the coast— hatred of the English by the French, hatred by all foreigners of the Chinese. His old friend had once even written a letter to the paper calling for greater Franco-English cooperation. Jason had helped translate Giquel's French into English, though he doubted the Frenchman even knew he'd been involved. It had been at the point months before when Giquel had been about to depart for France for medical leave and had decided to offer a few ecumenical comments to his fellow Europeans. Nevertheless, given the vehemence of intra-European rivalries on the Chinese coast, Giquel had requested that the letter be published anonymously.

As they ate, Giquel riddled him with questions, for the officer was unsure what was happening with regard to the larger war around him. Jason worked to sound as professional as possible. Giquel was increasingly in charge of the contingent and how he would react, were he to guess his real mission could not be predicted. Jason simply could not take the chance. Certainly, Giquel might be helpful. Weren't all Frenchmen supposed to be romantics at heart? But he couldn't chance it.

CHAPTER 20

HUZHOU

The next morning even before dawn broke, Jason sat bolt upright in the tent Giquel had assigned him. It was still dark, but he could already hear the sounds of the men stirring in the fields around him and cooks preparing breakfast. Emerging from the tent, he slowly made his way toward one of the cooking sites and sat down to a bowl of thin rice soup. More satisfying was the coffee that, though spurned by the Chinese, was quite popular among the Western officers and noncoms who worked with the contingent.

They were a motley assortment of men, almost the mirror image of those whom he'd met fighting alongside Ward and Gordon and the Anglo-Chinese Ever Victorious Army of Jiangsu. Among them was the usual batch of ragtag Chinese troops, numerous ex-Taipings, recognizable by their lack of pigtails, and the ever-present Filipinos who were so common along the coast. The only thing that made the scene somewhat different were the officers, for here, unlike in Kiangsu, they were French.

As he walked along, no one approached him. He was a foreign stranger, but these Chinese were familiar enough with foreigners not to be distracted by another white face. As was his habit, he kept his notebook at his side and spoke as often as possible to the men. He may not have intended to write another article, but he would need plenty of information if he were to carry out his plan. Already, he'd understood he would need some sort of pass to move closer to the front lines. Would Giquel and his superiors agree? He had no idea. Certainly, he'd go on in any case. But still, as they moved forward, some sort of official pass might be helpful, at least until he'd crossed into Taiping-held territory.

Happily, it took less than an hour to arrange it. He ran into Giquel as the latter was preparing to review the troops. Desertions were becoming more common as the struggle wound down and Giquel, distracted by the problem, readily agreed. Nothing more stood in Jason's way than the necessity of finding the right moment to push forward.

He spent the entire day wandering among the company. They had not seen significant combat in weeks, and most of the men were quite relaxed. The only disconcerting part of the afternoon was hearing screams coming from the perimeter of the camp. Apparently, some of the former Taiping warriors had gotten into a fight with a couple of Sino-Foreign contingent regulars. Two of Giquel's Chinese regulars had clashed with an aggressive pair of ex-Taipings and were badly hurt, their faces bloodied. At least one seemed to have sustained a potentially fatal slash on his leg. Jason watched closely as the camp physician worked to close the wound.

More interesting was the headquarters of the Gui Wang, another Taiping defector who was camped alongside Giquel's troops. Jason had not known the man in Nanjing, but he had often heard him referred to. Deng Guangming, the man's real name, was a notoriously brave follower of the Tian Wang, or at least had been. But here he was at least as well known as an opium addict. Jason had long known that despite the pretensions to the contrary, opium was terribly common among the Taipings soldiers and Deng's addiction well known.

Jason hesitated before entering the compound but did so recognizing that only among the former Taipings was he likely to find the information he needed.

Whether he should take the chance of simply asking the Gui Wang, though, was another matter. If he knew of Jason's friendship with Liu and his wife, the man might guess the real reason for his presence. Happily, though, the Gui Wang was absent and Jason ended up visiting with a young man who claimed to have been adopted by Deng. That turned out to be a lucky stroke, for the young Taiping, a fellow close to Jason's age, was at first especially talkative and more importantly knew all about Huzhou. Though as Jason asked more and more questions about the likely residences of important Taiping officials, he did notice the young fellow's eyes, to that point quite open, beginning to look suspicious. After a moment of uncertainty, Jason realized what the fellow's concern was, though nothing had actually been said. Of course, he had assumed Jason was more than a journalist, but rather than guessing his true intentions, he had understandably assumed Jason sought information on areas of the city likely to offer the best looting. Still Jason pushed on. The young man had known Wu's name, and had even speculated on his possible location within the city before becoming more uncommunicative. It was at least enough. He needed Liu's, not Wu's, location, but at least he was better off than before.

Jason left the tent more and more confident that he would indeed be able to find her if he somehow managed to get into the city itself. The rest of the afternoon was spent asking about the fighting in the southern parts of the city and the best way to travel. He even met some officers who'd been ordered to move on to even more forward positions the next morning. Quite readily they invited him to accompany them. Finally, after a long afternoon, for the heat was becoming unbearable, he prepared himself for dinner at Giquel's tent, where his old friend had promised an evening of champagne with several of the senior officers who'd been invited to meet the visiting journalist.

The next morning Jason again woke early, though unfortunately with a terrible headache. The stories and champagne had been excellent, and he'd indulged far more than he had wished. Nevertheless, there was nothing to do about it. It was time to move forward. The others would be leaving soon. It seemed best if he stayed with them at least until they moved closer to the city walls. Struggling against the pain in his forehead, he pushed himself as quickly as his headache would allow to dress and find the several officers who'd promised him company as he rode north. Happily, the officers, themselves looking considerably worse for wear, had remembered.

Three of them were waiting for him as he approached the camp's perimeter walking his horse along quietly in the early-morning light. The day promised to be a hot one, but at least much of the riding would be accomplished before the sun was at its peak. None of the men were interested in conversation, and for that Jason was relieved. The various foreign and imperial troops were now closing in on Huzhou, and Jason knew he would have to proceed forward on his own by the next morning if not by that night. How he would accomplish that was his principal preoccupation throughout the rest of the morning.

Finally, during the late afternoon, he announced he was heading off on his own. They put up some resistance. Several pointed out how stupid he was being, given the aggressive nature of the Taiping garrison that was hardly acting as it were under siege. Rather, Huzhou was almost constantly putting its besiegers to the sword. Nevertheless, the men had other things on their minds and offered only token objections. It was, after all, hardly their problem if some journalist decided to get himself killed.

Jason was relieved by their attitude. If they had really insisted on his staying with them, his task would have been all the more difficult. By late afternoon, having decided to abandon his horse to make himself less visible, Jason had approached within sight of the walls. Luck was with him; he'd chosen well. Although the sounds of rifle fire continued to be heard from several directions, all remained quiet around him. After some effort he found a spot to sleep for a time.

Hours later he awoke, unsure how much time had passed. The moon was still quite bright. At regular intervals groups of horsemen rode near his hiding place, patrols that consisted of both Taipings and Europeans. Jason did not recognize any of the Westerners, but he was hardly surprised by their presence, for he more than most understood that foreigners were fighting on both sides of the Chinese civil war. Realizing that he could go no farther till dawn arrived, he stopped. Settling down in a reasonably secluded spot, he waited. He found himself thinking back to the night he'd waited to near the coolie ship that had held Wu. How much had happened since then to both of them! In so many ways, the evening had a sense of déjà vu about it.

Many hours later, in fact not long before dawn, he had the opportunity he hoped for. One of the many mercenaries who'd attached himself to the Taiping cause happened by on horse with a small party, probably a scouting group. Though dawn had not yet broken, the moonlight was strong, and Jason easily recognized the man.

"Joshua Reynolds! Whoa there!" he called out from his hiding place, not revealing himself until the party had reined in their horses. There was no way of knowing how trigger-happy they'd become.

"Who goes there? Show yourself," Reynolds called out. Jason remembered the man fairly well, not too bright but a friendly sort. They'd spoken on several occasions in Nanjing.

"It's me. Jason Brandt. You must remember me from Nanjing."

"Of course I do. But you here…"

The long hairs who accompanied Reynolds were eyeing him suspiciously, which even Reynolds seemed to notice, for he turned toward them and told them in mangled Chinese that the stranger was a friend.

"It is true. I am a friend of your great movement," Jason added in his most polite and far more polished Chinese. There was no point in relying on Reynolds's language skills.

Suddenly one of the Taipings pulled abruptly forward, startling Jason, who fell backward toward the ground.

"I know you. You stood by when Roberts *Laoshi* had his audience with the Tian Wang."

So the man had been there. But was that likely to be helpful? Jason wondered to himself as the officer studied his face carefully.

"You are here to enter the city?"

Jason nodded. Then for a long moment complete silence, save for the sound of the horses shuffling in the early morning.

"He can ride with you," the man said.

At that Reynolds, without a word, motioned for Jason to climb aboard his mount. In less than a second, they were off toward the city walls, with the sounds of gunfire increasing to their left. It took only a few minutes to cover the distance and another minute to gain access to the city from those who guarded the gates. At first everything had gone so well that Jason thought he might be allowed to proceed on his own once within the walls, but that was not to be. Rather abruptly, he was ushered into a small building located near the inner gate.

"*Ching zuo.* Sit down," he was told and then left alone as he saw Reynolds and his companions walk their horses off toward some destination deeper into the city. At the door the officer had been told of Jason's occupation and the location they had found him but little more. When Jason had tried to introduce himself, he was rather abruptly told to remain silent. Happily, the uncertainty did not last for long. A few minutes later, he was ushered into the presence of another Taiping officer, who eyed him suspiciously.

"Why are you here? We know who you are. Are you not a friend of Roberts who insulted Prince Gan?" he asked, not with aggression but a serious tone that unnerved Jason.

"I have many friends. Commander Liu, whom you may know; as well as Wu, now a Wang I'm told. They will speak well of me if they are here."

"Liu will tell us nothing of you. He has gone to his ancestors, dead at Hangzhou, dead at the hands of the foreign mercenaries who even now attack us from the south. How do I know you are not a spy?"

Liu dead. At the man's words, a chill passed down his spine. He stood there trying to absorb the news, oblivious to the impatient stares of the officer.

Finally recovering from the shock, he turned to face him. "What of Wu? I'd heard he was here among you. Surely, he can help. Can I speak with him?"

At that, the man became quieter.

"So you wish to talk to the young scholar? He's well known among us, a real gentry become Wang. And of late a great deal more," he added as an afterthought.

Jason couldn't fathom what the man meant, though the note of irony was an obvious one. What could he mean? It was clear that he'd heard correctly. His friend had risen high indeed among the rebels. But what did the fellow mean?

"Is he here? I would like to see him. I am sure that the Wang would be pleased to see me. Perhaps even angry at those who might delay his reunion with an old comrade. One who once saved his life."

Might as well go for broke, Jason thought to himself. He'd come too far to fear chancing a subtle threat with a Taiping officer. Still one never knew.

A moment later, Jason understood that the gamble had worked. He was ushered out of the room and sent off with a lone soldier on foot toward the inner city. Nothing was said in his presence, but one soldier was hardly a guard. No, it was much more likely that he was being taken to Wu's headquarters. With any luck his old friend would know where she was. Or, he hated to think it, if she were still alive.

CHAPTER 21

WU'S COMPOUND

A few minutes later, they arrived at an attractive compound well into the city. There, while Jason stood anxiously in the narrow street, his escort banged on the gate, calling out for it to be opened. After what seemed an endless delay, the gates swung out, and after some consultation, he was ushered into the courtyard. His escort disappeared, obviously occupied with more important matters.

"Is the great Wang, Wu Sek-chong, here?" Jason asked the several older women, apparently servants, who stood gazing at him. Even while asking Jason wondered where the men were, officers appropriate to the rank Wu had attained - the beginnings of the entourage he had seen developing in Nanjing. The old women merely stared at him, looking quite astonished, and he thought to himself somewhat embarrassed.

"Wu Wang, is he here? I am a former student of his, a student and friend."

Still nothing and then finally, one of the women stepped forward, gave a slight bow, and gestured that he follow her into the building. A moment later, even before his eyes had adjusted to the limited lighting of the building, Jason realized the problem. The stench of opium was revolting. He knew it well enough from his time with the Guangzhou Sino-Foreign police. Was that it? Before he could think, he'd been directed toward a room in the inner recesses of the complex. There within a Chinese-framed bed carvings of exquisite lacquer around him lay Wu in a drugged state, the opium pipe at his side. Several complete opium balls, one at least eight inches in diameter, lined the corners of the room.

"Thank you," Jason said to the woman quietly and then gestured that he wished to be left alone with him. To Jason's surprise she departed. Wu had risen quite high in the Taiping world since they'd last seen each other. But now, if he was often like this, what was he now? Jason wondered to himself.

"Wu! Wake up. It's me, Jason."

Nothing. Wu lay there as if dead. If Jason had not seen signs of breath, he would have been certain Wu was dead. Sitting down to survey the room, Jason began to realize just how filthy the place really was, how much broken material lay scattered. Pieces of ceramic were everywhere.

"We've lost, you know," Wu said.

The words caught Jason off guard. One moment nothing and then Wu was awake.

"Wu. It's good to see you. I need to talk to you."

But then Wu seemed to fall back into his coma-like state. Jason reached forward and grabbed his arm. It was incredibly thin, much thinner than Jason remembered.

"Listen to me! We must talk," Jason yelled into his face.

His friend did no more than stare blankly at him. That one comment seemed to have been the supreme effort of the morning.

Jason was getting even more anxious. He had no idea how much longer the Taipings would be able to hold the city. He had to find Black Jade, and only his half-comatose friend was likely to know where she was. Grabbing a dirty vase full of filthy water, he flung it at Wu, only wondering at the last second if a squad of soldiers would run in to kill him. But as Wu slowly started to stir, the room remained quiet. Whatever help and leadership Wu had once offered the Taipings, he'd squandered it. His condition reminded Jason of those first months in Guangzhou, save that back then he'd not been an opium sot as well.

"Damn it, Wu, listen to me. I don't care what you do with yourself, but where is Black Jade? Where is she? We have got to get her out of here!"

At her name Wu's eyes cleared a bit. He stared curiously at him.

"Liu's dead, you know. Is that why you're here?"

Jason ignored him and started again more politely. "Just tell me where she is. You said it yourself. You've lost. But she can be saved. Is she here? I did hear Liu was—she must be close."

Wu slowly pulled himself up and started to smooth his tousled black hair.

"My fate has never been good. I insulted the Dragon Throne and then followed one who couldn't hold the Mandate of Heaven himself."

"Look. We can both get out of here. You're a learned man. We came only to learn, not to join. But now you must tell me. Please—"

"Your search was correct. She is here. In fact, not far from here. I have tried to help her in the days since Liu died, but she's changed, she's—"

"We can talk later. The foreigners are just south of the city. Governor General Zuo's army nears as does that of Li *Futai*. Will you take me to her?"

"You saved my life once." Wu was starting to waken fully.

"Let's go," Jason pleaded.

At that the young man set off at a quick pace. For a second Jason thought he looked again like his old self despite his haggard appearance, a look Jason had seen so often among opium smokers. As they arrived in the courtyard, the servants spotting

Wu stared in amazement. It was clear their master had stirred very infrequently from the inner recesses of the compound.

"Order two sedan chairs," Wu barked out with a tone Jason had never heard him utter. So much had happened in the two years since he'd left Nanjing.

Wu said nothing as he waited for the sedan chairs to arrive. Runners had left the facility and were expected to arrive shortly with bearers. Within five minutes, the chairs arrived. Neither was particularly impressive, and they were off.

"It will be better if we travel this way," Wu had whispered in Jason's ear, having noticed the young American's look of concern. Why sedan chairs? Surely they could travel more readily on foot or by horse, Jason thought to himself. But they could not speak, for each sat separately between the poles of the bearers.

Ten minutes later they had arrived at another compound. Within another minute they were inside. Wu clearly knew the staff, though they too seemed surprised to see him.

"What did you want to tell me?" Jason asked as they entered the inner buildings.

"You will know in a moment. I meant to say that you will have more trouble carrying out your plan than you might have imagined."

Before Jason had a chance to question him, they were in the room. On the other side of the chamber, in a lovely chair, partially blocked from view by servants, Black Jade sat. She seemed almost to be expecting him.

As he stepped forward, Jason understood what Wu had been trying to tell him. She was very pregnant.

"I am not as you knew me," she said with a voice as warm as he always remembered.

"You…" his voice faltered. He felt his brain freezing up. He had not even considered such an eventuality.

With a gesture, Black Jade indicated the servants were to leave.

211

"But, mistress, the widow of the great commander Liu cannot—" one older servant attempted to protest.

From over his shoulder, Jason felt a gesture from Wu. At that, the servants, led by the older T'ai-t'ai who had protested, filed out of the room and Wu with them to Jason's infinite gratitude. Both he and Black Jade waited for the room to clear, Jason near the entrance where he'd stopped and she sitting uncomfortably on a black lacquered chair near the corner.

"You did not expect to see me as I am. Did Wu not say anything?"

"I think he tried, but I was so anxious to see - you the imperials are so close. You are in great danger. But now, I don't know. I thought—"

"It was not, I presume, yet my fate to have children. Not my fate or perhaps not with my former husband," she said, smiling and to an extent apparently amused by the thought and then more sadly.

"But now Liu, my true husband, will not see his child either."

"I love you." There he'd said it, without thinking about it, without planning it. It had just come out. Almost immediately, he regretted having said it.

But Black Jade, clearly sensing his distress, stepped forward even closer, taking his hands gently in her own. She smiled into his eyes. He sensed she was both pleased and embarrassed. For the longest time, neither said a thing. Only the rather distant sounds of shelling entered the room. Then recovering herself, she said, "We will leave the city together. My child must live."

A moment later they were in the courtyard surrounded by astonished servants who soon realized what was happening. Many began to protest with considerable energy. How unseemly it all was. How against propriety against *li*.

"How quickly the truths of the Master return," Wu whispered into Jason's ear as they watched the burst of activity. "But you are right. You must get her out of the city. Take both sedan chairs; the runners have been paid well and seem content with the chance to leave with my chop mark to protect them. Your only problem will be passing through the military lines."

"You will come with us, won't you?"

Wu said not a word. At the question he moved from Jason's side and returned to the melee in the courtyard, calling for provisions for the trip, and for paper to write out the necessary documents. For several minutes he was quite active, though Jason could tell he was tiring; beads of sweat were forming on Wu's brow. How much longer his energy would last was unclear. At least something though was happening; there would be a chance to save her, to get out of Huzhou before the imperial soldiers arrived.

Within minutes the group was ready to depart. The sun had already passed its height and Jason was concerned about how much time they had before night fell again.

"We've got to go," Jason said, turning to Wu anxiously. "Get your own things. You can't travel as you are."

"My friend. I am not going anywhere."

"What? But I thought, Wu, listen to me. It's over. The Tian Wang is dead. There is nothing here for you."

"That is true. My fate has not been a lucky one. But it is my fate. I'll stay here anyway. I have nowhere to run. It will be safer for both of you if I don't travel with you. I am not unknown among the imperials, and you may see them first rather than your own people."

He'd said the one thing calculated to convince Jason to drop the issue. Jason hugged him, surprising, he could tell, both Wu and the others. Then he turned toward the sedan chairs, one of which already held Black Jade.

"Go!" hurriedly Wu handed one of the men the pass he'd written out and applied his chop, for he had, Jason now realized, arrived with the seal of his office on him. Perhaps the young man was not quite so lost as he'd thought. In any case Jason knew it would be invaluable as they tried to pass out of the city. They set out a moment later walking briskly toward the southern gate, where Jason felt it more likely they would eventually encounter Sino-Foreign troops rather than the imperial Qing soldiers.

Jason was certain that they would be safe if they could only get far enough from the city to dissociate themselves from the Taipings. How could any on the road recognize their origins if they were found well beyond Huzhou? Only the fact that Black Jade's feet had been unbound caused him concern, for they might be seen as a Taiping sign. But that seemed unlikely. Few, he reasoned, were likely to bother a pregnant woman traveling with a foreigner.

After what seemed an interminable time, they arrived at the gate, and as anticipated. Wu's chop had the intended effect. They were not questioned at all and passed easily from the city. Once beyond the walls, he was more relaxed but noted as well the increased nervousness of the bearers. The sounds of gunfire, while not in their immediate vicinity, were frequent. Were they afraid of the danger or of losing their sedan chairs? he wondered, knowing it was likely to be their only source of income. Still, none said a word. They merely followed his orders as he tried to direct them despite the diminishing daylight. Somewhat later, he thanked God for the bright moon that soon arose. Without it they would have been forced to stop far too near the walls for comfort.

Finally arriving at what appeared to be an abandoned village, the bearers halted. Black Jade, though she said not a word, was clearly exhausted, and Jason decided to spend the night in one of the empty buildings. As she was helped into the room and on to a pallet, he wondered to himself where the inhabitants must have gone. Fled the fighting, he assumed. There was no way of knowing, and he himself was too tired to consider more. After paying the bearers and telling them of his plans for the next morning, he fell exhausted on to a second pallet near her on the floor.

The next morning as dawn approached, Jason awoke to the sound of Black Jade's heavy breathing. He'd never seen a woman in labor, but it was obvious to even his untrained eyes that, that was exactly what was happening.

"Are you all right? The baby, it's coming?"

"You should not be here. It is not the place for you, a place for women. And my own husband..." Her sentence trailed off as a spasm seemed to rack her body, though she made not a sound.

Regaining her composure, she said, "If I could be taken somewhere where women might attend me."

Jason bolted upright, thankful for something to do, and ran for the door, now only somewhat lightened by the rising sun. To his horror as he exited, he saw what he should have expected. The sedan chairs and their bearers were gone. Black Jade's goods so quickly packed lay rifled upon the ground. Perhaps it was too much to expect such men to stay in the face of advancing troops, he thought to himself.

"They are gone?" she asked as he slowly reentered the room. If she were frightened, she said not a word of it. And then after a moment, she asked, "Our bags, are they gone?"

"Not gone. But everything important is. I am sorry." His answer, though, seemed to please her for some reason.

"The book, is it there? I need..." Again, she halted, catching her breath. Not waiting he ran outdoors and with the improving light began to look more closely among her scattered goods. At last he found it, the *Ta sheng p'ien, On Successful Childbirth*—that had to be it. It must be what she wanted. For a moment he studied the characters in the text. Almost six years of constant study had improved his reading ability immensely, but now he started to panic again. The vocabulary was hardly the stuff of the many works he'd read and practiced for so long. Now he was even more worried as he returned to the pile of goods. Thank God, it was there, his own well-worn Chinese-English dictionary. It was going to be a long day. She spotted the books in his hand as he entered the room, and her relief was obvious.

CHAPTER 22

CHILDBIRTH

Black Jade may have appeared calm, but Jason was terrified. Suddenly, long-suppressed feelings about his own mother's death flooded into his memory. The hours waiting outside with his father, the worried look of the physician who had hurriedly been sent for in the middle of the night, his own confusion, the adults' sense of panic mixing with his excitement about the new baby his parents had promised him, and then—that was what he remembered most—the look on his father's face as he'd told Jason of his mother's death. The death of the child itself, a tiny baby boy, a few days later had followed as if in a dream. And now Black Jade lay giving birth. And there was no one to help as even his mother had had in Hong Kong. Only Black Jade's own eyes, which revealed a remarkable calm, helped him control his emotions.

"It will fall as a melon dropping to the floor," she said quietly. "Here help me undo the sash."

Only then did he notice the tight cloth belt she was trying to remove from her body.

"What is that for? Surely it must have been uncomfortable?" he asked.

"Of course. But the child must be held tightly until just before arrival. Only thus is it safe. A too-active baby can put itself in danger."

He lay the sash out on the ground, trying as well as he could to clear some relatively clean floor space.

"How else can I help?" he asked.

"We must begin to review the *T'a sheng p'ien*. The Guanyin has heard my prayers, for the sedan-chair coolies thought our valuables consisted only of the trinkets."

Jason took up the book again and began to search its contents. Much of the vocabulary was indeed unfamiliar, but the dictionary turned out to be less necessary than he had imagined.

"My husband read it to me many times. I think I know its pages better than he knew the tracts of the Tian Wang," Black Jade said.

Indeed, it seemed likely, for the anonymous author clearly suggested to his readers that husbands study the book well with their wives. Thank God Liu had done so, Jason thought to himself, somewhat relieved by the detail he found available, though he wished as well that she were giving birth to their child rather than Liu's.

Sitting down beside her, stopping every ten minutes or so as her contractions came and went, they began to read the book together. Black Jade, in considerable discomfort, was happy with the distraction. Together, using his limited readings skills and her knowledge of the text, they were able to work their way through the material.

By late morning, the contractions were coming more and more frequently, and she was unable to continue. Jason, while massaging her legs and back, continued to press through the book, trying to understand as much as possible.

"Find something I can use to sit up," she said between clenched teeth. "The baby must be born as I squat." In a panic Jason surveyed the almost-bare room; there was nothing.

"I'll be back in a moment." Then running out the door, he dashed into several adjacent buildings, finding at last a pair of chairs, which he grabbed at a run. Carrying them as quickly as possible, for they were quite heavy, he started back toward the room where she lay. As he dragged the chairs, he was only half aware of hearing faint sounds of voices in the distance. But there was hardly time to investigate.

"Here they are," he called breathlessly.

"Put one on each side of me. They will be needed soon."

Again he sat down and took up the birth manual. Damn, there were too many pages, too many unknown characters. His panic was growing again; only vaguely did he sense that someone had entered the room and then quickly retreated. What could he do? Would she die? How could he keep the terror he felt from his face? But he needn't have bothered, for Black Jade's eyes remained tightly shut.

"You! Man—foreigner! Get out of here. We will deal with this!"

The voice caught him totally off guard. He swung around to see two old women coming in and then, after pushing him aside, bending over to examine her. Jason thanked God as he had never done. Then getting up, he kissed her on the forehead to the irritation of the old women, and left the room for the open air.

He spent the next several hours lingering near the door of the house, where from time to time women wandered freely in and out to examine the strange woman the villagers had discovered upon their return. Few approached Jason, but from those he did talk to, he came to understand that the peasants had abandoned their homes only as long as they feared the arrival of troops, of imperials or perhaps fleeing Taipings. That danger having passed, they had returned less than a day after their departure to find the village only slightly ransacked by fast-moving troop who'd clearly not stayed long enough to find the most important hidden treasures.

For his part, Jason was extraordinarily grateful they had returned. The old women attending Black Jade, he was assured, were very skilled in childbirth. All was said to be going well. Finally, after an interminable period, he heard the sounds of a baby crying, and to the astonishment of the assembled crowd, he rushed back into the room skillfully evading the efforts of several old ladies who tried to block him.

"You should not be here," Black Jade said quietly. "A husband maybe but another man; never, certainly not a foreign barbarian."

"You look beautiful. Are you all right?" he asked, ignoring her comment.

"I'm all right. The baby though, my husband would have been so sad."

He looked toward the infant, which looked healthy enough. Then, seeing his confusion, one of the older ladies, who'd given up trying to control the crazy foreigner, lifted up the blanket to show him. It was a girl.

"But I thought that among—"

"You are perhaps right," she cut in, "but it is still not as great a thing as a boy. Girls only leave the house. A girl will always leave, while the worst boy stays home to honor his parents."

"Well, maybe, but not for a long time. She is still beautiful. As beautiful as her mother!" he proclaimed happily.

At that the older women made another effort. This time the two of them gently nudged him toward the door. He made no effort to resist. Black Jade smiled and waved to him weakly.

Again, he took up his place outside, accepting after a time a bowl of soup one of the neighbors had brought him. His benefactor was an older man, about fifty, with an impressive moustache and a manner that put him a cut above the local peasants. Probably a low-grade literati, Jason thought to himself.

"The woman is going to be weak for a very long time. Her vital essence has been depleted. Her body is open to all sorts of diseases. These are things you can know nothing about," the man began, obviously leading up to something.

"Our women are always kept secluded until the first-month ceremony, but that is not possible."

"I understand. She is not from your village, though we do have some money. If it's not safe to travel..." The thought of staying in the village a month was not a pleasant one, but what did he know of such things? And she had to recover her strength.

"It is not that. Normally we could let you stay until the month had passed. But too many have seen her feet. Is she your woman? A Christian convert? The wife of a long hair? It could be very dangerous for us."

Jason did not answer him directly, and then after thinking a moment, he said, "I understand. I need to get her to Shanghai as soon as possible anyway. Can we stay a few days though, to let her rest?"

"Of course. But she stays in seclusion as well she should, and you must be hidden somewhere else. Enough danger has already come to this village." At that, the old man walked off, perhaps, Jason thought, to arrange somewhere less conspicuous for the young American to remain while they waited for the opportunity to leave for Shanghai.

For the next week, Jason spent his time sitting in one of the nearby homes only a partially welcome visitor the Deng family had admitted at the request of the village elder. As those around Black Jade were adamant that they not speak often, he spent his time looking through the several infant-development books available. Until a week before, he was sure he'd never given a moment's thought to babies, and now the subject absorbed him constantly. Liu was dead. There was no question of Black Jade's returning to her original village. No. She would go with him to Shanghai and stay there; at least he hoped she would agree, and the baby would be theirs. As he studied the various infant tracts, he was amazed at how much material was available, though he doubted his own mother would have agreed with most of what he read. He was particularly amused by a comment that babies that cried without reason had been possessed by negative elements introduced by night-flying birds. Nevertheless, during the following days, he came to really appreciate all the effort he'd put in to learning written Chinese. Certainly much of the advice seemed quite valid.

When he did wander out, and then only during the evenings, he was able to gain some idea of what was going on elsewhere. Huzhou had been abandoned by the Taipings and the city retaken by the imperials. The former had apparently fled to the east and were unlikely to appear anywhere near the village. It was altogether likely that life there would return to its previous calm. As each day passed, the villagers appeared less tense, and Jason was able to arrange the hiring of sedan chairs to begin the trip to Shanghai. Most of Black Jade's goods had been stolen, but his own money belt, which had never left his side, was intact, and it was enough to carry them via chair and boat back to Shanghai.

By the ninth day, all arrangements had been made, and they set out. Happily, no problems developed on the road. By early September, they were back in Shanghai, with Black Jade and the child established in a small room just down the street from Jason's boarding house.

CHAPTER 23

BUILDING A NEW LIFE

"But why do you look so concerned, Lao T'ai-t'ai?" Jason asked nervously as the old woman, a candidate *ayi*, or mother's helper, examined the little baby girl. Black Jade herself, though sitting quietly against the wall in a chair Jason had purchased for the sparsely furnished room, looked equally anxious. It had not been easy to find candidates for the position. Many of the Chinese were suspicious about working for a foreigner, and many more were unavailable, their families having left Shanghai now that the danger in the interior from the Taipings had passed.

"Look at the head. So little hair. And the baby laughs entirely too much. This will be a difficult child."

Jason couldn't tell if she were genuinely concerned about accepting the position or simply hoping for a higher wage. The foreigners were, of course, all thought to be rich.

If she really knew how much I made as a reporter, she'd be less certain, he thought to himself, though even his salary brought far more silver taels than she would ever see.

"Well? Do you want to work for us or not?" Black Jade's voice was as strong as ever, and now in the weeks since the delivery, she'd recovered some of that tone he'd so well remembered.

"Of course. I am sure I can please," the older woman answered.

"And the child. She is acceptable to you as a responsibility?"

"Yes."

The bargaining seemed over. "Then it's done. We'll arrange another room for you here," Black Jade said.

Jason was as delighted as he could be. Having someone to help Black Jade with the baby was important. Barlow had kept him busy since their return, and he knew it was hard on her to spend so much time alone with the baby in a city she was totally unfamiliar with. Now there would be more time for the two of them to explore Shanghai together.

Jason had still said nothing, but his plans were as grandiose as ever. It was too soon to suggest marriage, but he could certainly begin searching for a house, a home he was sure would eventually be needed. Hadn't the famous Frederick Townsend Ward, a fellow Bay State'r, married a Chinese? That would hardly be a problem. Only talking Black Jade into accepting him might be, and he hoped it would not.

Somewhat later, after they had agreed on the terms and the older woman had settled down to play with the child, Jason and Black Jade had a chance to talk.

"I have been looking at some land a few miles from the waterfront where I hope to build a home."

"Is it not expensive?" she asked, glancing back toward the new ayi, who was stroking the baby's arms.

"Not as it once was. The tea and cotton prices are down. And many Chinese are leaving as well for the interior. At least for a time we, uh, I can find something I can afford."

"A man should have his own home. Your own father would feel so."

At her mention of Reverend Brandt, he stiffened somewhat. For he'd not told her of the letter he'd received that morning. His father had decided to return to Boston. At the newspaper office, he'd received a small package, some money, and a short note suggesting that he write from time to time. The reverend had obviously not forgiven him. But at least, and for the moment that was important, he'd given Jason enough money, added to his own savings, to begin the search for a home.

"I've hired a sedan chair. Would you like to see the Bund—the Shanghai waterfront?"

She smiled and stood up ready to go. They were hardly lovers, but too much had passed between them to be shy. For the next hour, they walked along the Bund after having paid off the sedan-chair coolies. It was Black Jade's first time away from the baby, and she was taking in the sites with considerable enthusiasm. Jason had come to know the city well in the years since his arrival and was as proud of it as he could imagine. For here rather than in Hong Kong, where he'd grown up, was a city he himself had chosen. As they walked, he spoke to her of the many products found in the warehouses along the road and of the considerable ship traffic that filled the river. True, business had dwindled, yet the energy of Shanghai, always a constancy, was there nevertheless.

"This world is so different from China itself. The foreigners come here to create their own world. Do they not like my people?" she asked after a time.

"Some of them hate all Chinese. They're only here to make their fortunes. It's odd. These men will spend huge sums trying to learn French or German to work in Europe. But they never spend a moment studying Chinese. But they're not all like that; many really do care about China."

"As you do."

"It's different for me. I really don't know any other world. I'm as much Chinese as I am American. Even my father understood that, though he hated it."

"And will you make your home here forever or among your own people in America?"

There, she had given him an opening—one he'd hoped for since the beginnings.

"Where I live matters little, save with whom I live. If I could find a true wife. One I could love as a husband should love a wife…"

"Are there not many such women there?" She gestured away from the river toward the huge Western-style buildings cramped alongside each other on the opposite side of the road.

"But they can never be right for me. I need a Chinese woman."

"And in all of China, there are no families that would want you?"

She was teasing, but he hardly took it wrong.

"What I want is not an arranged marriage with a young girl but a real marriage with a woman, a woman like you." There, he'd said it.

"But I am not right. Widowed, rejected. I've had two husbands. One could not have sons. The other dead. I am bad luck. You don't need someone like me."

She was resisting but only with a smile. The real conversation was in their eyes. Finally, he'd had enough. Stopping, he took her into his arms. "You're going to marry me, as you should have done in the first place."

She said not a word but gently hugged him before disentangling herself. One simply wasn't physical in public, and certainly not in as open a place as the Shanghai Bund.

For a time, they were silent. Jason hailed one of the curious Shanghai rickshaws; actually, unlike elsewhere, they really looked and operated more like wheelbarrows, with the operator standing behind the occupants. Black Jade's face was showing the strain of physical exertion, for it was not many weeks past the birth, and hailing the coolie gracefully allowed the conversation to terminate for the moment.

A half an hour later, as they arrived again near the door of her rooming house, Jason began again.

"Black Jade, I have always loved you. You know that. I loved you before you ever met Liu. Loved you from almost the first moment we found you alongside the river. Surely you have known that."

"A woman should remain faithful to her husband's memory. Are not tales of virtuous widows told throughout the Middle Kingdom? If you are as Chinese as you claim, you know this as well as I do."

"Of course, but faithful to the memory and the family. But where is Liu's family to be faithful to? Some village in Guangxi, a family that knows nothing of you or even of his own life after he joined the long hairs."

"What you say is perhaps true, but ours was not a mere arranged marriage. We knew each other as women of my own village never knew their future husbands. And what of my daughter? I must think of her. Would you raise a child, and a daughter at that, who was not your own?"

There, she had said it. Jason was sure that was the real issue, for she had hardly been unwilling to question Confucian teachings before.

"A burden? She is the daughter of the woman I love. The child of my own benefactor among the Taipings. Of course, she would be our child. To love as my own."

Again, she said nothing but touched his hand discreetly before turning toward the door.

"I must go. Zhu Lao T'ai-t'ai should be checked upon." With a warm glance, she smiled back at him as she mounted the stairs. He was sure it would only be a matter of time.

Within an hour he was back at the newspaper's office, reading through the messages left for him by Barlow. The editor himself was absent as Jason knew he would be at that hour. He sat comfortably going through the mail. Of late, he'd taken to looking through the readers' letters and editorial comments when Barlow was gone. Although the editor continued to give him some of the best assignments, of late their conversations had become somewhat strained.

Jason's well-known sympathy for the Chinese and occasional barbs at the arrogance of the Westerners along the coast, which Barlow even agreed with on occasion, nevertheless did not always endear the paper to many of his readers. Barlow had been gentle enough, merely trying to get Jason to tone down his defensiveness regarding all things Chinese and, when that failed, simply editing out what he found unacceptable. Still it had sometimes proven easier for both of them to work through written messages. Neither of them wanted to alienate the other despite the occasional tensions present in their relationship.

The mail itself was interesting enough. Several readers had written him condescending letters, explaining his errors in judgment. He'd recently written an article detailing a murder by Western sailors of a local Chinese. According to the letters, he had erred in not explaining away the incident. Digging deeper into the pile, he found some notes from Barlow, suggesting he consider a series on some of the new Western-style dockyards the Chinese were trying to introduce. He found that an interesting idea, especially since his friend Prosper Giquel had discussed such efforts only a few weeks before in their last conversation. Another note, written a couple of days later, suggested he do a piece on the missionaries with a somewhat cryptic comment, suggesting that Barlow "knew" Jason would be sympathetic given his father's profession. Finishing the material, he left the office with a light heart. The work was always interesting, and he was certain Black Jade would eventually come around.

So sure was he that he took another few minutes to look through the real-estate advertisements that had come in. Working at the newspaper did have advantages, and he planned to use them as he searched for a suitable home for his future family.

CHAPTER 24
A PROPOSAL ACCEPTED

Over the next several months, Jason, although often traveling to other parts of China on assignment, spent as much time as possible with Black Jade and little Mei-ling, as she had named her daughter. Aware that Black Jade had no income save what he was able to provide, Jason went to the effort of establishing a small fund she could draw upon at one of the Chinese banking houses. He was absolutely determined that she did not feel herself forced to stay with him. She could hardly return to her parents' home dead to them for so many years, and as far as her family knew, a wife who had deserted her husband. The Taiping world she had made for herself was no more.

Her limited reluctance that had continued for a time was now completely dissipated. The famous Shanghai brothels clearly revealed how few options unattached Chinese women had. Still, his hope was that the fund would insure that were she to come to him as a wife, it would be by her own choice. She had said little as he'd explained the trust, but it was obvious she was grateful. Jason knew her well enough to understand how proud a woman she really was. His only remaining concern, for he was sure she did love him, was how much her concern about honoring Liu's memory would impact on her thinking. For Black Jade, despite her extraordinary independence for a Chinese woman, was at times as traditional as any he had ever met.

When he was in town, they most often spent their time along the Bund, watching the ship traffic, or walking among the growing Western-style buildings that continued to spring up near the river.

"Is this what Boston and London look like?" she asked once as they stared up at one of the larger buildings. "They are so much plainer than Chinese buildings; so few colors, so little to look at."

"Yes. At least, that's what one sees in the illustrated magazines. Actually I don't remember anything about Boston. I was too young when we sailed," Jason said.

"Maybe you really are Chinese," she teased. "Or perhaps a bit Manchu. You Westerners do come as they did, as conquerors."

They found a small noodle shop and spent more than an hour sitting there.

"Do you think they're studying us because I'm here?" he asked, noting the long stares they were receiving from the other patrons. There was not another Western face in the entire establishment.

"Maybe you. But perhaps I'm the real curiosity."

"What do you mean?" he said, and then looking around, he realized she was the only female in the room. Naturally, that was common enough in rural China, for few more than an occasional old woman ever ventured into public teahouses. But in Shanghai, it was more surprising, since he'd expected more toleration.

"I'm sure they think I'm a prostitute you're hiding from your fellow barbarians."

"How do you know about such things?" Jason asked.

"You think I just sit in the room while you're gone all the time. Oh, I'm proper of course; Zhu Lao T'ai-t'ai always accompanies us. But we do go on our little explorations. My mother would be as shocked as I can imagine. I don't think she went beyond our courtyard more than a couple of times a year, and then for only very short periods." She stopped, realizing he had other things on his mind.

"I do love you," he said quietly.

"And I love you, my future husband."

My God, he thought to himself, she'd said it! He was speechless. She'd finally agreed! He was absolutely tongue-tied. Then as he finally started to speak, she hushed him.

"Enough said. For now, we should go. We could upset the tale-teller if we stay much longer."

Indeed, she was right. A storyteller was preparing to begin one of the well-known tales of ancient military valor so common to Chinese audiences. It would have been rude to leave once the tale began.

They rose quietly. Though in reality, it was impossible to be discreet with a score of eyes on them. A rush of comment broke out as they left, but he was not able to hear it clearly.

Later they had parted at the door to her rooming house, without saying anything of substance. He had not even, as he often did, gone upstairs to play with Mei-ling or listen to Chu Lao T'ai-t'ai's gossip. True, the old woman, a Shanghai native, a relative rarity these days, could be fascinating. But Jason was simply too overcome to linger. Black Jade had gone up alone after wishing him luck with his work.

That evening, after a dinner alone in the rooming-house dining room, again something he'd not done for a long time, he went up to his room. There he sat on the bed lingering over his mail and editing one of his articles for over an hour. Finally, for it was starting to get dark, he extinguished the lamp and lay there allowing himself for the first time to really reflect on the day's conversation. Save finding a place for himself on the China coast, and the newspaper had already done that, he simply could never remember anything he'd wanted more than to be with Black Jade. As he lay there, visions of her as he had first seen her alongside the riverbed so many hundreds of miles to the south filled his thoughts.

He tried to remember his first awareness of her being the village gossip about the deserted husband the young woman said to have run off with her lover. Later Wu's own intolerance, even after she had told them her tale, came flooding back. He'd forgotten how much Wu had resented the decision to let her accompany them. For the young gentry, so very traditional despite his past, there had simply been no excuse to show her any mercy. A deserting wife, however justified, was beyond his comprehension. And Wu himself, what had become of him? Had he died at Huzhou or fled with the Taipings in their retreat?

The sound of the door opening made him catch his breath. The key had slowly turned in the lock, and her silhouette approaching the bed was as beautiful as he could ever have imagined. The few seconds she stood over him before disrobing took place as in a dream, and then with more reality, he felt her naked body against his. The thick black hair brushed against his face as he kissed her closed eyelids. For the longest time, they lay there simply embracing each other. Then slowly, she began to caress him, teaching him to touch her gently, massaging her head and brushing her lips with his fingers. Her confidence and experience aroused a passion in him he'd never felt before.

The following months went as beautifully as Jason had ever hoped. He was able to arrange a small marriage ceremony and continued to look for a piece of land to build on. The wedding itself, while limited to only a few guests, had been as much as possible a combination of Chinese and Western practices. Although marriages between Chinese women and foreign men were relatively rare, there were enough foreigners familiar with the marriages of the foreign contingent leaders, men like Frederick Townsend Ward and Henry Bourgevine, to avoid any sense of real scandal. Only the English, and especially those most familiar with India, tended to look down at his decision to formally marry Black Jade. Too much bitterness had grown up between the English community of India and the natives to have accepted such ties.

Having attended one of Black Jade's weddings only a few years ago, Jason himself experienced a sense of déjà vu, as his friend Prosper Giquel would have called it. Here at least he felt a great deal better about the ceremony as she became finally his own wife.

Several friends from beyond Shanghai had shown up as well. Giquel, as busy as ever, this time trying to establish a dockyard near Fuzhou, arrived with a small party as did, to Jason's great pleasure, Harry Parkes the consular official from the Guangzhou occupation commission. During their service together, Parkes had hardly spoken to him. But now the presence of the much-respected diplomat stirred a special pride in Jason. For it confirmed that he'd grown from the awkward boy who had run off from Hong Kong to be a respected member of the foreign community. Even Hedrick, of late established as an officer of a regiment in India, sent his regards.

If only his father had been present, but the man had long since left for Salem. The older Brandt's last letters had indicated a declining health, which was likely to terminate any future plans for a return. What the older man, despite his years in Hong Kong, would have felt about Chinese grandchildren was a thought Jason preferred not to even consider.

Within months of the wedding, two more events occurred, which were exceptionally pleasing. He finally found an appropriate site to begin building on, and even more exciting, Black Jade was again pregnant. Everything seemed to be coming together as well as it possibly could. They would have their own child, alongside the increasingly beautiful Mei-ling. Children who would grow up in their own home, away from the suffering their parents had seen so often in recent years.

That Jason would still have to travel the coast in search of stories was nothing alongside, knowing that there would always be a real home awaiting him. And Zhu Lao T'ai-t'ai had agreed to move with them to the new home. Jason knew, having spoken with her long enough, that they were as employers a particularly good find. They paid more than most Chinese families, as was common among the foreigners, yet understood their servants as most Westerners were simply unable to do. He'd even overheard Lao T'ai-t'ai bragging to other domestics in the area about her special master and mistress. That she occasionally hinted that the mistress had once been a Taiping and a high-ranking one at that seemed harmless enough. In one of the interior cities, it might have been a problem, but the Shanghai natives and foreign authorities had other concerns.

Finally, by late 1868 the house was ready. With as much fanfare as possible, for he was as excited as he'd ever been, Jason hired coolies to begin the move from their rented rooms in the American concession, a small building near the river, to the much larger home farther into the country. Black Jade had spent considerable time choosing the furniture, from the money he had originally set aside for her upkeep, and had produced rooms that, he thought, captured the best features of Chinese and Western furnishings. Just the sort of rooms he had always envisioned when he'd first realized that China, not America, was where his future lay.

CHAPTER 25

TIANJIN, 1870

"Why do you want to go to Tianjin so badly? I thought you were trying to stay put with your family after all these years of traveling the coast?" Barlow asked, slowly taking his cigar out of his mouth.

"Of course, I want to be with them. We've barely gotten used to the house, and little William is hardly even walking. But that's not a problem. We can all go for a while. I know a place we can rent for a couple of months. Besides there will be plenty of other things I can cover for the paper from there. It's easier to get to Beijing. You're always saying it's impossible to get real information out of the court. From Tianjin, I could do a much better job than I can from here."

"I don't like it. Everyone knows you side with the Chinese. You should hear the comments I get about your articles in my club. And now this idea—a major piece about Chinese attitudes toward the missionaries. They won't like it at all! The business community will claim you're only stirring up trouble."

"Me! Stirring up trouble? If you knew the way the Chinese have been talking you'd never say that. Look, the situation is getting more tense every day. The Chinese bookstalls are full of vicious material, and the comments among Chinese on the streets make that look tame!"

"But why Tianjin? Can't you write from here? There are certainly enough missionaries to talk to here."

"Sure, but I want to do something better. Shanghai is hardly a typical city. Even as a treaty port, it's different more and more Westerners all the time. Tianjin's much better, far more typical. And tensions there are running especially high. You remember the talk last summer when the French dedicated that cathedral right over a razed Chinese temple. I can talk to everybody make contacts among the gentry among the missionaries. People have to know how explosive the situation is. They have to understand how differently the Chinese see the missionaries."

"There you go again. Another one of your speeches. Do you really think anyone is moved by all your efforts to explain Chinese attitudes? I say that with all due respect," Barlow said.

"Look, I'll cover it absolutely objectively. No speeches, no slanders, just an attempt to explain. Even some of the missionaries have begun to translate the anti-Christian tracts. They understand that people have got to see what is happening."

"OK, OK, it's obvious you'll be no good to me unless I let you go. But no more than a couple of months. I want you back, at the maximum in three months."

Jason nodded enthusiastically.

"So when do you expect to leave?"

"In about two weeks. I already have a place reserved starting in May."

"Already reserved!" Barlow started to bellow, and then laughing, he said, "You're lucky you're the best reporter I have. Now get out of my office!"

Jason had known Barlow long enough to know when to tarry, and now was not one of those moments. Gathering the materials he'd brought, among them anti-Christian tracts produced by the local gentry, he scurried from the room. Black Jade and he had decided to have lunch at one of the teahouses, and he was anxious to tell her of the conversation. She had not, at first, been excited about moving north for the summer, but her own interest in Christianity had eventually involved her as well. For if Jason himself was not, despite his father's best efforts, a particularly involved Christian, Black Jade still retained significant feelings about the religious tradition she had absorbed in Nanjing. And if Jason had found Taiping Christianity to be awfully different from his family's, he knew that among the Chinese, including Black Jade, the differences had not seemed as significant.

Weeks later Jason found himself interviewing what he thought would be one of his best sources for the article.

"Everyone knows only the lowest sort of Chinese would become a Christian. Just think of it, to abandon one's ancestors to take part in the most horrid of rituals. Don't deny it. Everyone knows what goes on among them. And all that just for some rice and the supposed protection of the powerful foreigners."

The man had gone on for a long time, politely enough but vehement as well. It had not been easy to arrange the interview, for the aging Confucian scholar was a well-respected member of the local Tianjin gentry and one renowned for his dislike of foreigners. Only Jason's persistent efforts among the man's acquaintances had finally gained admission. And that, Jason was fairly sure, simply to satisfy the man's own curiosity about the Western writer said to be so fluent in a variety of Chinese dialects.

"Understand, I myself have nothing against the Christians. I don't even know if all they say about them is true. But the Christians should be more careful. They accept the lowest sort of Chinese. The sort most defiant of the authorities, and then they protect them whenever they get into trouble. As if such scum required conversion to the foreign god to arouse the officials. If the missionaries were more cautious about whom they accepted, respectable people would perhaps be less displeased."

"But are not the gentry the least likely to be attracted to the ways of the missionaries?"

"Of course. Our ways our different. The Sage tells us how to live. And without the hypocrisy of the foreigners. They have female slaves, you know, but won't allow a childless man to take a second wife to ensure himself a son. And have you read Wei Yuan? They told me you are an educated man. The Christians hate our customs just as their long-haired followers did. I assume you are familiar with the so-called Taipings?"

Jason said nothing, merely nodding as the older man, growing more excited, went on.

"They decry idols but hang the same things on their walls. The pictures of the dead god and his mother! It's hard to believe Chinese could follow such ways. There are other things I could say, but as a gentleman, I shall add no more. Merely tell your readers that we Chinese have our own ways. That the Christian god is not for us."

At that the older man signaled to a servant and, with some effort, was helped from his chair. His weight made the entire effort awkward, but it was accomplished, and after a moment of hesitation, the man left the room without further comment. Another servant then arrived and motioned Jason to follow. A moment later, after a few polite formalities, he was again on the street. Orientating himself, he headed for the north city gate toward the rooms he, Black Jade, and the children were occupying.

"Did it go well?" she asked as he entered. The children were playing with Zhu Lao T'ai-t'ai in the courtyard, and they had a moment to talk.

"It went fairly well. He spoke to me for more than an hour. Nothing really new. The usual accusations. Assuming the Christian communion is cannibalism and so forth. But the level of anger seemed worse than usual."

"Tell me exactly what he said. It won't offend me."

At that he began to reiterate the entire conversation in all its detail. He knew much of it hurt her, but nevertheless she continued to press him.

"It's all right to tell me. They can be very ignorant. I thought so among my first husband's people, and among the Taipings we learned of their weaknesses. And tomorrow where will you go?" she asked when he had finished the tale.

"I'm not sure. I am considering calling on one of the Catholic orphanages. They are often mentioned by the Chinese, and I'd like to get their thoughts on the situation. I may have even arranged an invitation, but it is not yet certain."

At the mention of the orphanages, she brightened up.

"May I accompany you?"

"Would you want to? Won't it be a problem?"

"No. Why would it be? Zhu can watch the children. I would like to meet the Catholic sisters."

"All right. We'll set off after breakfast."

⇒╫╪⇐

"You understand, monsieur, we are here only to do the Lord's bidding, and our orphanage only serves His purpose. I hope your newspaper will understand that," the aging nun said as they arrived the next morning.

"Of course. I am only here to try to understand more about your work, perhaps to help publicize the great accomplishments of your orphanage."

Sister Marie of the Sisters of St. Vincent de Paul had been almost as difficult to see as the previous day's gentry. For more than a week, he had been rebuffed in his effort to tour the orphanage. But finally, perhaps worn down by his persistence, they had agreed.

"Is it true that the orphanage is closed to the public? That might add to the controversy that surrounds your work."

"Closed? Of course not. We have many who come here for medical aid, and converts are often on the grounds. But we can hardly allow every commoner to enter. And the gentry would only come to find evidence of wrongdoing. But we are not 'closed' to the public. *C'est un mensonge.* I tell you, a complete lie."

"One often hears," he began carefully, for the subject was a sensitive one, "that many children who come to your institution soon die."

"Die soon? Of course they do. You know what the Chinese think of us. Only the most ill and abandoned would ever enter our doors. Naturally, many of them are near death. But *au moins*, we give them a chance to die within the graces of our Lord."

The mother superior was clearly feeling somewhat defensive. Black Jade, who had been sitting quietly alongside, gave him a nudge on his leg. She clearly preferred him to not press the woman. The nun was quite old and understandably strained by the effort to communicate, at least to a limited degree, in the several languages—English, French, and Chinese—that she shared with Jason. In fact, the sister had studied Chinese well, for on several occasions as he had turned to Black Jade to clarify a point made in French, she had intervened to offer her own ungrammatical but understandable Chinese version.

"Well, I believe I can thank you for your help. I now better understand your important institution. I'm sure that if the Chinese had a clearer appreciation of the good work you perform here, they would be more pleased with your presence," Jason concluded.

At that he started to rise, but to his surprise, the older woman crossed quickly over to them and, taking Black Jade's arm, suggested the beautiful Chinese woman stay a bit longer while Jason toured the rest of the facility.

"I'd like that," Black Jade answered, signaling him not to intervene.

"And now Father De la Place will give you a complete tour so you'll forget all the slanders about us," the older woman said, turning toward him.

Jason knew when he was being dismissed, and somewhat reluctantly left the room with the young priest who had been standing near the door for some time.

As he exited he noticed Black Jade and Sister Marie sitting near each other intensely discussing something, the details of which he couldn't hear. He would have liked to have heard their conversation, but the young priest was clearly anxious to distract him.

"So you're English. I was in London once."

"Actually I'm American, but my paper is English. I suppose my family once came from England a long time ago."

"That's better. We French hardly ever get along with the English. Even here in China, we are always having problems. Perhaps if Sister Marie had understood you were an American, you might have been invited sooner."

At that, the priest set off at a fast pace to begin the tour. The actual facility was not large, but it did include rooms not only for the clerics assigned there but for a number of converts as well. Walking among the graves in the cemetery, he noted how recent the majority were.

"Ah, you note the dates. There has been more illness among us than usual. But I don't think it is any less healthy here than in the Chinese city."

"That is probably true. But surely you know the Chinese accuse your people of kidnapping children who are killed here."

"I am, monsieur, very familiar with that charge and far worse charges that we worship with female fluids." He cleared his throat.

"Fluids that no man, certainly no priest, should even mention. But, of course, that is merely the ignorance of the masses. They even say we steal the eyes of their little ones. Had you heard that?"

Jason nodded. It was true that among the Chinese, the most vicious of slanders circulated about Christian practices. If the Chinese discounted the rumors, even by a hundredfold, still the missionary orphanages would be thought horrible places indeed.

"Of course, it is all nonsense. But the common people do believe much of it," the priest added sadly.

"They say the sisters, and I mean no disrespect, actually pay kidnappers for children."

"That is, of course, the worst slander." The priest was losing the casual attitude he had till that point maintained. "It is, of course, true that dying babies are sometimes found in the streets and brought here by the locals. But no more than that."

"But are those who bring them paid?" Jason asked abruptly.

"Of course not! Oh, perhaps the sisters will offer a few copper cash for the effort, but it is nothing. It is, after all, the children's immortal souls we are discussing. But we don't 'pay' for children. Only a token of gratitude for the effort made to bring the poor weak creatures to our door."

Jason said nothing, but he could easily imagine how such an attitude could cause misunderstanding.

"And do you feel yourself in any danger?" he asked.

"Not at all. The accusations we discuss are hardly new. I have served all over China. I have heard the same stories before. Even in the interior, there was never any real problem. And here in Tianjin with the consular authorities at hand? No. All is quite tranquil, I can assure you. And now, monsieur, I believe your beautiful wife is there by the gate ready to meet with you. It is true, as we have heard that she is a convert to the true faith?"

"She knows a lot about Christianity, certainly more than most Chinese."

"From your own father's teachings? Yes, we do know something about our guests before they are admitted."

"From my father and elsewhere." There was no point in going into her Taiping background. It was, after all, never a completely safe association to admit, especially among strangers.

"And have you seen enough, my husband?" she asked as they approached.

"I think so. At least for now. Shall we go?"

CHAPTER 26
RETURNING FROM BEIJING

O ver the next couple of weeks, Jason found himself very dissatisfied with the progress of his research. He had hoped to produce something of substance, something less superficial than usually appeared in the China coast newspapers—something that would really attempt to explain the Chinese perspective on the missionaries. But Barlow, having given his permission for the effort, seemed constantly to undermine it. Whether on purpose or not, requests, actually orders, kept coming from the newspaper's editorial offices to proceed at regular intervals to Beijing to interview various Chinese and foreign officials. Barlow had taken Jason's argument at face value and was taking advantage of Tianjin's proximity to Beijing whenever something important, at least as he saw it, came up. True, the capital was relatively close, but it still meant a several days' effort each time, and for Jason, so caught up in the important work he felt himself doing, those days were a complete waste.

As for Black Jade, at least Zhu was there to help with the children, and she herself had developed friendships among the sisters at the orphanage. Sometimes on the road, grateful that she had a place to spend her time, Jason wondered if his father would be more upset by his Chinese wife or the fact that she had drawn so close to the "Papists," as the upright New England protestant minister called them.

In fact, Black Jade was seriously considering having herself baptized by the sisters, an act Jason was ambivalent about. He himself was hardly religious but understood the attractions of such beliefs, and after all, despite all of his father's teachings, there was a sort of majesty to Catholicism that his own sterner New England religious background lacked.

One day late in June, as he was returning once again from another hasty trip to Beijing, he found as he approached Tianjin that the city seemed to be in some sort of an uproar. Crowds of Chinese were running around, yelling at the top of their lungs. Something had obviously happened, though he couldn't make sense of it. Suddenly, without warning, he was thrown to the earth. A second later he was rolling on the ground, trying to throw off a Chinese teenager who had tackled him. Jason, gasping for breath, for the fall from the horse had slammed his ribs into the roadway, struggled with all his energy to kick the boy away from him. Others were in the road, but no one intervened. The boy was quite strong. But slowly Jason's older, more experienced muscles prevailed, and he was able to push the young man off him. Then drawing his knife, he waved it at the boy. The teenager ran off without a word.

Jason stood there panting in the road, completely dazed. What had happened? His horse was long gone, as were his bags and the rifle normally tied to them. He had only his knife and the clothes on his back. Finally pulling himself toward the roadside, for his leg was badly strained by the struggle, he tried to understand what had occurred. Some sort of riot had broken out. But against whom? The Chinese authorities? The foreigners? And then he understood with a start. The missionaries! Bolting as upright as well as he could, considering the pain in his leg, he started off toward the area where the orphanage stood. The distance was considerable, and as he half ran, half walked, staying as much as possible from view, he finally began to understand that his guess was correct. Something terrible had happened. From buildings came excited talk of a shooting. The foreigners had killed a Chinese official the Christians finally punished? It all seemed so horrible. Black Jade! The children! He had to get to his rooms! Changing direction, he now set off much more at a run toward the rooms they occupied. As he grew closer, he calmed, for the street itself was quiet enough. No visible sign of rioting was evident. Finally arriving at the door, he flung it open. There they were. Both children happily playing on the floor at Zhu Lao T'ai-t'ai's feet, but the look on her face froze his blood again.

"Where is the mistress?" he screamed.

"I don't know," she said, her eyes frightened.

That was all he needed. He paused, only long enough to grab an extra pistol he kept in the room before running out once again into the streets. Now he was running as fast as he'd ever run in his life straight toward the orphanage. Had she been there? What could have happened? Whatever had caused the explosion seemed to have ended, for many of the streets were now deserted.

Suddenly to his horror, he came upon two Western corpses, both stripped and beheaded. One, a female, had been horribly mutilated. Her left hand, which had probably contained a ring, was now partially cut off. Steeling himself, he went on unaware that people in the streets were watching him. Whatever had happened, the madness seemed to have passed. At the orphanage itself, he found nothing but ruins, burned out with partially charred human remains strewn about on the street. From where he stood, at least a dozen or more bodies lay burned—men, women, some children, as many Chinese as foreign. He wanted to force himself to study each corpse, to find her among the dead, but it was impossible. The bodies had been so brutalized; it was horrible. After no more than a few terrible moments trying to study the remains, he fell to the ground vomiting in pain. After that he remembered nothing, save being dragged off by an English voice, which was insisting it wasn't safe to stay there. Marauding bands of Chinese, perhaps those who had burned the orphanage and killed the inhabitants, were still running amok, killing any foreigner or Chinese convert unlucky enough to get in their way.

In the hours that followed, he thanked God for Zhu's presence. She had consoled the children even as Jason himself had sat on the bed next to them trying to be with them. Happily, little William was too young to understand what had happened, but Mei-ling kept asking about her mother. What did one say to a six-year-old? Later that night word came from one of the neighbors that the authorities had ordered the bodies immediately cremated. That had been almost too much. He'd at least hoped to identify the remains and give her a proper burial, and now even that was impossible. Finding himself almost unable to breathe, he helped Zhu put the children to bed and then set off toward a nearby Western bar.

As he entered, the one thing that had always irritated him about the place now seemed reassuring. There was not one Chinese present. The owners, he never had understood why they'd chosen to settle in Tianjin, only employed Filipinos as servers, and the clientele consisted exclusively of foreign sailors and the few Westerners who lived permanently in the city. Walking toward the rear of the saloon, he took up a place near the back. Half an hour later, he was already half plastered as he sat listening to the angry conversations of the customers. The massacre was on everyone's lips, and studying them he realized they were each carrying far more weapons than one usually saw within the city limits. In one sense, he wished he were back in Shanghai. At least there he knew people,

people he and Black Jade knew, and he'd at least not be sitting there alone, hurting for her.

More than an hour after his arrival, he was momentarily drawn from his increasingly drunken stupor by the sounds of a disturbance near the front of the bar. Straining to see, for the light was poor and he himself was feeling awfully dizzy, he saw a young Chinese, one who even looked slightly familiar, arguing with one of the men who guarded the entrance. Jason couldn't tell what was going on, but a moment later, the young Chinese was abruptly shoved back out into the street whence he'd come. Another time, Jason knew he would have been incensed, but now he felt nothing, just a nagging desire to order another drink and a hope that he could forget the images he'd seen in the street so many hours before.

Much later, he really wasn't sure how, he managed to pick himself up and return to the rooms they'd rented in Tianjin. Zhu lay asleep on the floor in the first room, and beyond her both children slept fitfully in their beds. As he threw himself down on his own, he dreaded the thought of having to deal with the children's pain again in the morning. And they didn't even have the option he had in gin.

But the next morning broke quite differently than he'd expected. He awoke to the sounds of Zhu Lao arguing vehemently with someone at the door. Getting up to look, he realized she was trying to bar the door to the same young man he'd seen in the bar.

"It's all right, Zhu," Jason said as he gestured her to let him in.

"What do you want?" he asked, not feeling particularly pleasant, especially as he recognized the fellow. He was the second son of the gentry he'd interviewed the week before, the man who had accused the Christians of so many defilements.

"You know me?" the young man asked, looking relieved.

"Yes, what do you want?" Jason said.

"My father wishes to speak with you."

"What could he possibly have to say? I am not interested."

"Please. It is important. You must come with me."

"It's dangerous, master, a trap. These Tianjin people are monsters. Everyone in Shanghai knows it," Zhu cut in.

For a moment, Jason found himself amused by her regional prejudices, and then turning again to the man, he said quietly, "I have nothing to say to your father. No questions to ask. No reports to write. I think you should go. I have no interest in your father's explanations and apologies."

"Please, it is important that you come at once. You will understand later." He seemed almost to plead.

For reasons he didn't comprehend, Jason picked up his pistol and gestured for the young man to go ahead. Grabbing his jacket, Jason followed him out just as the children were waking. He felt uncomfortable about that, but it seemed important to go with the young Chinese.

At the bottom of the stairs, the fellow turned again toward him.

"All looks calm, but the great anger continues. Do you remember how to get to my father's compound?"

Jason nodded.

"Good. Then go there yourself discreetly. You'll be safe, but it is important that I not be seen with you. I'll meet you there shortly. Please remember to be discreet."

Jason, at first suspicious and then unsure what was happening, set off as the fellow had insisted. Somewhat later he arrived at the gate, which opened as he approached. They had obviously been waiting for his arrival.

Passing within, his last thought was whether it was a trap. Had he now left the children orphans? But once within the compound, the warm approach of the same young man who'd traveled more quickly reassured him. He was ushered into the inner part of the compound. "My father will be here shortly. Please sit."

The young man gestured toward one of the dark wooden chairs near the front of the room. It was the very chair Jason had sat in during the previous interview. No, the memories of the hate the older man had spewed were too fresh. He gestured impatiently that he would rather stand. The young man looked as if he understood and said nothing. For a moment, as Jason reflected on the earlier conversation, he fingered the pistol in his belt, imagining taking his revenge out on the older gentry himself. It was, after all, well known that the gentry were often behind the violence of the streets. His fingers were secretly fondling the handle of the gun when the door opened up abruptly as the older man walked in slowly.

"He knows nothing? You said nothing in front of the servant?"

"It was as you ordered, Father?"

Suddenly Jason felt completely disoriented. What was going on? Could…no. He dared not think it.

"Come with me. She is in the next chamber."

"My God, Black Jade? My wife. She's not dead? What are you talking about?"

"I'm afraid she may soon be with her ancestors, but she is not dead. Only nearly so. Come with me."

In another second they were at her bedside. She lay unconscious, a bloody wound across the right side of her head. He couldn't believe it.

"I don't understand. How did she come to be here? I thought she was…Why did you not tell me? Has she woken at all?"

"She is here because my son was…well, near the orphanage when it happened. He recognized her. You have not been here long, but your family is not unknown among us. He was able to bring her here. But there was great danger. Then and now. My family is respected. We don't want our role in any of this known."

Jason cupped her face in his hands, hoping for some reaction, but she only lay there breathing heavily.

"She has got to see a physician."

"That was our thought as well, but not here. There is too much possibility of talk. You must take her elsewhere. Have your own people see her or perhaps a Chinese physician. I can tell you that my first wife, who knows of such things, says she cannot live long like this. She may die after all."

But for Jason those words meant nothing. She wasn't dead yet, and he'd make sure he'd not lose her again. For the first time in longer than he remembered, he thought deeply of his dead mother, praying that she would help Black Jade to live. Begging her for help seemed more real than praying as his father would have insisted, and he felt better for it. Standing upright again, he turned to the second son.

"Can you get me a large sedan chair? Someway I can move her to our own apartments."

"It has already been ordered. They are waiting behind the compound for your arrival."

With that, Jason nodded and set off with some of the servants to find material to carry her in. Ten minutes later, he huddled alongside in the dark sedan chair, caressing her face and thinking back about the family that had saved his wife even as they had contributed to the hate that had almost destroyed her.

The next few days were hell. A string of visits by the one local Western physician seemed only to make him more depressed. The older man, a gray, somewhat odorous English physician, had been terribly pessimistic.

"If we can't get any water into her, she won't last the week," the older man had commented, looking discouraged.

"But what if we just pour something into her?"

"She'd choke on it. No. She can't remain like this for long. The wound's been cleaned, but how much damage she sustained is impossible to know. I'd not be hopeful."

Jason was hardly willing to hear such talk, especially after he'd already thought he'd lost her once. With a briskness he later thought he might regret, he ushered the man to the door, pressing his fee into his hand as he closed the door.

There in the living room, Mei-ling sat quietly, watching the scene, while from the window came the sounds of Zhu Lao T'ai-t'ai playing with William.

"Will Mommy be all right?" Mei-ling asked as he turned toward her.

"I'm sure she will be, honey. But she was very badly hurt, and we have to pray that she will recover soon. Can you do that?"

"Mommy taught me."

"Good. Then do it as hard as you can, love. Mommy needs it."

With that, he returned to their room to sit at her side. Later when Zhu returned, he slipped out for a time to arrange for a Chinese physician to visit that night. He'd seen enough of Chinese medicine to know that it was important that he try the traditional physicians as well. Having sent for one, he then spent time gathering information about the massacre itself and then returned to the apartment. It was important to send off a report to Barlow.

Hours later, after the Chinese physician had come and gone, he felt no more confident. The man had spent considerable time studying her tongue and feeling for the various pulses he explained were his diagnostic tools. Having satisfied himself regarding her condition, he'd applied acupuncture to various points on her body, but with little reaction. She seemed not to feel the penetration of the sharp silver needles at all. The physician looked discouraged. Jason had refrained from asking his opinion about her chances. Once the man left, he returned to his writing table to again take up to the newspaper piece.

Throwing himself into the article, not so much for the work but to explain to himself what horror had overcome his family and

Black Jade, he spent most of the night writing—explaining the stupidity of the French consul, for the first rumors were apparently correct. One of the consular officers, enraged over the accusations against the orphanages, had apparently shot a gentry official in front of a crowd, thus setting off the explosion. But that was hardly it. Even the stupidity of the sisters for paying vagrants to bring them dying children seemed not enough to explain the massacre, the murderous assault on his wife by the people for whom he had forsaken his own. How could it have happened?

He later remembered that night as the longest of his life. Finishing the article, he'd sat there staring into the whale oil lamp, studying the fire and thinking of the years since he'd met her... then later of the days in Nanjing when she'd helped him write those first articles. He even thought of those terrible hours when he attended her wedding, certain he'd lost her forever. And yet that had not happened. So much had occurred, but she had finally come to him as his wife and now...he looked over toward her, vaguely hearing a change in her breathing. But upon studying her more closely, all seemed as before.

Sitting down again at the desk, he took up the glass of gin he'd been nursing all night. From the window a very thin stream of light began to enter. It was almost dawn, and the bright sun of June was starting to appear. He thanked God that it wasn't hotter, for he'd been told several times that the faster she lost fluids, the more quickly she would weaken. He glanced anxiously at the sky, hoping for a reasonably cool day when suddenly he heard her.

"My husband. Is that you?" she said weakly.

He bolted to her side. "Of course it's me. I'm here. Feel my hand on yours."

"The children. Are they—"

"They are both fine—everybody's fine...Everything is now fine."

She began to close her eyes again. He was momentarily afraid. Would she drift off again never to awake? Should he force her to drink?

Then again her eyes opened once more.

"I'm going to be all right. Let me sleep a bit."

"Of course. Can I give you some water?"

"I'd like that."

She sipped a few ounces and then started to drift off again.

"Jason."

"Yes."

"When I'm better, can we go home?" she asked, her voice sounding somewhat stronger.

"Back to Shanghai, of course; we'll go as soon as you're well," he said.

"Back to Shanghai…yes, I'd like that," she said sleepily. "Or maybe even to America. William is half American, and he should know your country as well."

"We'll go wherever you want. I love you."

"I love you," she said as she fell back into a light sleep.

ABOUT THE AUTHOR

Li Bo is the fictional pen name of Steven A. Leibo, a professor at the Sage Colleges in New York. Leibo specializes in international history and politics with a focus on China and Asia.

Leibo is an associate in research at Harvard University's Center for Chinese Studies and has published extensively on China and Asia. He is also a commentator on Northeast Public Radio.

Made in United States
North Haven, CT
10 January 2023

30869209R00143